DEMON UNDERTOW

MARK SUTTON

hope**again**
books

To: Ron and Linda. You are godly people and great friends. Thank you for enriching my life in so many ways.

CHAPTER ONE

Not quite a bird; certainly not human. The grotesque, malformed figure flew across the face of the newly-rising moon. It thrived on privacy. Fed on darkness and shadows. Grew fat on fear. Black, leathery wings beat steadily as the Dark Lord's servant searched methodically for its prey somewhere far below. Evil worked best if never noticed, but the creature had little worry as it flew over the beach, moving inland toward a thick glut of houses, stores, automobiles and restaurants. Physical eyes could not see into its realm; no man or woman would find the demon unaided. Its effects, however, would soon prove quite devastating to the inhabitants of Hidden Beach . . . .

Everything depended on finding the right instrument. One of Satan's most powerful captains had chosen him for this important assignment. The target, according to the captain's explanation, had already become a disquieting influence in the area. Neither temptation nor discouragement had proved effective against him so far; the target could not be moved from his chosen path. So, he had to be destroyed.

The demon looked with a vision that saw not just flesh and blood, but emotions, weaknesses, lusts. They fairly shouted at the dark spirit to be used. All could be exploited, if one dangled the right bait. Carefully deployed, it would eventually reel in the intended prey. That prey would then be honed into a deadly instrument. And, finally, the instrument would remove the target. It might take some time, but that was acceptable. The demon was willing to wait until he found the perfect vessel. What was not acceptable was failure. He shuddered and faltered in his flight for a moment. Punishment, pain and, worst of all, banishment awaited the demon if he could not neutralize the target.

Something tugged at his attention. The misshapen figure folded his wings and dropped like a stone. Once below the skyline, he slowed his descent, landing with a clumsy lurch. The demon looked around, oriented himself and began to move forward. At this point, caution took over. He slipped from bush to tree, from shadow to the alley of a building. Human eyes could not see him, but there were other forces roaming the earth. Their senses were keen, and they opposed the demon and his kind.

Just past a brick wall on the side of a non-descript house, the goal beckoned. The demon trembled with desire. But prudence had to be maintained: go slowly, hide, be safe.

He walked quietly through the wall, examined his surroundings, then smiled. Black spikes in the demon's mouth momentarily revealed themselves. Then he closed his mouth, unfurled his wings, and floated to the back of the dwelling. His prey awaited.

The man sat on a couch watching a baseball game. He displayed no reaction as the demon walked straight through the television and then crouched before him, eye to eye. Clouds of emotions swirled unchecked about the man as he sat silently. Above all the other emotions, the demon could see anger covering the man tightly, cutting off anything remotely resembling contentment or happiness. Those emotions would become the strings of the demon's latest puppet. He would never realize what he had become until it was too late.

The demon opened his mouth and a thin, sharp projection slowly emerged, unwinding, stretching, then separating into two deadly snakes. One slithered toward the man's left temple. The other moved across his face, down his neck, not stopping until it found a location where the heart beat right beneath the skin. The demon paused for a moment. Everything depended upon what happened next. He focused hate-filled eyes on the man, then gave a violent twist of his head. The two snakes pierced temple and chest simultaneously, penetrating the brain and the heart.

The man stiffened for a moment. The demon still crouched, absolutely motionless. The two snakes had linked to the intellect and the emotions. If the man couldn't bring himself to fight now, he would soon be the demon's tool, ready to be honed, used . . . and destroyed.

His future, unseen to the man, hung before him, ready to tip either way. The slightest act of will to shut out the bitterness, and all might still be saved. The demon watched intently. But after several long moments, the man relaxed, turned off the television and closed his eyes; anger, resentment, bitterness flew about him like wasps. The crouching figure smiled. It reminded the demon of watching Judas at the Last Supper as Satan entered him. Then he leaned forward and released a flood of poison into the snakes. They opened their mouths wide and bit into heart and mind once again. Evil coursed through their fangs and into the man. He shuddered as strange thoughts and attitudes swept over him.

"Yes," he said out loud after awhile. "Of course. That's what I'll do." The long-harbored anger had given way to a new resolve. He'd been frustrated for a long time; now, he had the beginnings of a plan.

The demon smiled one more time, letting the snakes crawl

back through his mouth and into their dark, welcome nest in his stomach.

Time to begin the destruction.

CHAPTER TWO

"Henry, where's the dog?"

The wiry man whirled around from his desk and looked out the office window. Just in time, he saw a wagging tail disappear into the church.

"Thanks, Jenna. I've spotted him. Gotta go."

Henry hung up and started for the worship center on the run, his thick brown hair flopping down over his eyes. As he rounded the corner from his office, a metallic clang and a strangled yell greeted him. The pastor slowed immediately. No reason to hurry now. He'd blown it once more.

"Pastor Watchman, this is it! I've had it. You can have this job and this church. I'm too old to have to put up with this anymore."

Chaos confronted Pastor Henry Watchman. His custodian, a tall, willowy man now stooped by age, took pride in the job he'd held for thirty-plus years. At the moment, however, Raymond looked ready to have a stroke. The once-beautiful wood floors of the church had pools of water scattered everywhere. In between each pool, muddy paw prints made a connecting trail. The prints led in a circle to an overturned bucket and a golden retriever with a happy grin. The dog was the only one here who looked happy, Henry noted.

"Two hours of work. Hard work. Gone down the drain because of that dog of yours!"

Here it came again, Henry thought, and I deserve it. "Raymond, I'm sorry. This time, we really thought the yard had been made escape-proof. Titus must have somehow dug under the fence." He tried to shame the dog by looking fiercely at him. It didn't work. Titus wagged his tale ferociously.

"Get the dog out of the church, Reverend. This will be my last day to work here, and I don't want to leave a dirty floor as my legacy."

"You can't mean that, Raymond!"

Pastor Watchman knew he was groveling, but it didn't matter. He needed someone to clean the church. "Every time Titus escapes, Jenna and I find the problem and fix it. We've raised the height of the fence. We're closing all the holes and putting railroad ties around the bottom to keep him from digging out. This will probably be the last time he gets . . ."

"You said that last time, and the time before that," Raymond muttered. He watched as Pastor Watchman grabbed the dog's collar and began leading him out of the church. The dog's feet slid about in the puddles of water, creating more scuffs and mud to be cleaned up. Just before the two penitents left the building (actually, only one of them could be remotely termed a penitent; the dog was still having a good time), Pastor Watchman turned for one last plea.

"Please reconsider, Raymond. You're as much a part of this church as are those wood floors you clean so well each week." Henry winced as he said this. Tactical mistake to call attention to the floors again.

Raymond's face got even redder. "I've had it, Reverend Watchman. The more this church grows, the harder it is to keep it clean." He pointed a shaking finger at Titus. "If you don't keep this dog out of the church – and if you don't get me some help around here — I'm gone." The ancient custodian looked at the ground for a minute, reflecting. "I'll give you a month. If the dog comes back, he'll be cleaning the floors. If you don't find someone to help me, you can consider this my four-week notice."

Henry could see the custodian beginning to calm down. The stooped shoulders relaxed. Raymond's color improved. Finally, the old man grinned a little. "I'm too old for this, Pastor. I really do need some help." He gave a dry laugh. "Know it's wrong, but even here in church, that dog makes me so mad I could cuss."

Henry Watchman allowed himself a small smile in return. "The dog will stay in the backyard from now on. And I'll do my best to find some part-time help." He paused, and his voice firmed. "But don't curse, Raymond. You know I *hate* profanity."

After putting Titus back where he belonged, this time attached to a long chain, Henry shook his finger at the dog. "You listen about as well as some of my church members!" he said. Titus whined and lowered his head. The pastor softened his tone. "Yeah, I know it's hard for a puppy not to dig." He looked around the backyard. In the back right corner, farthest from the house, a small hole could barely be seen behind a bush, in spite of the bright light shining from the carport. "I'll fix it tomorrow, Titus," Henry said. "Until then, you're back on the chain gang." The recaptured convict wagged his tail and jumped up to be petted. Henry laughed and ruffled the dog's fur behind his ears. "Oh, Titus, if only everyone were so quick to forgive."

Inside the church, lights began to go out as Raymond finally decided to call it a day. Henry hurried back to the church and caught up with his custodian. "Don't bother closing up, Raymond," he called out. "I'll be here another couple of hours."

The old custodian looked at the clock on the back wall of the worship center. "Pastor Watchman, it's nearly 10:00. You've had a long Sunday, and you're planning to work till midnight?" He shook his head. "I'm sorry I lost my temper while ago. No matter what kind of hours I put in, they're nothing compared to what you do."

Henry waved the apology away. "Forget about it. You were right to be upset. I have to keep Titus in his doghouse, or you and Jenna will put me in it!"

Raymond grinned. "I'm not the one to worry about, pastor. Whatever you do, keep the missus on your good side." He put up the last of his cleaning tools and opened the back door. "See you in the morning."

Henry went back to his study. Sunday *had* been long. Over the years, however, he'd discovered that the best antidote to all the sermons preached, people counseled, and decisions made was to work late, until the adrenaline had subsided. Jenna was the one who'd suggested he end the day with a long run on the beach. It cleared his mind and body, getting him ready for the new week.

Just before midnight, he picked up the phone and called his wife. "You sure you're okay with my running this late?" he asked.

On the other end of the line, Jenna laughed good naturedly. "That run is really a gift to me. It makes you calm, tired, and easier for me to handle! Seriously, go jog on the beach. It will be good for you.".

CHAPTER THREE

"No luck tonight. Might as well try to get some sleep."

The aging man picked up a recently stolen leather tote and moved toward sand and darkness. He looked up at the sky and nodded at what he saw. Not much light meant more protection for him.

Waves reflected only dull silver as a thin moon rode wisps of clouds far above. Normal sounds faded to nothing in the constant roar of surf meeting a dark shore. Lights had been banned along Hidden Beach, Florida to protect nesting turtles. Prior to the blackout, turtles moved too far inland, following the bright lights of civilization. Screeching tires and crushed shells had alarmed both tourists seeking a worry-free vacation and ecologists who wanted to protect the endangered species. Now, only the waning moon illuminated parts of the beach. Protected by the shadows and the surf, nesting turtles inched forward to lay their eggs and return to the sea. Beside them, the man named Terrence quietly moved into a protected patch of sand between clumps of sea oats, ready to bed down for the night.

Terrence had always thought of himself as clever. In his younger days, he'd made a pretty good living as a pool hustler. It hadn't even been necessary to move from place to place to hide his identity. Every week fresh tourists poured into the bars in his area, flush with money and ready to prove they were the best. Terrence always smiled and politely took their money. Age and alcohol, however, finally combined to rob him of a steady hand. The cue stick began to shake, ever so slightly. The smooth, silky stroke would sometimes show a hitch. The wins – and the money – dried up. He'd had to find another way to earn a living.

That's when Terrence turned to his current line of "work." He discovered a way to use the hand-eye coordination that had made him a good pool player . . . even if it was outside the law. Terrence targeted hotels up and down the southern Florida coast. He simply stationed himself outside a row of rooms and watched the first three floors for activity. When the tourists left their rooms to swim, dine or shop, Terrence hopped over the railing of a first-floor room and climbed from balcony to balcony until he reached his target. He never climbed too high. Terrence liked money, but he was also careful. Too much height, one misstep and a fall made for a fatal combination he'd rather not risk.

A quick tug on the sliding glass door of the just-vacated room usually proved to be enough to gain him entry. Most people never thought to lock those doors. He'd discovered that in a small hotel room, it took only a moment to find the cash and jewelry left behind. Terrence would move to the other end of the strip after several successful robberies, spend the night in a cheap hotel, and start the process again the next day.

This past year, however, pickings had grown slim. His body, older and not as limber, confined him mainly to the first floor. The decreased revenue meant Terrence could no longer afford even the cheapest motel rooms on a regular basis. But he knew how to hunker down and conserve money until better times came around. Take, for example, his "home." The beach provided him lodging and a place to bathe that cost him not a penny. A nice designer swimsuit -- stolen from one of the first floor balconies of the beach-front hotels – made him look like a tourist. The showers placed at the entrance to the beach by each hotel encouraged their guests to wash the sand off feet and bodies before re-entering the building. By moving a hundred yards or so up the beach each day, Terrence had a different place to shower every morning during the summer. On the rare occasions an over-zealous employee confronted him and asked for his room number, Terrence would always pick a number out of the air . . . and then name a hotel directly adjacent to the one where the employee worked. The response that he had passed up his own hotel was always given politely. Both Terrence and his accuser would have a laugh about it, and off Terrence would go, clean and, sometimes, richer. It still amazed him how many hotel guests left their wallets and keys under a towel while they swam.

Terrence prepared for bed. He had already watched the weather channel in one of the hotel lobbies and knew the thin clouds held no rain. The petty thief had developed the knack of sleeping with what he called "one ear open." Even in a dead sleep, he could hear the motor of the beach patrol's vehicle long before it got to him, and Terrence made sure he was up and walking by the time the spotlight swept over where he'd been a few minutes earlier. He knew that guests looking from the hotel verandas onto the dark sand couldn't tell the difference between clumps of grass and a person. Easing down onto the protected he'd chosen Terrence opened up a bag and unfolded a beach towel recently stolen from a nearby hotel swimming pool. Time to go to sleep.

Midnight. He had already sat up and started to stuff the towel into his bag before completely waking. Terrence rubbed the sleep from his eyes and looked around. No beach patrol. But he must have heard something. "I wish those egg-layers would get finished and leave," he said in disgust. As he settled down once more, the shadows seemed to waver and a scuffling sound reached his ears. He looked around for a turtle. Terrence wasn't giving up his place for some stupid animal's nesting ground, ecologists or no ecologists.

He never saw the knife. Coated in a black substance, the blade reflected no light. It slashed once and missed. Fear rose up in Terrence like a wild beast and he struggled even as a strong arm tried to force him down onto the sand. The last thing Terrence felt was a terrible rip across his throat, accompanied by the whispered words, "I have to start with someone." He wanted to ask, why me? Instead, nausea rushed across him like a tidal wave. And then failed hustler and petty thief Kylie gasped for air, gave in to the growing darkness and collapsed on the now blood-sodden beach towel.

To the naked eye, the alley looked like any other. Nearly all of the lights in the area had long ago gone out, and the lone bulb still working only made the shadows more pronounced. Roaches scurried about in the darkness, feeding on the mounds of trash overflowing a battered garbage bin. The stink of sweat and urine combined with the garbage to form an overwhelming stench.

Around the corner, on the main street where traffic, both auto and pedestrian, poured by shops and bars, the world looked entirely different. Any fantasy seemed possible to fulfill in the electric atmosphere of loud music and laughter coming from restaurants and clubs of all types. One entrance managed to stand out above all others. Combining high tech and over-the-top gaudiness, the LadyZ-N-Waiting strip club seductively invited anyone and everyone. Bright lights winked at passersby, as if to say, "We know what you want. It's okay!" Pictures of the strippers adorned the windows. Beautiful women, seductively dressed, opened the doors for those intrigued enough to enter. Liquor, dollars and temptation flowed freely in the club for the well-dressed patrons.

A back exit into the alley, however, revealed the true nature of the club. When someone ran out of money but refused to leave, that person was no longer a customer, but a problem. The alley functioned as a place to take care of those "problems" quietly and unobtrusively. After all, no one wanted the strip club's paying clientele to feel anything less than welcome.

The back door opened, and bright lights and loud music flooded the alley. A bouncer for the strip club stood in the doorway of the rear entrance for a moment, holding a struggling figure, while at the same time trying not to gag at the smell. "You're drunk and you've started asking customers for money to buy more drinks," he said, flinging the figure out the door and pointing a finger at him. "Don't come back until you're sober and have enough money to pay for the action." The bouncer slammed the door and locked it, returning the alley to its normal darkness.

The drunk lay sprawled on the rough pavement for several minutes; his limber state had actually saved him from any serious injury. He struggled to his hands and knees, where he promptly threw up. Somewhere in his alcohol haze came the thought that the alley smelled no worse, even with what he'd done. He rolled away from vomit until he could feel the wall behind him. Using it for support, he finally managed to get himself erect, straightened his clothes as much as possible, then fell against the garbage bin. With a great effort, he pushed off the bin and staggered from the alley. Another bar awaited him just down the street.

Silence, except for the muted thump of the bass from inside the club, settled on the squalid strip of concrete. From time to time, someone would venture off the main thoroughfare and down the side street fronting the alley. Once they got a whiff of the stench permeating the entrance, however, all would turn their heads and hurry past.

The hour grew later. Finally, in the deep stillness of the early morning, one of the shadows wavered for a moment, then began creeping forward. The demon looked intently at every inch of the squalid area.

As he moved to the back of the alley, the demon walked slower and slower, eventually stopping before one particular spot. He nodded to himself, then disappeared into the wall. Several minutes passed before the creature eased back into the alley, a cruel smile on his face. He had just found the perfect . . .

A thin, vertical, glowing bar appeared before the demon. Panic rose like a flood in his throat, and he took a step back, ready to flee. Before he could do so, however, a tall, powerful being filled with silver light burst into the alley and grabbed the monster.

"Shi'intor, I see you still recognize a portal from Heaven!" boomed the angel.

The demon managed to wrench his arm free from the steel grip. After the original scare, he had calmed a good bit. No demon became an advance scout without showing courage and a willingness to fight, when necessary. Shi'intor had to admit, however, that he would rather face anything other than the figure before him. Celestial light poured from the angel effortlessly, banishing every shadow in the area. The whole alleyway turned a bright hue of silver.

Claws sprang up from the demon's fingers. He pulled a sword from beneath his shadowy cloak and stood, waiting. "Come on, Toldin, I eat angels like you for lunch every day," he snarled.

The angel ignored the sword and focused on the demon's eyes. "I know you're in Hidden Beach for a reason. I'm here to make sure you don't overstep your bounds."

"You can't stop me," Shi'intor said. "There are many in this community who can't wait to give me control of their lives."

Toldin nodded sadly. "Yes, I know Satan is the prince of this world, and many will follow him. You and the Fallen Dragon's other foul spawn have *limited* freedom to touch lives. You will not ruin everyone you please. Those who have said yes to Christ are not yours to ruin."

Shi'intor sneered and raised his sword. "And if I refuse?"

The angel drew his weapon and swept it toward the demon's chest. Shi'intor just managed to fend off the attack. Then with a snarl, the demon backed into the alley wall and disappeared.

CHAPTER FOUR

"Anderson!"

The sound ripped out of the big man and quieted the whole room. Police officers busy writing up reports paused and looked up. Those booking the usual petty thieves and drunks fell silent. They all knew Jinx Monroe, captain of the Hidden Beach Police Department, had a reputation for loyalty to his personnel.. But if one of them disobeyed him, what little bit of patience he had went out the window. When that happened, most looked for cover.

"Chief, he's not here."

Maria Da Silva, an Hispanic detective as strong as Monroe, and certainly in better shape, happened to be one of the few who weren't *too* intimidated by the chief. "You sent him to one of the garages that help the tourists who visit the speedway. Checking out a fight between some irate customers and a mechanic, if I remember." Hidden Beach prided itself on being far enough away from Daytona to miss most of the craziness, yet close enough to get some of the racetrack's spillover.

Jinx Monroe's face only got redder. "He left four hours ago! He could've crawled there and back by now."

"I'm surprised you didn't make him try that."

The whisper barely reached the chief's ears. He rushed around the desk with a suddenness that made the cops take a step back in alarm. Monroe grabbed the shoulder of the man nearest him and squeezed . . . hard.

"Did you say that, Thompson?" Monroe asked in a voice gone suddenly pleasant.

Sgt. Hank Thompson winced and tried to pull away. The huge hand held him in a grip the policeman couldn't hope to escape. "Come on, chief. It's just a joke. Anderson gets everything done so perfect, I just thought you . . . you might want to give him something he couldn't succeed at."

Monroe slowly let go of Thompson's shoulder. He smiled and patted gently the shoulder he'd almost turned into ground meat. "Sorry, Thompson," he sighed. "I don't know what's wrong with me lately." The chief rubbed his eyes. "We gotta get on top of things here, with the tourist season moving in."

The door that led to the back parking lot clicked as someone slipped in. Hank Thompson looked in that direction, grateful to have a new point of focus. Just inside the door stood the youngest detective in the department's history. As usual, Maria noted, the man's black hair lay perfectly in place. The pants, crisp and starched, revealed a shirt carefully tucked in. The polished shoes gleamed, as if reflecting the blackness of the detective's hair. Today, the short sleeves looked as if they would burst under the pressure of biceps they were trying vainly to contain.

"Shouldn't all of you be working, instead of staring at me?" He asked the question in a neutral, controlled voice. Everything about Vincent Anderson spoke of control.

In three steps, Jinx Monroe covered the distance between him and his detective. "Anderson, where have you been?" he shouted.

Anderson's expression never changed. He stood his ground as if a boss well over six feet and weighing 280 pounds were not standing within ten inches of him. "Chief, I've been doing what you asked me to do." He pointed a well-manicured finger at Monroe. "But the old car the department gave me – the one that's randomly broken down on most of the detectives who've used it – broke down again."

The detective continued to look his superior calmly in the eyes. "The mechanics at Dale Levinson's garage asked me if I wanted them to take a look at the car. Turns out the only things wrong with it were a bad sensor marked for recall and a required reflash of the transmission control module. Problem solved. And they got it done in three hours." He gave a small smile. For Anderson, that meant the right edge of his mouth moved up about a millimeter. "The car runs better than the day it came off the assembly line. And it didn't cost us a penny."

Monroe refused to be mollified. "Yeah, but why didn't you radio in and let me know your situation? You could have been wounded and bleeding to death somewhere, and we wouldn't have known."

Vincent Anderson's head turned slightly. His gazed fixed on the dispatcher. "Shirl, where's the message I called in?" His voice, still calm, galvanized Shirl into action. Pieces of paper flew everywhere as she searched frantically through what had obviously become an impossibly cluttered desk. Then she held up a message.

"Oh, Chief, Vince did report in. He had no problems, and we had several other things going on, so I just forgot to tell you."

All the anger drained out of Jinx Monroe's face. His body slumped slightly. "These guys are gonna kill me," he muttered. In a trance, he shuffled toward his office. "Monroe," he said, more to himself than anyone else, "those . . . those . . ."

"Chief," warned Anderson, "watch your blood pressure."

The door into Monroe's office closed softly. After a moment, the precinct resumed its normal activities.

"You got away with another one."

The words, spoken clearly for everyone to hear, could have

only been meant for Anderson. A patrolman, Eric Batts, strolled by him, never looking in Anderson's direction.

"You got a problem, Batts?" the detective asked.

Batts insolently turned and faced Anderson. The redheaded police officer could at best be termed bulky, with muscles turning to fat. His shirt hung half out of his pants and a mustard stain covered a significant portion of his front. "You think you're so much better than the rest of us, Anderson," he sneered. 'Climb the old ladder so fast that you knock the rest of us off, right?" He reached out to punch Anderson's arm. Instead, the detective snapped up his hand and caught the offending fist, immobilizing it. The hand squeezed tighter and tighter until Batts jerked back and rubbed his own hand.

"Keep your hands off me, Batts." Anderson's voice never raised. His face showed no anger.

"You watch your back, 'Jinx's pet.' Yeah," Batts hissed, seeing the detective's reaction, "that's what everyone calls you when you're not around. So, watch it. We take care of our own."

Vincent Anderson turned away. He figured the best way to deal with people like Batts was to ignore them.

It proved to be a big mistake.

CHAPTER FIVE

A bird's-eye view of the Hidden Beach community would reveal the original town with later, additional layers adding to the size and complexity of the inhabited area. According to local tradition Henri de Lyon, an emigrant from France and the founder of Hidden Beach, had built the center of the town to resemble the "Etoile" in Paris. Encircling the Arc of Triumph, the French believed this vast oval had been made for the purpose of encouraging as many automobile accidents as possible . . . and it succeeded well. The star-like configuration of roads branching off from Hidden Beach's center was an insurance adjustor's nightmare. Not only did it make defensive driving difficult, it also made it easy to get lost. Trying simply to make a block and get back to one's original position proved nearly impossible, with no road able to parallel another. Later city planners had tried to impose order on the newer parts of the community, adding streets that actually ran perpendicular to each other. This created a "charming mish-mash of styles" (according to one guide book) that served to bewilder the tourists who ventured away from the beachfront strip and into Hidden Beach's interior.

The church Henry Watchman pastored lay closer to the beach than to the town's center. Its comfortable parsonage provided a boundary for the parking lot that lay between the two structures. Both buildings gleamed white under the bright sunshine, and in the rare moments when no cars passed, the constant roar of the ocean could be heard. A steeple shot straight up from the side of the church, its cross at the top able to be seen for miles around.

For the moment, the church was empty, which also reflected the state of Henry Watchman's stomach. The preacher had gone home for a snack.

"Henry, you've got that glazed look in your eyes again. What's going on?" Jenna Watchman's slightly plump figure was a counterpoint to her husband's trim, athletic build. Friendly green eyes looked out at the world from under blonde hair, and a face creased with smile lines. Henry called his wife "Mother Earth," because Jenna believed that if she could just give everyone enough love – and food — it would cure their ills. This time, however, her eyes squinted a bit in concern. "Don't let Raymond's threats to quit bother you. He'll be all right."

"It's not that, exactly," her husband sighed. "I'm more worried about Raymond's health. That last heart attack left him pretty weak. His emotional strength is iffy, too. For his own sake, I need to find him a replacement soon."

Henry walked over to the counter and started to pick up one of the deviled eggs his wife had arranged on a plate. She slapped his hand. "Leave those alone. They're for the women's study group this evening." Jenna pointed with the wooden spoon in her hand. Globs of mayonnaise flew toward Henry. He ducked, managing to avoid three or four. But one, bigger and lower flying than the others, hit him on the cheek. He wiped it away with his finger and popped it into his mouth.

"Mmm!" he grinned. "I love it when you preach at me."

Jenna snorted. "Honestly, the way food seems to find its way to your mouth, it's amazing you're the thin one around here." She waved her husband toward the kitchen stool. "Sit there and tell me what else is going on. You're worried about more than Raymond's job."

"You're right," he admitted. "Yesterday's sermon still bothers me."

"What do you mean? I thought you did a good job."

"Your opinion isn't shared by everyone. A couple of the members came by this morning and told me they thought I needed to preach on subjects more important and 'lofty' than profanity." Henry shook his head in frustration. "The truth be known, I think my sermon hit those men a little too close to home. Profanity was only a small part of the sermon. They seemed to miss the whole focus, which was to let everything you say in your daily relationships reflect your walk with Christ."

Jenna's eyes narrowed. "Who were they?" she demanded, waving her hands in frustration. "Don't they realize our culture is becoming cruder by the day? We're not letting our children have an innocent environment to grow up in. People can't express themselves except with four-letter words, and *those men have the nerve to accost you?*"

"You should have been the preacher, honey." Henry smiled at his wife and took the spoon out of her hand. "But right now, let's put the spoon down and get busy wiping off the walls. The spackled look, even with mayonnaise, doesn't go with the rest of our décor." He took a seat on one of the stools and frowned a bit. "The men were Ralph Johnson and David Jones."

"Isn't Ralph in the contracting business?" Jenna asked.

Henry nodded. "Yes, and he's around profanity all the time. David . . . he's just got a bad attitude. You know the man carries no weight in church opinion."

"To tell the truth," Jenna replied with a smile, "having him against something usually helps you get it passed in council." She came over to Henry and began rubbing his shoulders. "Why are some people what my grandpa called 'aginners'? They're against everything that's good and sensible."

Henry puckered his lips. Here came a joke, Jenna thought. Her husband had the ability to find humor in most situations..

"In David Jones' case, it might be because of his name and how close he lives to the ocean. If he's been called 'Davy Jones' once, he's been called it a thousand times. By now, he just growls when someone says it."

"Well, his wife tells me he growls quite a bit at home. Their daughter really suffers from his temper."

Henry grimaced. "I can see that." His eyes widened a bit as a thought struck him. "Is there any physical abuse you're aware of?"

"No, just verbal. But you know that can be bad enough. A constant wave of profanity and negativity hitting you daily can warp any child's self-image all the way into adulthood." She shook her finger at her husband. "That's why he's complaining about the sermon. He knew it hit him squarely where he lives."

Henry held up a hand in mock surrender. "Jenna, you're preaching again." Then he turned serious. "Let's add them to our personal prayer list, and ask God to begin healing their marriage and their family."

As they talked, neither Henry nor Jenna saw the misshapen figure of the demon rise from beneath the floor. His teeth glinted darkly in the kitchen light as he advanced on the couple.

CHAPTER SIX

Tourist season announced itself in different ways to different people. For the shops selling bathing suits and T shirts, the sound of cash registers opening and closing suddenly went up dramatically. Home owners living close to restaurants began shutting doors and windows, trying to keep the blare of music around the clock from intruding. For detective Vincent Anderson, tourist season could actually be *felt* in the police station. A palpable rise in the excitement/tension level hovered around everyone . . . even the chief.

As if aware of Anderson's thoughts, Jinx Monroe opened his door a crack and looked toward Vincent and the detective sitting at the adjacent desk. "Da Silva, Anderson. I need the two of you."

Maria Rodriguez looked at Vincent and shook her head. He knew she wanted him not to cross the chief right now. The two of them walked into the office and started to sit down.

"Don't bother," Monroe grunted. "There's been a report of a dead body down on the beach. I want the two of you to see what you can find out." He grimaced and then glanced up from the phone message. "We try to keep drugs out, but it's difficult. In any case, murders don't help our image with tourists."

The chief lowered his voice. "The owner of the motel closest to where the body was found would like the motel kept out of the papers, if possible. I'm sure you two understand."

Anderson frowned and opened his mouth to respond, and Maria put a warning hand on his arm. He paused for a moment, then said, "We'll get right on it, chief."

"And this time, Anderson, if you're going to be late, make sure you get through to me, personally." Monroe's face began to turn red. "You understand?"

The detective never moved a facial muscle. "Yes sir. I understand." He wheeled around and glided out of the office.

Monroe sighed again. He was probably using up his daily quota of sighs early, he noted. "Da Silva, take care of him. He's good, but not as good as he thinks he is." The chief stood up. "I don't want things getting out of hand."

Maria's face split into a big grin. "Don't worry, sir. 'Mamma Maria' will take care of him and he'll never even know it."

The chief stared sightlessly at the desk for several long moments after the two detectives had left. "The boy may not even know it, but he's gunning for my job," he mumbled to the empty office. Then he grimaced at the unintentional pun and got back to work.

———

Maria turned the car down a side street leading directly onto the beach and parked beside the "Nite's Sleep" motel. Painted in blue and white colors that had faded from the combination of wind, sand and salt, the motel had obviously seen better, more prosperous days. Its clientele consisted of those who came to Hidden Beach to relax, but whose desire for a vacation exceeded their bank account balance.

The afternoon sun pushed hard at the two detectives as they exited the car. Maria noticed Vincent ignoring the heat, and wondered if he ever felt anything at all. *Everyone is driven by something*, she mused. *We just haven't found yours yet.*

The figure coming toward them across the parking lot certainly felt the effects of the summer day. A small, rotund man, he seemed about to drown in the circles of sweat staining his Hawaiian shirt. "I'm the manager. The one who called about the . . . the *incident*." He motioned for them to follow him around the side of the motel and into the pool area fronting the beach. Several heads raised themselves off of towels and beach chairs to see if anything exciting might be happening.

"Over here," the manager whispered. "Try not to look too official," he added. "Maybe you could smile some while you talk to me. Kinda like we're just friends, and you stopped to see me during a lunch break."

"We're not friends, and this is official." Maria winced at the words as Vince stared down the manager.

"Come on, Vince. Lighten up." She patted his shoulder and tried to get a smile out of him. No luck.

"What's your name?" the detective continued in a no-nonsense tone.

"Sessions. Arnold Sessions," the manager replied. Maria could see the sweat stains growing on the man's shirt. Vince could certainly handle this in a better way. A couple more minutes in that vein, and their witness would be so nervous there'd be no more information forthcoming. She decided to step in.

"Mr. Sessions, it took a great deal of courage to do your civic duty and call us. I really appreciate your willingness to cooperate with the police." She watched Vince grimace and Sessions relax.

"Of course we'll try to be as discreet as possible." She gestured vaguely toward the beach. "But, could you show us where you found the body?"

The three of them wound their way through the pool area, carefully stepping around groups of tanning tourists intent on raising their chances for skin cancer later in life. Arnold led them down a flight of steps and out onto the beach. Talk would be easier to keep private here. The pounding of the waves ensured only those within a few feet would be able to hear anything said.

They walked about fifty yards further up the sand. Maria could see a piece of what looked like black tarp lodged against the wall separating the motel from the beach.

"The body's under here," the manager said. "If you don't mind, I'll wait in my office 'til you're finished. You can ask me any questions in private." He started to turn away, but only got a few steps.

"Don't leave, Mr. Sessions. That's an order." The manager turned to see Vincent staring at him with cold eyes. "I have a number of questions that need to be answered right here."

Maria eased into Vincent's line of vision and frowned at him. "Umm," he added belatedly, "I realize this is difficult, but it will help us a lot if you remain in the vicinity."

Oh well, it's a start, Maria thought.

"Are you the one who found him?" Vincent continued.

Sessions started sweating again. "Yes," he admitted. "I come down this part of the beach every day. Make sure our portion stays clean. You wouldn't believe how many beer cans I pick up. When I think of the lawsuits we could have from cut feet, it makes me . . ."

"Please, Mr. Sessions." Maria could see Vince beginning to lose patience. "What time did you find the body?"

Arnold shook himself, as if trying to get up the courage to talk about the incident. "I got delayed because of trying to oversee repairs to a couple of rooms some partiers trashed last night. I got out here about noon. Lots of cans to pick up. When I saw the tarp, I thought at first some bum had copped it – excuse me, I meant no insult -- for a shelter. I didn't want to get assaulted or anything, so I just kicked easy at the end of the tarp and then jumped back." He shook his head. "Nothing happened. I started to kick at it again, when the wind blew up a corner." Arnold's eyes got a faraway look. "That's when I saw the blood."

Maria nodded to Vince. They put on gloves and carefully lifted the tarp.

A sharp intake of breath came from behind them. Vince ignored it. "Whoever did this had quite a bit of strength." He pointed at the knife protruding from the corpse's chest. "The guy struggled, but the killer overpowered his victim. 'X,' whoever he is, held this guy down, slashed his throat and then buried the knife in his chest, all the way up to the hilt." He paused for a moment. "Of course, the victim probably never felt the blow to the chest. He'd already pumped most of his blood out onto the beach by that time."

The sound of retching could be heard from Arnold.

"Vince, I think I know this guy." Maria stooped to get a closer look. "He's a small-time con and petty thief. Name's Terrence Dunnigan. I've arrested him several times." She turned to Arnold. "This Terrence has probably stolen from several of your guests this summer and you never even knew it."

Arnold, pale but still sweating, stammered, "You . . . you don't suppose an angry guest got revenge, do you?"

Vince shook his head. "No, only angry managers do things like this." He quickly held up his hand, palm out. "Just kidding, Mr. Sessions." Arnold's pale face showed he failed to appreciate the humor.

"Tourists normally don't kill over stolen swim suits and a little cash." Vince ran his fingers lightly over the chest wound. "It could be about drugs, but I don't think this guy ran in that circle – Maria, look at this."

She could see him pointing to a small piece of white paper held to the corpse by the knife. Vince lay down on the sand and eased his head over to where he could see the underside of the paper. He stiffened momentarily, then sat back up.

"What is it?" Maria asked. Vince's face had flushed bright red and his breathing sounded ragged. She'd never seen this much emotion on Vincent Anderson during his brief career at the department.

"Who else has seen this body, Mr. Sessions?" Vince asked in a strained voice.

The manager shook his head. "I've tried to keep this as quiet as possible. No one else even knows about it . . . yet."

Vince turned toward Maria. "Make sure no one has the opportunity to examine this body until it gets to the police lab."

"Me? What are you going to be doing, Vince?" Maria's tone turned cold. "And since when did you start giving the orders?"

"I . . . I've got to check something out." He started walking back to the car.

"Vince, get back here," Maria yelled. "We've got more work to do."

The detective kept walking. "You can take care of the rest of it. I have somebody to talk to." He got into the car and started it up. "And don't worry, I'll call the chief and make sure someone picks you up."

"Vince!" Maria found herself shouting at a car already a block away. She slammed her fist on the wall in frustration. Wheeling around, she found herself face to face with a sweating, trembling motel manager. Maria took a couple of deep breaths to calm herself. "Let me get someone to come pick up the body. Then we'll go back into your office where we can talk in private." She smiled a smile she didn't feel. "Your office is air-conditioned, isn't it?"

That did the trick. She could see Arnold thinking about the cool air already. He nodded. "As soon as you're ready, detective."

CHAPTER SEVEN

The demon shuffled toward the couple, intent on attack. Henry and Jenna continued talking, oblivious to imminent danger, planning how to help a troubled family. The demon slowed his advance and after a moment, stopped completely and raised his head, sniffing the air. A strange scent, an aroma of long-forgotten splendor . . . Several seconds passed, then the demon shook his head. Nothing.

He turned slightly, angling toward Henry Watchman. The mouth opened; a black tongue emerged and transformed into its snake form, slithering down to the floor and toward the unsuspecting pastor. Anticipation flooded the demon. Shi'intor's mission might be completed even more quickly than his superiors had envisioned.

Something shot past his vision, and before the demon could respond, a silver hand reached down and throttled the snake. "They are not yours!"

Yanked off his feet, in great pain now, the demon thrashed about as his captor dragged him outside to the car port. There, Heaven's messenger let go of the demon. Once the pressure had vanished, the pain began to subside and his freed tongue quickly went back into the dark mouth. Shi'intor had greater concerns than a bruised tongue, however. Righteous anger covered the angel like a garment as he loomed over the demon. Shi'intor grunted and rapidly backed up several steps. Toldin seemed to pulse with God's glory. He put his hand on the sword strapped to his side, ready to dispatch this enemy of Heaven.

"Wha . . . what are you doing here?" the demon stammered. "I'm only interested in the man. I promise to leave the woman alone."

"You. Promise." The angel's eyes bored into his adversary. "Your master is the father of lies, and you're just like him." He took a step toward the demon. "Leave both of them alone."

Shi'intor began to gather his wits. He had been chosen for one particular reason: he would not scare easily. The servant of darkness slowly shook his head, dingy scales fluttering with the action. "You know what I sense," he said. "There may be an open door for Satan in the human's life right now." Obsidian eyes, little more than slits, narrowed as he prepared to attack.

The angel raised his hand. "Heaven is aware of what you know. In spite of that, the pastor is not yours."

"That's impossible!" the demon thundered. "Look at what he's done. By all rights, I should have access to him!"

Toldin refused to give ground as the demon began advancing. "Henry Watchman may yet fall under your influence, but there is nothing here for you right now. You have the right to try to tempt him, but you may not assault and ruin him."

"Then I'll assault you," snapped the demon. A scaly fist whipped toward the angel, but before it could connect, the angel grabbed the fist with his own hand and swung the creature around and to the ground. Even as Shi'intor hit, he was rolling into the throw, coming up against Toldin and pushing hard. The angel stumbled for just an instant, then recovered enough to pull out his sword and slash at the demon. Shi'intor barely managed to block the attack with his own hastily-drawn sword. They stood face-to-face, panting with exertion.

"You will not ruin Henry Watchman," the angel said once more.

"Maybe not now." The demon looked at Toldin appraisingly and begin to disappear. "But you've noticed I am getting stronger."

CHAPTER EIGHT

Lamar Johnson watched his clientele carefully. The owner/manager of "Miracle Beach Gym" knew his workout facility couldn't boast being the biggest or the newest. But he'd carved a niche in the fitness world by paying attention to his members, constantly working the floor, giving encouragement, correcting faulty posture during workouts. "Lamb," as most people called him, looked more like a lion, or, because of his skin, more like a black puma. Several body building awards lined the shelf in his office, won in the years before he left competition voluntarily, disgusted with the rise in steroid use. A gentle demeanor and quiet humor served to make everyone feel at ease in the giant's presence. His size and ripped physique, however, assured a well-run, orderly gym.

"Reverend, how's it going?" The minister, forty minutes into his workout, smiled and nodded. Lamb's eyes followed Henry Watchman as the minister flowed through his exercises. Some clients were in love with themselves, glued to the mirrors and their images. Others talked almost incessantly, working their mouths more than anything else. Watchman, however, always seemed to be in a "zone" when he began his workout. His reps and weight levels would have been difficult for anyone, but

Watchman never let up. He seemed incapable of idle chat during these times and, truth be known, his intensity caused others to leave him alone until he finished.

"Lamb." His assistant's voice carried over the sounds of weight machines and treadmills.

"Whatcha need, Billy?"

"I have a husband and wife who are interested in joining. They want to talk to you."

Lamb nodded to Watchman and moved off to take care of the couple. He gave them a quick tour of the facility, introducing them to several other members. By the time he'd answered their questions and explained the dues and rules of the establishment, they were ready to join.

"Billy will help you with the paperwork," he told them. "For your first sessions, I'll personally be helping you design a workout and checking to make sure you're following proper form."

The man smiled and shook Lamb's hand. "Thanks for the time. We're excited about being here – and, quite frankly, we're a little scared. We've never done this before." His wife nodded in agreement.

"You'll fit in well here," Lamb said. "A lot of our regulars were just like you at the beginning. That's why I try to take a personal hand in helping you get familiar with all the machines." He gestured to the chairs in his office and they sat down. As the couple started the application process with Billy, Lamb stepped back out into the gym.

He nearly collided with Henry Watchman. The minister had showered and was on his way out the door. "Henry, got a minute?" Lamb asked.

Watchman looked at his watch, then nodded. "Sure, Lamar, my next appointment isn't for another hour."

Lamb grinned. Only a very small group of friends could get away with calling him by his first name. He motioned for Henry to join him in the small coffee bar. They sat down at a table, and

Lamb looked over his shoulder to make sure Billy still sat occupied in the office.

"I don't want to put too much on you, Henry, but I've got a favor to ask."

Henry nodded. "What's up?"

Lamb lowered his voice. "You know that Billy got married about six months ago?"

Henry nodded again.

"The other day, Billy's wife, Cherie, came to see me and my wife. She looked hysterical and it took us a long time to calm her down. Seems she discovered Billy's been going to a certain strip club downtown. She said Billy had been irritated all the time for the last couple of weeks, and she couldn't do anything to please him."

"How did she find out about the strip club?" Henry asked.

"The night Cherie came to see us, she'd followed Billy to the club. She wouldn't go inside at first, but after an hour, she'd had enough. So she marched inside, confronted him and some stripper, and got herself and Billy thrown out. When they got home, Billy became furious, according to her. Told her he didn't appreciate her butting into his personal life and refused to discuss it any further."

Lamb shook his head. "I'll be honest, Henry, I'm not sure how to handle this. Billy doesn't know that I know, and I'm afraid if I confront him it will fall back on Cherie and make things worse." He looked up at Henry. "Could you maybe talk to Cherie and, if he's willing, to Billy as well?"

Henry motioned toward the office. Billy had completed the paper work and headed toward them. "I'll talk to Cherie and get back with you. If Billy's willing to discuss this, I think I can help them."

"Thanks, Henry." Lamb smiled and shook his head. "Muscles I can take care of, but marriages are another thing."

As Billy moved toward them, a man brushed by, excused himself, and sat down at the table next to Lamb and Henry.

"Reverend Watchman," he said. "My name's Vincent Anderson. I've seen you here several times."

"Just call me Henry," the pastor responded. He took a closer look at Anderson. "Am I mistaken, or did I see you at church last week?"

Anderson nodded. "I'll try not to use any profanity while you're here."

Henry flushed. "Well, at least you listened to the sermon. That's more than I can say about some of my members."

Anderson stood up. "If I don't have to work this Sunday, I'll be back." His eyes seemed to bore into the minister. "Everyone needs a moral reminder from time to time . . . even you."

"Especially me," Watchman affirmed. "I can't lead people any farther in their spiritual life than where I am myself." He smiled a smile he didn't feel. "I'll look forward to seeing you again."

"You can be sure of that . . . Henry." Anderson turned to walk away, then stopped. "By the way, I never see you doing any aerobic exercises here, only weights. Yet you're in excellent shape. Just curious, but how do you do it?"

Henry paused before answering. "I didn't know you were watching me so closely, Vincent. But, you're right. I prefer running on the beach. I like the solitude, and the beauty makes me run longer."

Anderson finally smiled back. "Running on the beach? That's one reason to go there, I suppose. But what do you do in the summer? It gets awfully hot out there."

"If I don't have a meeting, I'll run at night," Henry said, not feeling comfortable with the personal nature of this conversation.

"Yeah, I thought maybe you'd say that. In fact, weren't you out there late Sunday night?"

Something washed over Henry Watchman; something unclean that made him want to take another shower. "Vincent, how'd you know that? I guess I should be flattered that you seem to be taking such an interest in me."

Vincent waved a careless hand. "You'd be surprised at all the people I'm interested in. But no, no. It's nothing like that. I just happened to be down on the beach at about the same time. You didn't see me, but I passed you jogging in the other direction." He turned to leave once more. "See you in church next Sunday."

"What was all that about?" Lamb wondered.

Henry shook his head. "He's wound pretty tight, wouldn't you say? I don't want to be around when it finally comes loose."

————

Jinx Monroe's voice cut through the police station's hubbub. "Anderson, Da Silva, get in here!" Anderson, already close to the chief's office, stepped aside to allow Maria passage in front of him. Monroe motioned them impatiently toward the chairs, at the same time getting up to close the door. Da Silva raised her eyebrows at Vincent, but said nothing. The door to the chief's office seldom stayed closed.

"You guys want any coffee?"

That got another raised eyebrow from Da Silva. The chief *never* offered any of the private stock of coffee he brewed in his office. Both detectives accepted the coffee, and silence filled the small office for a minute while the three sipped from their mugs.

"Well, this is certainly pleasant, chief." Anderson put down his coffee and gave a stiff smile. "I could get used to this every morning when I come in. If you could have it ready tomorrow . . ."

"Cut the crap, Anderson." The chief's face began to redden. "I'm just trying to be polite. I know how all of you talk about me when I'm not around." Monroe rubbed his eyes. "Just trying to make things a little more pleasant, that's all."

"And we appreciate it, chief," Da Silva broke in.

Monroe swung his head around and glared at her. "Like I said, cut the crap. Anyway, hope you like the coffee." He pulled a folder from the stack on his desk and handed each of them several photos. "Now, down to business."

As the two detectives flipped through the pictures, their captain continued to talk. "Terrence Duggan is the name of the deceased. Autopsy tells us there were no drugs in his system. He's a small time thief who stayed far away from the dangerous, high-profile crimes." Monroe gave them an additional photo. "This is one of the craziest reasons for a crime I've ever come across."

Maria Da Silva noticed two things. First, the photo showed a piece of paper that had the words, *"Use profanity and you will DIE!"* scribbled on it. Second, she saw Vince's mouth tighten as he looked at the same photo.

"This is the paper 'attached' to Duggan's chest by the knife," Monroe explained. "I'm assuming the killer wanted to send a message."

"Maybe he wants notoriety, chief," Da Silva interjected. "After all, there are some crazies out there who'll do anything for attention."

Anderson began shaking his head even as the chief said, "Well, he or she is not going to get it. We're not releasing this to the press. No one knows about the message but us. We'll see how keeping a lid on the contents of the note affects the killer."

"Chief." Anderson leaned forward slightly in his seat. For Maria, who knew Vince as well as anyone – which wasn't much – this meant the detective had gotten hold of something. "I went to church Sunday."

Monroe looked startled. "Good for you, Anderson. Good for you. Now, back to the subject at hand . . . "

"Excuse me, sir." Vincent held up his hand to apologize for interrupting. "This has something to do with the case."

The chief sighed again and reached into the drawer for a couple of antacids. "Go ahead, Anderson. Enlighten me."

"Sure chief." Vincent paused. "Uh, you know that if you'd

drink less coffee, you wouldn't have to pop those antacids so often."

Jinx Monroe's face turned a beet red, and Maria reached over and squeezed Vincent's leg *hard*.

"Anyway," he continued on hurriedly, "I happened to go to Hidden Beach Community Church last Sunday morning. The pastor is one Henry Watchman."

"Come on, get to the point," Monroe said. "If the killer didn't walk up to you, introduce himself and confess to the murder, I'm really not interested. My church going stopped a long time ago."

Marie watched as Anderson inched forward a bit more in his seat. This was going to be good. "Chief, that's almost what happened. Watchman preached a sermon with the title 'Profanity: The American Sickness.'"

"And for that, you want to charge a preacher, a respected member of this community, with murder?" Monroe shook his head in disgust.

Anderson continued in spite of the interruption. "The only person who would commit this kind of murder has to be a religious fanatic. Like, maybe, a preacher. This morning, while working out, I saw Watchman. We talked for a few minutes. He doesn't know I'm a detective. He admitted to being on the beach late Sunday night." He paused, and a tight smile flitted across his face. "If we can pinpoint him on that part of the beach where the murder occurred, then I think we have a strong suspect."

Jinx Monroe hadn't become chief of police by being slow or unwilling to make decisions. "It sounds far-fetched to me. But this is already a strange murder." He swiveled toward Da Silva. "I want the two of you to question Pastor Watchman. See what you can find out." His throat tightened, as if he'd swallowed something distasteful. "Good job, Anderson," he muttered. "Now, you guys get to work."

CHAPTER NINE

Lunchtime. Jenna Watchman watched her husband wolf down the enchiladas, refried beans and Spanish rice. She shook her head. The man's metabolism had to be running at an all-time high. He'd eaten a huge breakfast that morning, but now Henry acted as if he were starving.

"Have you no shame?" she asked, smiling. "Couldn't you slow down at least a little and talk to me in between bites?"

Her husband looked up from the plate, fork poised to enter his mouth. "Sorry, honey. You're right. It's just that after working out, I get so hungry." He looked embarrassed. "Plus, I was thinking about how to take care of a marital problem."

Jenna frowned.

"Not ours!" he added hastily. "If I can get permission, I'll share with you what's going on with a young couple I know. I'm going to need your help with this one."

Jenna knew Henry relied heavily on what she called her "mothering ability" to help him in counseling situations. What she lacked in formal education Jenna more than made up for in her seemingly endless well of compassion. That, coupled with a strong vein of common sense, helped her shed light on situations Henry couldn't have handled well alone.

A whining sound began outside the den window.

"You haven't played with Titus today," Jenna reminded her husband. "Remember what happens when he gets bored."

Henry sighed. "I simply don't have time right now. Maybe this afternoon." He pulled the den curtain aside a fraction of an inch and peered out. "It looks like the fence is holding Titus for the moment. Maybe we're finally to the point where he can't get out."

"Don't bet on it." Jenna patted Henry on the back, trying to add a little comfort to her words. "Prisoners could take escape lessons from that dog."

They went back into the kitchen and began to clean off the table. Jenna appreciated this quality, among several others, about her husband. Their schedule could be crowded, but he took the time to spend moments like these with her. She'd told him early on in their marriage that women needed time and a lot of communication with their spouses. It took awhile, but Henry had finally learned that lesson.

Titus's whining became a low rumble. Car tires could be heard crunching on the gravel in the driveway.

"Who's that?" Henry asked. Jenna took a quick peek out the window.

"It's a couple of policemen . . . wait a minute, correction: it's a policeman and a policewoman."

"Law enforcement personnel," Henry corrected, grinning.

Jenna snorted. "Whatever. You've had much more contact with that world than I have."

The doorbell rang. Henry stood up, stretched, as if trying to make his food digest faster, and moved toward the door. "I'll get it."

Jenna saw a look of surprise flit across her husband's face as he opened the door and greeted the man and woman. The female, big and strong enough to take down any criminal Jenna had ever seen, seemed pleasant enough, but tightness covered the man accompanying her.

"Pastor Watchman, I'm Detective Maria Da Silva and this is . . ."

"Vincent Anderson," Watchman interrupted. "I've already met Detective Anderson, though he neglected to tell me his profession."

In the background, Jenna frowned. Something definitely felt wrong. She lay a hand on her husband's arm. "Aren't you going to introduce me, Henry?"

Watchman shook himself and turned toward Jenna; for a moment, he'd forgotten all about her. "Of course, honey," he said. "Detectives Da Silva and Anderson, this is my wife, Jenna." Henry felt himself being pulled back from the door. "And, I've forgotten my manners. Won't the two of you come in? We just finished eating, but we'd be glad to get you a glass of tea."

"We'll come in for only a moment," Maria said. "We need to ask you a few questions and then we'll be on our way."

Vincent and Maria sat down at the table in the small kitchen, and Henry sat on one of the stools by the bar. Jenna began getting ice out for the tea.

A dark, shadowy fog oozed through the kitchen window. It hardened and took on the form of the demon assigned to Hidden Beach. Moving to a spot beside the police officers, he surveyed the four humans. The servant of Satan, the great tempter, looked for weak points where he could turn the situation to his advantage. The demon had been tempting for millennia and could quickly find where a person would be most vulnerable.

He nodded. The male police officer held the key. Shi'intor stepped over to his side and raised his mouth to the man's ear. *"You know what he did,"* the demon began whispering. *"Ruined your life . . . his fault for everything . . . knew and didn't care . . . a criminal hiding as pastor."*

"Pastor Watchman," Maria began, "could you tell me where you were last Sunday evening between 9:00 and midnight?"

"What's this all about, detective?" Henry asked. I'd like . . ."

"Just answer the question, Watchman." Vincent leaned forward as he spoke.

Maria's face tightened. "Vince . . ."

"We don't have all day for this, Maria," Anderson interrupted.

"Making you look like a fool . . . doesn't care who he hurts."

Anderson stood up and took a step toward Watchman. "Answer the question, *reverend*."

Jenna watched in alarm as her husband also stood up. He did seem to be staying calm, however. "I would really like to have a better understanding of what is going on here," he said. "I certainly don't mind answering any questions you have, but I deal with confidential information on other people all the time. I must be sure I'm not getting ready to hurt anyone by what I say or be forced to compromise any of my members."

"Just stalling . . . will get away again . . ."

"For the last time, Watchman, answer the detective's question – or else." Vincent's voice held a ragged tone Maria had never heard before.

Henry Watchman simply shook his head. "I must have more information before I tell you anything."

Vincent's lips drew back in a snarl. It started low in his throat and grew louder and more intense. Then he raised his right hand and threw a punch at the pastor.

Henry Watchman never raised a hand, never stepped back. He simply moved his head a fraction of an inch and let the fist sail by. "Let's calm down a bit, here, Vincent," he said. "I'm not refusing to cooperate. All I want is a little assurance no one will be compromised by what I tell you."

For her part, Maria couldn't believe what she'd just seen. "Vince, that's it. You and I need to step outside for a minute and talk." She grabbed his arm, but he shook it off and lunged for Watchman. Knocked off balance, Maria tumbled out of her chair and hit the floor. Pain blossomed in her elbow, as well as in her heart. She could see a lawsuit coming. And in the midst of the frenetic scrambling and lunging, Maria heard Jenna say, "Henry, try not to hurt him." Hurt him? The pastor's wife was worried for the detective?

The speed with which the pastor responded to this new threat, however, made Maria temporarily forget her pain. She'd seldom seen a man move so fast. In comparison, Vincent seemed to be moving through molasses. Somehow, Watchman easily avoided the onrushing detective and the flailing fists. He slipped under Anderson, slapped the heavily muscled arms aside and came up behind his attacker. Then, when he could have attacked Vincent's back, Watchman stopped. The pastor glanced over at Maria for help.

Vincent whirled around and reached for his gun.

She might be on the floor, but Maria wasn't helpless. The big detective rolled over in desperation and hit Anderson in the knees. He went down for a moment, then started struggling immediately to get back up. But when he regained his feet, he faced a furious Maria Da Silva also beginning to stand. She slammed into her fellow detective and pressed him against the kitchen wall. He tried to move his partner, but her weight against him proved too great. She began pressing a powerful arm of her own against his throat.

"Vince, that's enough!" she shouted. "Do you want to lose your job and everything you've worked for?"

He looked at her, a wild look in his eyes.

"What's gotten into you?" she asked in a quieter voice. "I've never seen you like this."

Vincent took a couple of deep breaths and then his body relaxed. He reholstered his gun and snapped the flap. She eased up the pressure on his throat and moved a foot away from him, still watching her partner like you'd watch a lion in the same cage with you.

"I'm sorry, Maria. I'm sorry. But I know what he really is." Vincent pulled a handkerchief out of his pocket and wiped his face. His body sagged visibly, as if all the energy had been sucked out. Then he turned around, walked slowly out of the house and got in the car. He never looked back at Henry or Jenna, never said a word of apology or explanation.

Maria rubbed her elbow and winced. There would be a nasty bruise growing there within the next few hours. It promised several days of discomfort. That discomfort, she thought, was nothing compared to what awaited them when she and Vince returned to headquarters.

"Here, take this." Jenna had gone to the freezer and gotten some ice cubes. She wrapped them in a hand towel and offered the homemade cold pack to Maria. "Put it on your elbow immediately, and it should keep the bruising and swelling to a minimum."

Maria ducked her head in embarrassment. Most people would be yelling police brutality and looking up their lawyer's number about this time. "I . . . I'm so sorry about what happened," she stammered. "Detective Anderson is never like this. He always stays in control, no matter what the situation."

Henry Watchman smiled and patted her shoulder. "I used to be a headstrong young man. I know what it's like to lose control." He looked at Jenna for a moment, and something seemed to pass between them. "You don't have to worry, Detective Da Silva. Neither Jenna nor I will say anything about this incident."

A huge weight seemed to lift from Maria's shoulders. Maybe things were going to be okay after all. The least she could do for this couple would be to tell them the truth, even if it proved to be unpleasant. "Pastor Watchman, I know someone will still have to come by and question you about Sunday night. But I can assure you the next time won't be anything like this one." Maria turned to go. Jenna's next words, however, stopped her.

"We'll be praying for both you and Detective Anderson. The fault of what happened here doesn't lie with you. Neither Henry nor I want you to get in trouble over it. If we can back you up in any way, let us know."

"We don't want Anderson to get in trouble, either," Pastor Watchman added. "But if he loses his temper like that with someone who's not able to defend himself, you'll have a death on your hands and a ruined career." He fixed Maria with his eyes. "If I can help him in any way, just call me." He smiled briefly. "And, as I said earlier, I have no problem telling you all about my Sunday night activities."

———

Maria drove. Without a word, she'd shoved Vincent into the passenger seat, started the car and savagely popped the car into gear. Gravel flew from the tires as she drove away from embarrassment as fast as possible. But there was a problem: embarrassment seemed to be keeping pace with the car. She couldn't outrun it.

"What in the world were you thinking, Vince?"

At least she'd waited to say anything until they were well away from the house. Maria hadn't been too sure about her partner's being able to keep his mouth shut. She needn't have worried. Vince had said nothing from the moment he'd walked out of the house.

Maria looked at him out of the corner of her eyes. His skin looked pasty and he slumped in the seat. "Vince, you've got to say something to me before we get back to the chief. We don't want to walk in there unprepared."

Silence.

"Vince!" Maria yelled. She hit the top of the dashboard with the flat of her hand. The slap caused Vince to flinch. He put his head in his hands.

"He's a murderer, Maria."

She shook her head in frustration. "C'mon, Vince. I've watched you deal with murderers before. You're cool, under control. What's the difference here?" She nudged him to try to get Vince to look at her. "Ever since you saw that body, something's happened to you. You're losing control."

"He's a murderer," Vince repeated. "A cold-blooded murderer."

And then Vincent Anderson closed his eyes to try to stop the tears, but the flood was too great, and his body rocked back and forth as he wept in the Florida sunshine.

In the back seat, one arm draped over Vincent's shoulder, the demon howled with laughter.

———

Billy Lawrence finished drying off, dropped the wet towel on the bathroom floor and reached for a clean shirt. The discarded towel, huddled in a sodden mass, looked at him reproachfully. At least, that's what it seemed to be doing. He paused, thought about it for a moment, then picked up the towel and hung it neatly over a bar until it could dry enough to be put in the clothes hamper. Billy looked around the clean, sparkling bathroom. Six months of marriage had certainly changed his habits . . . at least, some of them.

"Lunch is about ready, Billy. Can you be dressed in five minutes?"

"No problem. I'll be right there." Billy shook his head. Six months, and already the excitement of being with Cherie was fast disappearing. Sure, he loved her – or, he thought he loved her. He wasn't sure what love was anymore. Her head on his shoulder at night, the arms that embraced him when he came home, the stability he had finally found in life – all that was wonderful. But . . .

He put those thoughts out of his head as he walked into the kitchen.

Cherie had put out baked chicken, green beans, and rice with gravy. Water, filtered, filled the glasses. Billy smiled. She knew he only drank water. It looked as if he'd converted her, a lifelong tea drinker, as well. Maybe both of them had changed for the better during their brief stint together.

"Honey, Lamb's wife called me while you were in the shower. They wanted to know if we could go to dinner and a movie with them tonight. What do you think?"

Billy could feel a flush beginning to creep into his face. He heard the slight shaking in Cherie's voice that betrayed her real intent. "Come on, Cherie, why don't you say what you really mean." He looked at the floor, unable to face her. "You really want to know if I'm going back to that club tonight."

"No, Billy, I swear that's not it. They really did just call and invite us."

Billy was silent for a long moment. Cherie seemed unable to breathe. Then he said, "Sure, let's go. For tonight, anyway, I've got nothing else to do." He finally raised his head to look at her. The smile he tried to put on his face was forced and pitiful. He thought it probably looked just like the smile coming from Cherie.

They sat down to eat in silence.

CHAPTER TEN

Change can be both exciting and cruel, even for a town like Hidden Beach. An area about three blocks off of the beach and a world away from the town's center had once claimed most of the tourist dollars. In the '80s, souvenir shops fighting for prime land jammed up against one another, greedily swallowing the money that flowed in a seemingly unstoppable torrent. Two elements held the key to the area's prosperity: the main road these stores fronted, and an old bridge with a "split personality." Almost every hour, traffic stopped when the bridge opened to let boats continue down the intra coastal waterway. As the cars idled and their occupants turned more impatient, the stores became a place to escape both the heat and the boredom. The locals called the area "Dollar Town."

At the turn of the millennium, Hidden Beach began construction of a new bridge. Wide enough to hold four lanes of cars and high enough to allow boats free passage at all times, the bridge spelled trouble for stores in "Dollar Town." The main road went a different direction – and so did the money. Souvenir shops slid toward bankruptcy; restaurants closed; rent fell sharply. Into the vacuum came enterprises used to dealing with the desperate. Pawn shops replaced restaurants. "Loans 'till payday" appeared on windows. Drug dealers and their followers now gave an ironic twist to the name "Dollar Town." Some people actually felt the new strip clubs beginning to take over represented a step up for the area. Those with a discerning eye, however, knew better.

None of this mattered to the tall redhead. Her body swayed seductively with each step she took in the late afternoon sun. A narrow waist and lush figure threatened to split apart the revealing tank-top and shorts. Wanda Lemming waited for the hoots and whistles she knew would be forthcoming from a group of men standing on the other side of the street.

They did not disappoint her.

"Hey babe! Come across the street and I'll give you a surprise," one of the braver of them called out.

Wanda had learned a long time ago how to deal with these types of males. She stopped, turned and looked them square in the eyes. "Boys, I'll bet I can give you a better surprise." A seductive smile moved across her lips. "I'll be on stage and waiting for you at the LadyZ-N-Waiting tonight, beginning at 10:00." Wanda pursed her lips and blew a kiss. "You won't be disappointed," she purred.

The young men laughed and punched one another. "We just might be there," the spokesman called out. "You better be ready."

The tall redhead stuck her hip out and wiggled it at them. "You'd better bring money. I'm expensive . . . but I'm worth it."

The whistles followed her through the next block, all the way to the strip club that had her name as the latest headliner. She turned down the street beside the LadyZ-N-Waiting, walked to the back, then made her way down the narrow alley behind the club. A burly man stood beside a rusty, creaking door. "Good afternoon, Ms. Lemming," he said, stepping back so she could enter.

Wanda smiled again. This time, however, she meant it. "Hello, Tony. It's good to see you." Tony treated her with respect. No other man did, she thought bitterly. Wanda wished she could find more caring guys like him. But even if they existed, she knew they'd never be interested in her.

Wanda Lemming had learned some hard lessons in her relatively young life. One of the hardest had been pounded into her early: she couldn't attract the good men. Sure, their eyes might lock onto her during a five-minute dance. For those few minutes, she might even have them in the palms of her hands. But after the show, they always went home to the "good girls," and Wanda went home alone. Men came and went in her life.

Her shoes clicked on the tile floor as Wanda walked to her dressing room. Once inside, where no one could see her, the smile drained from her face. Her body slumped and she put out a shaking hand to support herself. "I don't know if I can do this anymore," she whispered to no one.

Everywhere she looked, mirrors showed her reflection. Twenty stunning redheads gazed back at her. *Thank goodness, the mirrors can't show how I hurt*, she thought. *But they can't reveal the way out of a dead-end life either, or show me how to change all this.*

Wanda had learned to trust only in herself. Her mother and grandfather had made sure of that years ago. She leaned against one of the walls, careful not to let the peeling paint get on her, and closed her eyes.

"Wanda, get your lazy self in here right now!"

The words slammed into the 10-year-old girl and caused her hands to begin to tremble. She struggled to get a brush through her tangled red hair. It seemed to get thicker and more unmanageable each day. Again and again she fought to bring some order to those tresses. She'd get fussed at for taking too much time in the bathroom. But Wanda knew a worse scolding awaited her if she appeared without her hair perfectly brushed.

"Wanda!"

Her mother's tone now held a hint of panic in it. The little girl could figure out what that meant. Grandfather was driving up. She hurriedly put the hairbrush away, slipped on her shoes and ran into the front room.

The ramshackle house Wanda, her mom and her grandfather lived in had needed a fresh coat of paint for more than a decade. The wood had rotted in several places. Some roof shingles had long ago blown off and now the house rewarded its apathetic owner with multiple leaks when it rained. Inside, the frayed carpet revealed deep stains from standing water and neglected food spills.

Wanda slid to a stop beside her mom just as the front door opened. The two of them looked at each other. The stench of stale alcohol hit them even before the man appeared. Wanda's mom moaned, "Oh no. Pop's drunk again."

His big frame suddenly filled the doorway. He staggered into the room and fell heavily. Wanda's mom managed to partially catch him. Wanda rushed over to help her carry/drag him to the tattered couch. Her grandfather was snoring before they could get a pillow under his head.

Wanda's mom sighed. "We're lucky this time," she said to her daughter. "You get on to school now. I'll handle him when he wakes up."

"What about breakfast?" Wanda asked as her tummy rumbled.

"You shoulda thought about that earlier, you lazy girl!"

Wanda's eyes began to glisten with tears. "But I already put some clothes on to wash like you asked. That didn't leave me any time to fix breakfast."

"Then maybe you'll get up earlier next time," her mother hissed. A wicked smile crossed her face. "You oughtta be glad I'm teaching you these lessons while you're still young." She swatted Wanda hard on the bottom, pushing her out the door. "Besides, when you're hungry, you learn more."

As she walked, Wanda dried her eyes. She wasn't going to let any of the other kids see her crying; it showed weakness. And even at this young age, Wanda knew when others saw you look weak, they attacked. She'd show her mom how tough she could be. One day she'd ...

"Wanda, you in there?"

The doorknob rattled. Wanda stood up, straightened her back and forced a smile on her lips. Some things never changed. It didn't pay to let the owner of the LadyZ-N-Waiting see you cry, either. "Sure, Mr. Jamison," she breathed seductively as she opened the door. "I'm always here for you."

CHAPTER ELEVEN

Chief Monroe stuck his head out into the corridor and looked around until he spied a rotund, rumpled patrolman. Eric Batts must have felt someone's eyes on him, because he turned around to face the chief's office. He'd obviously just come in the station, because he still wore the usual mirrored sunglasses. Monroe silently crooked his finger at Batts and then stepped back into his office. Batts grunted as he made an effort to get out of his chair. He pushed his sunglasses up on top of his head and grinned inside as he made his way toward Jinx Monroe's office. The patrolman knew most of the police officers were watching him in his efforts. The others could think he was out of shape, and they could look down on him for it. But Batts also knew how deceptively fast he was. Most of the morons he worked with didn't know how much of an athlete he'd been in high school. The weight certainly slowed him down some, but his reflexes still proved remarkably quick. He kept those reflexes his own private secret. He had used that secret, when needed, to his advantage . . . and he would do so again.

"Close the door, Batts."

Eric eased into the office and stayed standing. It never paid to sit down in the chief's office without an invitation.

The demon Shi'intor pushed through the door and moved toward a corner of the room. This conversation, he thought, should prove interesting! Any information now would help him in his mission to ruin Henry Watchman.

"Tell me about Robert Jamison and the LadyZ-N-Waiting."

No invitation to sit down, Batts noted.

"What do you mean, sir?"

Chief Monroe frowned in exasperation. "I hear Jamison may be using his girls for more than dancing. Some people in the neighborhood say prostitution is on the rise, and most of them point to that strip club as the source." He looked up at Eric Batts. "For some reason, I can't remember exactly why, it seems to me that you and Jamison spend a lot of time together." He stood up unhurriedly until he towered over the patrolman. "What do you know about the prostitution?"

Eric Batts held up his hand, as if to ward off his chief. "Sir, you know I don't try to hide anything from you."

Monroe snorted at this.

"No, sir," protested Batts. "Here, I'm telling you the truth." He swallowed the bile rising in his throat. "I don't deny knowing Jamison. And I . . . I may have heard some of those same rumors about prostitution. But I don't know anything for sure."

To Batts' relief, Jinx Monroe seemed to buy it.

"Okay, for now I'll take you at your word," the chief growled as he sat down again. "But I want you to go see your friend Jamison and give him a message from me." He stopped to make sure Batts was looking at him. "Let him know that if I find *even one* girl prostituting herself, I'll close his whole operation down so fast he won't know what hit him." He shook his head in disgust. "I hate those strip clubs anyway. They don't make our city a better place." Monroe stood up once more. "Get it done quick, Batts."

Eric Batts gave a convulsive nod. "I'll get on it as soon as possible, sir."

"I'm assuming that 'soon as possible' means as soon as you

leave this office. Am I right?" The chief tried to take some of the sting out of his response by smiling. It didn't work. Eric Batts blanched and nodded so hard his glasses fell off his head and clattered on the floor. As he bent over to pick them up, his shirt-tail came out.

Good grief, Monroe thought, the man's going to disintegrate on the spot! He forced some calm into his voice. "Take a minute to get yourself presentable before you leave," he said. The patrolman nodded *a third time*. He must have figured anything else he said would only get him in deeper trouble. Monroe maintained an impassive face, but inside he allowed himself a small moment of pleasure. He'd already deduced Batts and Jamison were trying to get a fledgling prostitution ring started. This should nip it in the bud. Batts might be greedy and unprincipled, but he didn't have a death wish.

Monroe came around his desk, opened the door for Batts and ushered him out. Then he looked around for his next victim. When the chief found him, he called out, "Anderson, we have a mess to fix. We might as well go and get it over with."

Batts, for his part, quietly let out a sigh. It was always good to get the chief's spotlight of attention onto someone else.

The demon nodded in satisfaction. His choice of the LadyZ-N-Waiting as a nexus was proving correct. He growled with plea-sure as he contemplated whose life to ruin next, using the damage to help bring down Henry Watchman.

Shi'intor turned to leave, when a movement in the opposite corner of the room caught his attention. He looked around, and instinctively drew his sword. Not fifteen feet away stood the angel!

"How long have you been here?" the demon demanded. What he really wanted to ask was, "Why didn't I see you until just now?"

Toldin advanced a step. "Long enough," he stated. "My even being here should tell you how much I know about your strategy." He advanced one more step. "Watch yourself, demon. You tread on dangerous ground."

"You're the one on dangerous ground," Shi'intor growled. "Lust, greed and lies flow into me every moment I spend in Hidden Beach. I'm growing stronger by the minute. You, on the other hand, have made a poor decision in choosing to fight me in such a corrupt place."

Toldin laughed. It startled the demon, because it was so unexpected. "You, Shi'intor, dare to talk to me of poor decisions?" The angel gestured toward heaven. "Do you remember when you were an angel of light? Can you still recall the beauty of heaven, the holiness of God's throne room, the divine love that constantly enveloped us?"

Shi'intor's face darkened as those ancient memories returned with painful clarity.

"When you and the others rebelled, I still remember my amazement as I first saw the ugliness of sin change you forever," Toldin continued. "We fought, Shi'intor, and you lost that day . . . as you will lose again." The angel advanced a third step. "Your poor decisions ruined you then, and they will defeat you here.

Shi'intor grimaced, but gave ground as the angel moved toward him. He nearly choked from his fury at being reminded of what once was. " My growing strength cannot be stopped," he hissed. "Soon, angel, I will no longer retreat and disappear." The snakes writhed in his open mouth. "Ssssoon."

The books lining Pastor Watchman's shelves covered a plethora of subjects. Everything from evangelism to systematic theology, from prayer to church growth awaited him. At the moment, however, none of them held inspiration for next Sunday's sermon. His mind kept drifting back to the lunchtime encounter with Vincent Anderson. That man seemed to hate him; yet they'd never met before the previous Sunday morning!

He sighed and opened his Bible. If not inspiration for the sermon, perhaps he could find some comfort and peace. Psalms had always been a good place to look.

Henry thought of David. The man who'd written most of the Psalms might have been a king with lots of talents and riches, but he'd also had huge problems. David's poetic prayers to God during those trying times had, in turn, blessed untold numbers of individuals going through difficult moments.

The passage from Psalm 9:9-10 beckoned to Henry: *"The LORD is a refuge for the oppressed, a stronghold in times of trouble. Those who know your name will trust in you, for you, LORD, have never forsaken those who seek you."*

Pastor Watchman closed the Bible and bowed his head. "Help me to remember you are here with me, God, especially in the tough times. And, thank you for always loving me," he prayed. After a moment, he gave a rueful shake of his head. How quickly one could forget all the promises of God! Focusing on life's present circumstances, instead of relying on God's faithfulness, condemned you to losing your joy and letting doubt get the best of you.

The ringing of the phone pulled him out of his reverie.

"Henry." Jenna's voice sounded strained. "You need to come home right now. Detective Anderson is back, and this time, the police chief is with him."

"I'll be right there."

Henry breathed a quick prayer for calm and wisdom as he started across the parking lot. A police car sat in the driveway, and he saw people slowing down in their cars to gawk as they passed. The members would certainly have something to talk about this week!

Henry walked into the kitchen and encountered Detective Anderson and the chief sitting at the table, drinking tea. Anderson held himself stiffly erect. The other man looked relaxed. He and Jenna were talking about traffic problems during the tourist season.

"Yes Ma'am," the chief admitted. "You're right that we don't have to put out officers to check speeding during this time of the year. It's hard enough just to get up to the speed limit with thousands of cars on roads designed for a few hundred at a time." He looked up just in time to see Watchman enter the room.

"Hello, pastor," he said. "I'm Jinx Monroe, chief of the Hidden Beach police force." The big man stood up and put out his hand. An easy smile still flickered on his face. Behind him, Vincent Anderson reluctantly stood up, as well.

Henry put a smile on his face he didn't feel. "I guess I should feel flattered. Neither Jenna nor I have ever gotten this much attention from the police before."

"I don't believe that," Anderson muttered.

Chief Monroe glanced casually at his detective and Vincent shut up.

"We're here for two reasons, Pastor Watchman," Monroe continued. "First, Detective Anderson has something to tell you."

The detective turned red. Henry couldn't be sure if embarrassment or anger had been the cause. "Pastor and Mrs. Watchman, I'm sorry for my attitude earlier today." Vincent paused, and his mouth looked as if it held something bitter. "Regardless of how I feel about someone's guilt, I admit I acted without provocation." At this, he actually hung his head in shame. "I've been guilty of unprofessional behavior."

Henry moved next to his wife and put an arm around her shoulders. "As we said to Detective Da Silva, there's nothing to forgive. We work all the time with people under pressure." Henry looked Vincent directly in the eyes. "If God has offered us His grace and forgiveness, we'd certainly be lacking if we didn't offer that same forgiveness to others."

To Henry's surprise, Vincent looked as if he'd been struck. He turned pale and grabbed the table for support. "Chief Monroe," he said in a strangled voice. "Can I wait outside in the car?"

"Detective Anderson, I need you here with me right now."

Jinx Monroe's smile never wavered. He motioned toward a chair. "I know it's not my house, Pastor Watchman, but would you sit down and tell me where you were Sunday evening?" He held up a hand to forestall Henry's question. "And, yes, I'll give you an explanation first."

Henry sat down. "Go ahead," he said. "I'm ready to cooperate in any way possible, as long as I don't compromise any of my members."

"I don't think this has anything to do with your members, pastor . . . unless they're thieves and con men," Chief Monroe chuckled. Then he turned to Vincent. "Give the Watchmans a quick recap of what happened Sunday night."

"Yes sir." Vincent cleared his throat and managed to look Henry Watchman straight on. "Sometime around midnight – maybe even as early as 11:00 p.m. — someone killed a man by the name of Terrence Duggan on the beach next to the Nite's Sleep Motel. When the motel manager found the body Monday morning, slash marks covered his throat." Vincent nodded to Chief Monroe. "I think that about covers it."

Monroe nodded. "We've learned that you were on that part of the beach sometime during the late hours of Sunday night. We'd like to know why you were there and if you saw anything out of the ordinary."

Henry Watchman paused a long moment. "First, I can affirm that I was jogging on the beach at about 11:00 Sunday night. I do it all the time. Second, I'm sorry, but I saw nothing unusual or suspicious during that time. " He felt Jenna moving closer to him. She placed a protective hand on the back of his neck. "However, I am wondering why this simple explanation couldn't have been given to me the first time the police dropped by."

Vincent Anderson flushed again. Chief Monroe, however, remained unfazed. "Pastor Watchman, do you care about your people? Do you want the best for them?"

"Of course," Henry said.

"In the same way, Vincent Anderson cares deeply about the law. He takes quite seriously his duty to protect citizens from criminals and predators." He nodded at Vincent. "Detective Anderson is one of our finest police officers. In this case, his zeal for the law led him to make some assumptions that have caused him embarrassment." Here, Monroe frowned. "And, when something reflects badly on one of my people, it affects the whole force."

Henry stood up slowly. "Again, chief, you don't have to worry about us. This story will go no farther." Then, he grinned at Vincent. "Detective Anderson," he said. "You were out there on the beach. You could be a suspect – or a witness – just as much as me."

He'd intended it to be a joke, but the detective's mouth tightened. Henry also noticed the chief's forehead furrow ever so slightly. Did he actually suspect Vincent?

"We'll be going, Pastor Watchman." The chief nodded to Jenna. "Mrs. Watchman, thank you for the tea and the time." He and Vincent exited the house, got into their car and drove off, accompanied by the frantic barking of Titus.

CHAPTER TWELVE

As he drove slowly out of the church's parking lot, Vincent could feel the chief's eyes burning into him. "Chief, thanks for taking up for me back there. I still think that 'reverend' is as guilty as . . ."

"You pull a stunt like that again, Anderson, and I'll bust you so far down a new recruit will be above you in rank. Do you understand?"

The words, delivered in an affable voice, still got their message across. Vincent stiffened, but only said, "Yes sir. I understand. It won't happen again."

"Good." Monroe's tone became businesslike. "I want you and Detective Da Silva to put a tail on this preacher. Whatever you do, don't make it obvious. I want the two of you in plain clothes and an unmarked vehicle – wait a minute. Make that two unmarked vehicles. In this summer traffic, one of you could easily lose him, and I don't want you having to turn on a siren to catch up. That would blow your cover."

"How soon do you want us to start, chief?"

"Be on him by 9:00 this evening," Monroe said. "I really don't think he's the one we're looking for, but if Watchman is somehow the murderer, he's probably not ready to stop killing.

Whoever he is, we didn't publicize his note, so his cause didn't get the notoriety he'd hoped."

"So you think he'll kill again?"

The chief nodded. "It might be two days; it might be three. But he – or she – will probably murder again. Right now, the preacher's our only lead. If it happens to be Watchman, I want you and Da Silva there to stop him before he succeeds."

Jinx Monroe rubbed his face. "The last thing we need to ruin the economy further is the fear of a serial killer at the height of tourist season." He grabbed Vincent's bicep. "Get the killer quick, Anderson."

A grim smile flickered over Vincent's face. "I'll do my best, sir."

"Anderson . . ." The chief paused until they'd gotten to a stop light and the detective could fully look at him.

"Yes sir?"

"Get in control of your emotions. I know I've said in the past that you should loosen up some, but the pendulum has swung too far in that direction. I need that 'self-contained' detective back."

Monroe could see Anderson's shoulders straighten a bit. "You don't have to worry about me anymore, sir. I won't embarrass you or the force again."

The chief grunted. "Good. Retirement's been looking awful good the last few days. I want to enjoy work a little more and worry about you a lot less."

CHAPTER THIRTEEN

Everyone has moments that significantly change the course of his or her life. An accounting student attends a concert, falls in love with what she's heard, and changes her major. A man sits down next to a woman in a coffee shop, strikes up a conversation and finds his life mate for the next forty-five years. In reality, few individuals realize the true import of what they're doing at the time. It is only later, looking back – sometimes with regret – that they see how their lives veered off in a completely different direction. Henry Watchman had already had one such incident . . . and it still haunted him. The phone call coming into his house Thursday afternoon would prove to be another turning point, though he had no way of knowing it.

"Pastor Watchman?" The woman's voice sounded hesitant.

"Yes, I'm Henry Watchman."

"I'm . . . I'm Cherie Lawrence. I think Mr. Johnson at the gym talked to you about me and Billy."

Henry Watchman waved a hand to get his wife's attention. "Yes, I've been hoping you'd call."

"Pastor Watchman, I don't know what to do or where to turn. I feel so guilty for not being a good enough wife to keep Billy at home. Now, I'm afraid I've lost him to a . . . to some stripper." Henry could hear her crying. "I'm so embarrassed my friends will find out."

"I understand how you feel," he said. "And I want you to know that talking to someone like you're doing now is the first step to getting this problem taken care of." He paused to lift up a silent prayer for wisdom.

"Cherie, could you take a few minutes to come and talk with my wife and me right now?"

Renewed crying came from the other end. "Oh, Pastor Watchman, I don't want to bother you or your wife. But you're so kind to offer."

Henry sighed. Why did people think they were bothering him when they shared their problems? After all, didn't the apostle Paul say that we should bear one another's burdens, and in so doing fulfill the law of Christ?

"Jenna and I would love to see you," he assured Cherie. "Can you come now?"

A small hesitation, then – "I'll be there in fifteen minutes. Thank you so much, Pastor Watchman."

Henry hung up the phone and turned to Jenna. "Two steps taken with the Lawrence couple. Cherie's coming for help, and she's allowing you to be a part of the counseling process." He looked around the spotless kitchen and dining room, his blue eyes twinkling. "You'd better clean up this mess before she gets here."

Jenna threw an oven mitt at him as he ducked out of the kitchen.

————

Maria pulled her cruiser to the side of the road and parked in front of a brown stucco duplex. Home! It had been a difficult, troubling day. She walked slowly to the front door, reached for the doorknob and sighed when it turned easily and the door swung open. The detective sighed again. Her mother never learned. "Mama, where are you?" she called out.

"Where else would I be this time of day? Come into the kitchen; I've got something new for you to taste."

Maria sighed for a third time as she entered what her mother referred to as the main room of the house. Maria worked out regularly, but her mother's delicious temptations threatened to win the battle of her waistline. The counter before her contained five platters of food. The scents of cheese, tomatoes, onions, chives, peppers, beef, pork and chicken swirled seductively into her nostrils. Maria's stomach growled appreciatively.

"Mama," she said, "did we invite the whole police force over for dinner tonight?"

A squat woman with sharp, piercing brown eyes glanced up briefly at Maria before returning her attention to the dough she kneaded with sure hands. Only strangers called the woman her given name, Etelvina. Her friends had shortened it to "Vina." But for Maria, since she was a child, it had always been "Mama." Maria wasn't fooled by the brief glance. She knew her mother could see far beneath the surface of almost anyone she met. She decided to pounce first.

"Mama, how many times have I told you to lock the door, especially when I'm gone? Someone's going to come in here one day and either steal our stuff, hurt you, or do both."

A snort was the only reply Maria got.

She tried again. "I'm serious. If you could see some of the people I have to deal with each day, you'd not only lock the door, you'd also put several more locks on it. I'm just trying to protect you, but you keep refusing to . . ."

"Mi Hita, everyone around here knows me," Vina interrupted. "And anyone with eyes to see knows there's a police car parked in front of our house every night." She gestured toward the Empanadas with a flour-covered finger. "Try one." She continued kneading. "How can my friends come in the house if it's locked? Besides, I can't keep track of the key! It's easier and friendlier to just leave the door unlocked." She looked up at Maria and her face split into a huge smile. "Besides, you're here each night to lock it up and keep me safe."

Maria snorted in return; two could play that game! "Mama, your food's good; your logic's not." She threw up her hands in defeat. "But I give up . . . for right now." A platter, warm from the oven, beckoned her. She took it, put several flautas in the middle and surrounded them all with paella and frijoles. After pouring a diet cola (the only way she could rationalize her descent into "nutritional oblivion"), she carefully balanced the plate on her arm, put her drink in the same hand, and opened the back door. She placed the plate and drink on a small table, then sat down in their small Florida room and surveyed the back yard.

"What's bothering you, Mi Hita?" The voice floated gently from the kitchen.

Maria smiled. She couldn't hide much from her mother.

"It's Vincent, Mama. The guy who's always been known as 'Mr. Cool and Controlled' is beginning to unravel. And, I can't figure out why. It worries me."

Vina's head appeared around the corner. "Everyone – no exception – has at least one weak spot in their life. Some bury that weakness deep in their soul and cover it with as many things as possible. But, it's still there." She sat down beside Maria. "Don't you count him as a friend?" she asked.

Maria nodded. " I may be the only friend he has," she confided. "He doesn't let many people inside his life. And I'm not sure I'm anywhere close to understanding him."

"A true friend stands firm when everything falls apart." Vina waited until her daughter was looking directly at her. "Whatever it is, stand firm for Detective Anderson."

Maria nodded. "If he'll let me, " she said.

————

"Vince, whatcha got over at the house?"

Maria and Vincent had decided to split up their surveillance. Because of the constant coming and going of Pastor Watchman, sometimes seeing people at his house, sometimes working at the church, Maria had stationed herself behind the Hidden Beach Community Church, keeping tabs on who entered and left, and how long they stayed. Vince had parked his car up the street from the Watchman's house.

Vince's voice crackled over the radio. "Since that Lawrence woman left while ago, it's been quiet."

Night had begun to creep into the town. Lights flickered on and a steady stream of cars moved away from the now darkened beach, headed toward homes and hotels.

"Marie, you want to get us something to eat?"

"Why me?" Marie shot back. "You know the way to the BurgerBarn."

Vincent's laugh came loud over the radio. "'Cause I've gone for food the last two times. You ought to have some of the fun."

Maria grinned. "Okay, what do you want?" She got his order, started the car and drove off. "If there's a change, call me immediately," she said.

"No worry."

Night. Darkness. Shadows. The demon looked forward to the sun's going down. Yes, the encounter with the angel had caused him momentary fear. But that was earlier in the day. He felt more powerful in the absence of light; emotions seemed to run stronger as the hour became later. As he floated above the community of Hidden Beach, the feelings of despair, jealousy, lust, depression, and a thousand other negative thoughts made their way to the demon, feeding him, making him stronger.

His tongue darted out, tasting everything. Shi'intor could see the night's events starting to unfold. If things worked out right,

Satan would claim another soul in the next few hours. Three individuals, though they knew it not, would play key roles in this drama of evil.

The demon sighed with pleasure. Time to get started!

———

The dressing room seemed smaller to Wanda with the other women jostling against her, elbowing each other for space in front of the mirrors. The pounding of an electric bass could be heard coming from the already filling club. Another audience waiting to be fleeced by us, she thought, applying the final touches to her makeup. She'd done this so many times, it was now automatic. The women around her talked to each other of boyfriends and bills. The muted music circled around and between the words. Wanda, listening to it all, let her thoughts drift back, back . . . .

Eleven years old. Wanda started out the door to meet friends at the mall.

"Where do you think you're going?" her grandfather slurred. He reached for her shoulder, but the young girl, knowing what was coming, had already stepped back out of reach.

"Think, Pops," Wanda said. "You and Mom already agreed I could go to the mall if I promised to be back by 9:30." She knew alcohol could do strange things to a person. She hated how it changed the people closest to her, and promised herself she'd never let it take over her life.

The old man swiped at her face with a drunken lurch. Again, he missed as Wanda side-stepped the blow. "I didn't say you could go out dressed like that!" he said. "Look at you. That body of yours would tempt any man. And you're flaunting it on purpose!"

Wanda blushed. That particular subject always gave her a sick feeling in her stomach. Though only eleven, her body had begun to mature much more rapidly than had her emotions. It wasn't her fault looks and catcalls from the older boys had started coming her way. She didn't like them or want them. In truth, she still felt and acted like a little girl.

Wanda hated to hear her grandfather talk like that. "No, I'm not!" she shot back. "You just don't know what's in style. You haven't so much as even looked at a women's catalogue since the 1940s."

Wanda ducked under her grandfather's clutching hands and slid out the door, running as hard as she could. Two blocks away, her best friend, Jennie, and Jennie's mom would be waiting to take them to the mall.

"You come back here, you slut!"

Wanda ran from her house, her grandfather, and especially from the hateful words. But she'd discovered the words stayed with her, no matter how far or how fast she ran.

Those words had made a powerful impact on her over the years, Wanda thought. Bitter tears threatened to spill over onto her costume. She looked at her image in the mirror one more time. *Yes, grandfather, you raised me to be a slut, alright. Wherever you are, I hope what you kept pushing me to become has made you happy.*

The volume of the music swelled as a door opened and in walked Robert Jamison. Several of the women were completely nude, but neither they nor Jamison attempted modesty. After all, thought Wanda, if everyone sees us naked, why does it matter if it's onstage or in the dressing room? Anyway, she'd stopped thinking of her body as being a part of Wanda Lemming a long time back. In her mind, it existed simply as a tool to get what she wanted . . . except for one troubling thing. She'd begun thinking over the past several weeks that it just might be she'd paid too high a price for things that didn't satisfy like she'd always dreamed they would.

The woman who'd embarrassed herself the other night, for example. That was true love. And Wanda knew she had unwittingly played a part in perhaps destroying the marriage and hurting true love. How could she continue to . . .

Jamison came over to her and stroked a hand seductively down her back. Wanda's blood ran cold, but the emotion never reached her face. She placed two soft lips on his cheek and left lipstick there. She knew he'd not wipe it off. The kiss would be worn as a macho badge of conquest that would only enhance

Jamison's reputation among his clients. It would also represent hope to some of them that they might receive the same treatment . . . and more.

"Wanda, you been tired lately?"

Here it comes, she thought. "No sir. I've been here every night and worked all my rotations." She looked him straight in the eye. "I can guarantee you're not getting complaints from the customers."

"Nah, of course not. I know you're a pro up on stage." He lowered his voice. In the din, no one but Wanda could hear his words. "But you and I both know you ain't working the crowd like you was last week. Somethin's happened. No lap dances, no drinks with the customers. You just dance and then disappear." Jamison grabbed her arm and squeezed at the bicep. "I pay you almost double what the other girls get – and I expect more out of you . . . beginning tonight."

He stepped back, released her arm and smiled again. In a louder voice, he said, "Girls, some of you are kinda new. You may be wonderin' exactly how to conduct yourselves off stage. Tonight, Wanda Wonder is gonna teach you." His massive head swung around to look at Wanda. "Ain't that right, honey."

The time's not right. You're not ready to leave all this money just yet. Don't confront. The thoughts seemed jammed into Wanda's head. She looked around at her audience and slowly rotated her hips. "Tonight, ladies, I'm going to teach you how to make money!" Squeals of delight surrounded her. She damped down the nausea and despair, ignored Stanley Jamison and stepped out the door and into her every-evening nightmare.

CHAPTER FOURTEEN

The house was supposed to be a "starter," small and a little run down when Billy and Cherie had first spied it. It nevertheless looked like the start of dreams for the then newlyweds. They purchased the place, moved in and immediately began a transformation. Billy scraped off old layers of peeling paint and applied fresh coats of beige and white to the outside. Cherie cleaned the inside . . . inside out. She carried out what seemed to her two-hundred trash bags full of dirt and neglect. At night, the young couple would sit on the front porch in the evening breeze, listening to the ocean and talking about the future. For both of them, the smallness of the house didn't matter. It put them closer together. "Cozy" was the term Billy used to use about their house and their marriage. Not any more.

Billy hesitated as he got ready. He'd promised Cherie they would go out together, and he wanted to please her. But when he thought about the other possibility for the evening, his heart started pounding. He flushed, thinking about what he wanted to happen.

The demon sank through the roof and settled beside the human. He not only hated marriages, Satan's messenger had need of the young man. The heavy chain running from the newlywed's loins to a collar about his neck revealed everything. The dark creature tugged lightly on the chain and watched the man's emotions turn toward another woman. Unbridled lust would bludgeon the hopes and the marriage of the young couple.

"You work hard for your money," the demon whispered seductively. *"You deserve some time doing what you want."* His mouth opened wider, and the snake-like tongue tried to pierce the ear. The human shook his head, as if trying to get rid of a fly. The demon withdrew his tongue. Not quite ready. However, the human's resistance grew weaker by the day. Soon, the man would belong to Satan. *"The woman is trying to control you,"* he continued. *"Show her who's boss. After all, you have desires that just one woman can't fulfill."* He tugged one more time on the chain.

"This house is just too small for me!" Billy fumed. "I need some space, and I can't wait any longer. See you later."

Cherie couldn't believe this turn of events. "But Billy, you promised we'd go out with Lamb and his wife this evening. They've already made plans. Besides, you know I talked with Pastor Henry and his wife this afternoon. They said it was good for us to spend time as a couple with other married couples."

Billy swung around, his hand already on the doorknob. "Quit trying to control me, Cherie!" His voice trembled with anger. Muscles bunched under his tight fitting T-shirt and a flush covered his face. "I'm a man, and I'm going to act like one. I don't need some crazy preacher who doesn't know anything about life trying to tell me how to run mine!"

"But Pastor Watchman and his wife have a lot of common sense. And . . . and they care a lot about both of us. Come on, Billy, let's follow their advice."

Her husband shook his head. "Maybe another night, Cherie. But tonight, I'm outta here." His voice raised as the anger resurfaced. "Don't ask where I'm going, and don't try to follow me!" He opened the door and started for the car. "And one more thing. Don't wait up 'cause I'll be late."

Cherie tried to keep her emotions checked as the door

slammed in her face and the sound of squealing tires came from the driveway. She picked up the phone and dialed the pastor's number.

"Pastor Watchman, I . . . . " She could get no further. The tears began and would not stop.

———

Vincent Anderson felt off balance. Up until now, his adult life had been one of incredible control. Emotions always in check. Dry humor used sparingly to keep *others* off balance. Moving steadily toward his goal of becoming one of the youngest police chiefs in Florida. Now, everything had changed. His life, his emotions, his career – all spinning out of control. Everything centered on Henry Watchman as the cause and he had to be stopped. "Maria might be fooled by his refusal to fight, but not me," he muttered to himself.

A bubble seemed to surround him right now. It had begun shrinking and the increased pressure threatened to crush him. Something bad was about to happen. He could feel it.

———

"I know Billy told you not to follow him." Henry Watchman spoke in as calm a tone as possible. "You're not going to. Jenna and I will take care of your husband this evening, Cherie." He looked up at his wife for confirmation as he said this. Jenna nodded.

"Do you know Daryl and Jocelyn Sanders?" he continued. Cherie said she didn't. "I want to bring them in on this. You and Billy are going to need a couple who've been where you are right now. They worked through their problems, and they can help both of you."

"Can they be trusted, Pastor Watchman?" Cherie's voice

carried an uncertain note. "I don't want any more people to know about this than necessary."

"I promise they are close mouthed. They'll talk to you and Billy, and to Jenna and me; but it ends there. Daryl is a retired sheriff's deputy," Henry Watchman explained. "He'll meet us in front of the club and go in with me to help in case there's a problem."

Jenna gestured for the phone. "Cherie, I need you to do something for me right now," she said. "It's very important, and the success of what we're going to try will depend a lot on your completing this assignment."

On the other end of the phone call, Cherie managed to pull herself together for a moment. "What in the world can I do?" she asked.

"Henry and I need you to get on your knees immediately and pray for us. You must do this until we call you back."

"I . . . I'm not used to praying, Jenna." Cherie's voice quavered a little, but at least she'd begun to get hold of her emotions.

"I want you to pray for several things." Jenna paused. ""Get some paper and a pen."

After about thirty seconds, Cherie came back to the phone. "Okay, I'm ready."

In the other room, Henry Watchman made a call on his cell phone. "Daryl? It's Pastor Watchman. Do you feel up to helping me make an intervention on a wayward husband at the LadyZ-N-Waiting strip club? Great. Meet Jenna and me in front of the club in twenty minutes. I'll fill you in there. Please ask Jocelyn to pray for us. And, thanks."

CHAPTER FIFTEEN

Toldin flew above the LadyZ-N-Waiting strip club. He would rather be almost any other place, but the angel felt something important was about to happen here. The lives of quite a few people hung precariously on the edge of eternity. Whatever the cost, Toldin would do his best to save as many as possible. He winced as emotions of lust and greed, combined with lies and desperation, rose to buffet him about. If only the men and women below would take the time to understand how much more life could hold for them! "You are created in the Father's image!" Toldin said softly to unhearing ears. "You have settled for a lie that will turn sour in your stomach and poison you."

A young, well-built man got out of one of the cars in the parking lot and began making his way to the strip club's entrance. Shi'intor, the demon of Hidden Beach, strode along beside him, one arm around the young man's shoulders, the other tugging lightly on a chain. Righteous anger flooded the angel as he realized what was occurring. How many more lives would this demon ruin! How much more pain would these people have to endure? A confrontation here would be difficult. No prayers ascended from this place to strengthen him. Nevertheless, Toldin knew he had to try something. The angel streaked toward the two, drawing his sword as he descended. The closer he came to the club, however, the slower he moved. Sin, palpable, seemed to reach out and tear energy from his body.

The demon looked up in time to see the attack from above. He grinned cruelly as he let go of the chain and drew his sword. "Not so easy now, is it?" he gloated. Shi'intor reveled in the evil swirling around him. It made him feel invulnerable. In this place of moral filth, the angel seemed to be moving in slow motion. With a vicious swipe, the demon's sword batted aside his opponent's thrust. Shi'intor drove a fist into Toldin's chest that threw him against the club's wall. As he came in contact with the club, the angel cringed and moved away immediately, as if burned. His sword, however, he still held before him, pointed at the demon.

Shi'intor never stopped walking with the young human. He turned his head to look at the weakened angel. "You're not welcome here, Toldin," he flung back over his shoulder. "Go back to your do-gooders and useless churches." He and the young man came to the entrance and passed through, leaving the angel alone.

———

Vince straightened up. Pastor Watchman's car had pulled out of the driveway and headed for the town's center. He waited until three cars had passed, then eased into the flow of traffic. "Maria," he radioed. "Watchman's left the house. I'm a few cars behind. We're headed South. Try to catch up with us. I'll let you know if he turns."

"Vince, I'm not going to turn on my lights unless it's an emergency."

" I agree," Vince replied. "If something starts to come down, I'll yell. By then, there'll be no reason to lay low. Come with lights and siren blasting."

"I'm probably about ten minutes behind you in this traffic."

Maria sounded frustrated. "For right now, you're on your own. Be careful."

"Okay, Mama." Vince grinned in the darkness.

Pastor Watchman's car continued straight down the strip. Soon, it left the beautiful hotels and resort condominiums behind and moved into Dollar Town, the seedier area of Hidden Beach. The car pulled up to the LadyZ-N-Waiting strip club and stopped across the street. In the bright street lights, Vince could see Mrs. Watchman behind the steering wheel. She and Pastor Watchman had their heads bowed, probably praying. The detective grunted. The preacher might fool his wife, but he couldn't put anything over on Vincent Anderson.

Another car pulled up, and a familiar figure got out and joined the Watchman's in their car. *What's Daryl doing here?* Anderson wondered. The former law enforcement officer had a good reputation as level headed.

He tensed when the car door opened. Unbelievable!

"Maria." Vincent thumbed the mike. "Hurry to the LadyZ-N-Waiting. The pastor of Hidden Beach Community Church has just walked into a strip club." Then, "Shirl, did you catch what I just said?"

"Got it, Detective Anderson."

"Tell the chief what's going on. I'm headed in to keep an eye on that preacher."

"Vince! Vince! The chief asked that he not be disturbed. He's meeting with two city council members and . . . ." Shirl's voice echoed slightly in the now empty car.

———

The deejay's amplified voice boomed out over the crowd, accompanied by pulsating music. "Aaand now, LadyZ-N-Waiting is proud to present the female wonder you've all been waiting for – Wanda Wonder!"

The already loud music rose in volume as a long leg appeared from behind the curtain. The rest of Wanda's scantily clad body followed, and cheers and whistles surrounded the "exotic dancer." As she went through her routine, Wanda focused primarily on the men at the edge of the stage. She knew that's where the money would come from. Looking each one in the eye in turn, she gave that patron, for that moment, the impression he mattered more to her than anyone else in the world. She would do anything he wanted . . . and then her gaze moved on.

The practiced, seductive moves came automatically to Wanda. Thank goodness, she thought. Putting her body on auto-pilot seemed to be the only way for her to get through the dancing these days. She continued with her eyes making the rounds of the stage-side customers – and then Wanda Wonder faltered. The music continued, but she didn't. Arms at her side, she stopped in front of one man.

"Hey, what's goin' on?" someone shouted.

"Come on, Wanda. We don't want to have to 'wonder' what you've got," another called out, laughing.

Wanda ignored them. She bent down in front of a well-muscled young man in a tight fitting shirt. "Billy, what are you doing here?" she asked. "After your wife made a fool of herself the other night, I can't believe you'd come again." Billy drew back in shock. "I came back because of you! I could tell by the way you looked at me that we might be able to get together. I . . ."

He never got to finish his thought. An iron hand clamped Wanda's shoulder as a bouncer pulled her off the stage and another girl quickly took her place. "Hey, you let her go!" Billy jumped up to follow the bouncer and knocked over two tables in the process.

"Watch where you're going, Bub," one of the men said.

"If you don't want your face punched in, you'll shut up and get out of my way," Billy snarled. He started to push his way past when two people jumped him from behind. As he fell toward the stage floor, he could see more bouncers on their way. Billy determined not to go down without a fight. After all, Wanda might be watching. He wanted her to think him a hero. *Her* hero.

Then Billy could see nothing else. Someone pinned his arms behind him. A strong pressure on the back of his neck forced him into a painful, unnatural position. His ears began to ring and he could feel darkness closing in.

"Gentlemen, if you'll get off this man, I'll take him home right now and get him out of your way."

The voice sounded familiar, but Billy couldn't place it. When the pressure on his head finally eased, however, he looked up to see the last person he would ever figure to be in front of a girl stripping. His heart seemed to stop, and he managed to stammer out, "Pastor Watchman?"

"Hello, Billy." Henry Watchman looked around, taking in his surroundings. Two bouncers and a customer had Billy Lawrence held fast. His face, even in the dim light, had turned red from embarrassment. Wanda Wonder had disappeared, but the girl up on stage, while continuing to dance, had a smirk on her face as she took in Billy's predicament.

"You remind me of Jonah," Pastor Watchman said. "Running from God isn't easy, Billy. It hurts you and it hurts those who love you. And right now, it looks like you're hurting pretty bad."

Robert Jamison could be seen wending his way through the tables toward the stage area. He motioned for the bouncers to move their captive to the back and far side of the club. Henry Watchman and Daryl followed. They maneuvered Billy into an alcove that sheltered them from the view of other patrons. Once there, Jamison stepped around the corner for a moment, held up a hand and motioned toward someone. Henry turned a bit and groaned. Coming toward the group, his face grim, Detective Vincent Anderson prepared to crash the party.

"What in the world are you doing in a strip club, Pastor Watchman?"

Henry noted that at least Anderson seemed to have his anger under control. He started to respond when Jamison squeezed between the two men. "Forget that. What are you going to do about this man starting a fight and trying to ruin my business?" The owner pointed a shaking finger at Billy. "I want him arrested and charged with disorderly conduct!"

Billy struggled in the grip of the bouncers. "If your goon hadn't manhandled Wanda, this never would have happened."

"Excuse me, gentlemen." Heads turned to look at Pastor Watchman. "Mr. Jamison, I gather you're the owner of this club." Jamison nodded. "I don't think you really want the negative publicity your club will get in the local newspaper. I can see the front page now: 'Violence breaks out at the LadyZ-N-Waiting.' Underneath that might be something like, 'Brawl makes customers wonder if they can be safe in the club.' Do you really want that?"

Jamison thought about it for a few seconds. Then, with a curt nod, he turned to Billy Lawrence. "Get out of my club and don't ever come back. A hysterical wife one night, your preacher this evening."

"He's not my preacher."

"Shut up!" Jamison said savagely. "The bouncers at the door will be instructed to turn you away if you try to enter again." He turned to Vincent Anderson. "Detective Anderson, could you *please* escort this man out of my establishment and make sure he doesn't cause himself or me any more embarrassment."

The detective looked at Billy, then at Pastor Watchman, then at the ceiling. He finally sighed, turned to Billy and said, "Come quietly, no fuss, and you can go home . . . with an escort. From seeing you at the gym, I know you're not normally a troublemaker. Make one problem for me as we leave, though, and you'll be in jail before you can turn around."

"I'll come with you, detective. But could I have a private word with the preacher first?" Billy could see a frown beginning on Vincent's face. "It won't be more that fifteen seconds."

Henry Watchman moved off a few paces and Billy quickly

whispered in his ear. "I'm not leaving unless you promise to see about Wanda."

"Now, Billy, I don't . . ."

"No sir, that's the deal. If I hadn't come tonight, she wouldn't have gotten in trouble. Now she's going to probably lose her job, and all because of me." Billy pleaded with his eyes as the detective came to lead him away. "You've got to help her."

It didn't make Pastor Watchman happy at all, but he said, "Okay."

———

Maria could see the front doors of the LadyZ-N-Waiting pushed open forcefully. Vincent Anderson accompanied a young man up the block toward her, keeping a hand on his arm to guide him. She rolled down her window. "What's up, Vince?"

The detective pointed at his companion. "This is Billy Lawrence. Billy, you're getting ready to have a police escort from detective Maria Da Silva. She'll follow you home, to make sure you get safely to the right destination."

Billy visibly tensed. "Who says I've got to go home? I'm not a criminal and I've got rights." He twisted his arm away from Vincent.

The detective grabbed him again. "You'll do as I say, or you'll go to jail. Remember what Watchman said? He's the only reason I'm not cuffing you and taking you down to headquarters right now."

Well!, thought Maria. We've had some excitement inside the club. But, she wondered, how in the world did Vince come to be on the side of the preacher? As Billy finally agreed to go to his car, she took the opportunity to ask her partner that very question. "Everyone gets something right once in a while," Vince said in response. "I watched Watchman calm down a tense situation in there. I gotta admit he did well." Vince glanced back at the club door. "I'll stay here and follow the preacher. When you get Billy home, give me a call."

Maria smiled. As Billy's car pulled out of the parking lot, she put the cruiser in gear and eased away from the curb. "Vince, was that really so hard to say?" she called back. "You know, admitting Watchman did something right. The earth didn't swallow you up and life still goes on."

Vince's eyes narrowed, but Maria had already rolled up her window and headed down the street.

"What the . . . . What's that crazy preacher up to now?" The detective saw a figure dart away from the preacher's car. Vincent started for the alley behind the club, trying to catch up to Henry Watchman.

CHAPTER SIXTEEN

Henry Watchman and Daryl followed the other two men out of the club, giving them a few seconds head start. The pastor wanted to honor Billy's request about the stripper Wanda Wonder, but he also knew that with his reason for being in the strip club gone, and with Daryl possibly on his way to Billy's house, the time had come for him to be out of a place that could ruin his reputation.

He and Daryl crossed the street and quickly filled Jenna in on what had taken place. "If I read Jamison right, he's getting ready to fire Wanda."

Jenna's eyebrows raised slightly. "Oh, so you're already on a first-name basis with a stripper?"

She was secretly pleased to see her husband blush. "Jenna, look, I don't know her last name, and I certainly don't want to call her Wanda Wonder!"

Daryl chuckled softly. Jenna reached up and poked her husband's nose. "Henry, just kidding. I know you." Then, she turned serious again. "What were you saying?"

"Anyway," Henry continued, "if she loses her job, Jamison will bring her outside, in the alley, to fire her. At least, that's what I think. He'll not want to do it in the club, even in his office, where she can still make a stink in front of the other girls." He started for the alley. "You stay here and guard the car. Hopefully, Daryl and I will be right back."

"Wait, Henry."

Pastor Watchman stopped. "What is it?"

Jenna pointed at a group of men just down the block. "Those men might be completely innocent. But they've been watching me pretty steady now for the last ten minutes. I'd feel safer if Daryl stayed with me, unless you really need him."

Henry smiled at his wife. "Good thinking, as usual." He turned to his friend. "Daryl, could you keep an eye out for my wife? And could you keep the other eye on the end of the alley?"

"Take off, pastor," Daryl said. "Those boys will stay where they are as long as I'm here." He pointed at the group. "Some of them know me from a couple of years back. They probably don't want to renew acquaintances."

Watchman nodded and took off at a run for the alley.

Jenna stuck her head out the window and called to him. "If she needs a place to spend the night, we can put her up in the guest bedroom."

———

Deep in the shadows, Gin McFain felt a little safer. Blind for the last few years, he'd learned to eke out an existence through begging on street corners in the neighborhood. Tonight, though, things had taken a turn for the worse. The tough economy had finally made its way down to Gin's level. "Donations," as he liked to call them, were down. Unable to make the rent for the last two months even in the cheapest motel he could find, he'd been kicked out by the landlord.

"Don't panic, Gin," he whispered to himself. "Panic don't help nobody." He eased farther back into the bushes on the vacant lot. Tomorrow he'd find something else. Gin wiped his eyes absently as he thought. They ran most of the time, now, and sometimes itched ferociously. Only the alcohol that had given him his name eased the pain. A once large, well-built man, life and liquor had reduced him to an almost empty husk. Thick, disheveled black hair and a face that had not seen soap in days gave mute testimony to the power gin had over him.

The sound of something metal falling in the street caused him to flinch.

"You stupid idiot!" The words, though spoken in a low tone, seemed to come from right in front of Gin. He froze. After a moment, the voice continued. "Slow down. You still have time to get it right."

Someone talking to himself, the frightened beggar thought. But the voice . . . he'd heard it somewhere before.

————

Mary Connors leaned over and expertly twisted a hidden knob as she began her nightly ritual of turning out lights. She moved easily through the house. Her 70-plus years hindered Mary very little, she thought, giving a wan smile. The hundreds of flowers, plants and fruit trees that demanded her attention assured her of more than enough exercise. Though the house comprised three levels, these days Mary only lived on the main floor. She did manage to keep the upper levels clean, but she was finding it harder and harder. Not because of the energy; she still had that. But lately, she'd found a nagging question buzzing in the back of her mind: *Why bother?*

Mary and her husband, Jake, had purchased the house a full fifty years ago and had never moved or sold, despite the generous financial offers from several large condominium outfits. The two of them had hoped to have children, but that hadn't happened. So she and Jake had poured their lives into their marriage, their church community and this house. Jake had wisely bought as much land as possible around them. Now, acres lush with vegetation effectively hid the house from the increasing crowds along

Hidden Beach. Comfortable in their sprawling house, she and Jake had looked forward to their retirement years.

The house darkened a bit more as she extinguished the next lamp. It felt a lot like her life.

Colon cancer. It's amazing how two little words could so change someone's world. By the time they'd heard the words in connection with Jake, the disease had spread throughout his body. Within four months of the diagnosis, he died – and so did Mary's future, or at least that's what it felt like. She'd finally realized that with the passing of her husband three years ago, loneliness had become a regular companion. Her church family was dear to her, but they weren't there every day. And neither plants nor flowers could take the place of the man she called *the best part of my life*.

"Heavenly Father, could you please help me?" Mary prayed as she walked through the house. "I don't want to be selfish, but I want to feel whole again." She bent to turn out another lamp. Darkness came on steadily. "I give you this house and my life, God," she said. "Use me however you want. I just need to know I'm doing something that makes a difference."

She turned out the last light and moved quietly into the bedroom. Outside, myriads of leaves rustled in the evening breeze.

CHAPTER SEVENTEEN

"C'mon, Wanda, You can't be serious! Do you realize how much money you're giving up if you do this?"

Wanda Lemming couldn't look Jamison in the eyes. Standing just outside the club's back entrance in the alley, she focused on not caving in. "You were here when Billy's wife walked in the other night. She risked everything for her marriage, and I'm the one that's helping break it up! Mr. Jamison, I can't do this anymore."

"What do you care for their marriage anyway?" Jamison retorted. "Remember, marriages come and go all the time. It's really about money. That's all that counts." His face turned ugly. "And I'm not going to let you take money out of my pocket, Wanda. You're staying."

Something welled up in Wanda Lemming. A brief surge of hope, courage . . . she didn't know what. But it enabled her to say, "You're wrong. I'm quitting – right now."

Jamison grabbed her around the neck with one hand and pulled her up against him. "No one leaves Robert Jamison, Wanda. No one." She looked around wildly, hoping Tony might still be by the door. But, no, Jamison had told him to take a break.

The club owner pulled back his fist to smash Wanda's jaw. "What ...?" An incredible pain blossomed in Jamison's neck, right below his left ear. He gasped and let go of Wanda.

"Leave her alone, Jamison. She's free to leave you and this slime you call a business."

Jamison turned to see Henry Watchman standing in front of him, shielding Wanda. "Did you just hit me?" he hissed.

"I didn't want to," the pastor said. "But I couldn't figure any other way to stop you from doing something both of you would have regretted later."

A red haze filled Jamison's eyes. He'd had his share of fights, some in back alleys like this one. He stepped forward and launched a right hook guaranteed to take down this meddlesome preacher.

It never landed.

Instead, Jamison's head snapped back as two of the hardest, fastest punches he'd ever had the misfortune of receiving came out of nowhere. They staggered him, and he grabbed at the open door for support as he went down. Several teeth felt loose. When he could finally sit up, he saw the preacher headed down the alley with Wanda Lemming. Running to meet them, Detective Vincent Anderson was unsnapping his holster and yelling, "Watchman, what are you into now?"

"Get them, detective." Jamison mumbled as loud as he could through a bloody mouth. "Arrest them! I want to file a complaint!" He cleared his throat and yelled louder, "Tell that tramp she's evicted from her apartment as of right now if she leaves!"

Detective Anderson turned to look at Jamison, then stumbled, but not from the rough bricks in the alleyway. Instead, an explosion that rained glass and car parts on the club out front claimed everyone's attention.

———

Jenna shielded her eyes from the blast just up the block. When she risked a glance at the scene, she could see the remains of a car on fire. Out of the alleyway came Detective Anderson, her husband and Wanda Wonder. She heard her husband yell at the detective. "Don't worry, I'm not going anywhere! I'll put Miss Lemming in the car with my wife, then come back." Vincent Anderson hesitated only a moment, then turned in the opposite direction toward the fire.

Jenna unlocked the door and Henry motioned for Wanda to get in the front seat by her. "Jenna and Daryl, this is Wanda Lemming. Miss Lemming, this is Jenna Watchman, my wife and Daryl Sanders, a friend and an elder in our church." He smiled briefly. "Believe me, Jenna will take care of you, if you'll only let her." A turn back to Jenna. "She wants to quit her current line of work. She's also just lost her apartment, if Jamison means what he says, and I think he does. Take her to our house and see if you can help her." He took a moment to caress her hand, then ran back to the scene of the explosion.

Jenna put her arm around Wanda. "You're a brave young woman," she said. "I know things may be moving awfully fast for you, but we're all going to take a moment to pause and ask God for protection."

"What are you talking about?" Wanda asked. These people had to be some sort of fanatics. Was she safe here?

"I'm sorry," Jenna said. "I should have explained. We are going to pray." She looked closely at Wanda. "Haven't you ever prayed?"

Wanda, remembering her desperate prayers as a young girl, nodded. She wasn't sure her prayers had ever been heard by God, but she figured prayer was, at the very least, something harmless.

Darryl and Jenna bowed their heads and closed their eyes. After a moment, unsure of what might happen next, Wanda decided to keep her eyes open. She wanted no more surprises this night. She listened as her new protectors asked God to take care of them, of Wanda, and of Henry Watchman.

If she could have seen what was happening in front of the club, Wanda would have probably joined in the prayers. Zooming through the roof of the LadyZ-N-Waiting, the demon Shi'intor flew about in a rage. That Henry Watchman! Who would have believed a pastor would ever go into a strip club to rescue someone? Billy had escaped the demon's claws for the moment. The stripper, however . . . . Shi'intor looked down the street. With other-worldly eyes, his vision penetrated the darkness and he spied Wanda in the car with two Christians. "Christians!" he muttered. "That will have to be stopped now."

But even as he turned to attack, a silver glow began surrounding the car. Toldin appeared, larger than ever. His wings encompassed the three occupants of the vehicle, protecting them.

"What's happened?" Shi'intor wondered. Even from a distance of a hundred yards, the demon could see his opponent had become too strong for a frontal attack. He gnashed his teeth in frustration and looked around wildly. Surely something could be done to rescue this night. As his eyes swung past the alley, something -- or someone -- pulled at his vision. Shi'intor peered closely at the dark shadows, then smiled and disappeared into the cloud of black, oily smoke coming from just around the corner of the alley.

———

The car lay on its side. The force of the explosion had thrown it up in the air and onto the grass. The front doors lay hundreds of feet from one another, blown completely off. Glass glinted everywhere, easy to see in the light of the flames still licking at the vehicle. Vincent Anderson moved in cautiously, getting as close to the burning automobile as possible. He didn't think anyone inside it could have survived, but he had to check. Putting up an arm to shield his face, he edged toward the fire. After a careful search, his heart beat easier; no occupants.

"Anyone in there?"

Vince whirled at the voice coming from just behind him. "No," he sighed, "but Pastor Watchman, you do seem to have a knack for being in the wrong place at the wrong time."

Henry Watchman wasn't smiling. Sweat dripped off his chin and blood stained his hands from the short fight with Robert Jamison. His gaze, however, was clear as it pierced the detective. He said, "Funny, you seem to show up every time, as well."

Out of the side of his vision, Vince caught some movement. He walked slowly into the vacant lot beside the flaming car. Drawing his revolver, he parted some bushes. A man with filthy clothes and dirty, matted brown hair lay on the ground. "Help me," he said. "I . . . I think I'm hurt pretty bad."

"Watchman, come help me for a minute."

No answer. Watchman had disappeared.

Detective Anderson swore. This was becoming a night from Hell. He radioed Shirl and, when she answered, said, "I've got a car explosion in the 1600 block of Sandstone Avenue. I also have an injured male, unknown at this point, with multiple cuts and contusions. He's bleeding a lot and needs immediate attention."

"I'll call an ambulance right now," Shirl said. "And, Vince? Maria reported in a little while ago to tell us where she's headed. I've called for some backup; you don't need to be there by yourself."

––––––––

Excitement filled the demon. Still, however, he moved cautiously. No reason to alert the angel if he was still nearby, watching for an opportunity to interfere. After he'd left Jenna's car, Shi'intor had used the smoke from the explosion to hide his true destination. Slipping through dark, seldom-used alleys, slithering down long-forgotten tunnels, he had found and followed Satan's latest tool of destruction.

At last, a door opened and the man eased through, gently

shutting the rusted door behind him and crouching down behind a garbage bin. He peered at the figures on the other side of the bin. The reality of what he was about to do began to sink in. He'd never really believed it would be possible to get this far without someone seeing him.

The moment seemed to rush at him. What if he were seen? What if the target cried out? How could he be sure of succeeding? He froze as the implications of what he contemplated swam before his eyes.

Beside him, unseen, the demon snarled with anger. "Time to show who's boss now," he said, menace filling his voice. "I will *not* have this evening ruined further!" The tongue/snake shot out of the demon's mouth faster than eyes could follow and pierced the man's ear.

"You miss the killing," he hissed with persuasion. *"You can't afford to let him live."* The human shook violently, but stood silent, still refusing to move.

The demon forced the snake deeper, all the way into the man's brain. *"Look at the possibilities. It's just another step toward getting what you want. You deserve it."*

The man drew a knife from beneath his coat and advanced several paces. The demon reclaimed the snake and stepped back, watching with anticipation. Mission accomplished.

———

Embarrassment and fury washed through Robert Jamison. He'd make that preacher pay – and through the nose – for everything. Watchman had not only taken his headline stripper, the pastor had also robbed him of his pride and dealt his manhood a serious blow. An arrest would be only the first step. The lawsuit that followed might ruin both Henry Watchman and his holier-than-thou church. Jamison smiled ferociously. Yeah, that should do the trick!

Footsteps coming from the other end of the alley caused Jamison to turn.

"Hello, Jamison. Tough evening?"

Jamison squinted, trying to identify the newcomer. As the figure finally edged into the circle of the doorway's dim light, he felt his blood pressure go up once more.

"I already told you once you shouldn't . . ."

"Yeah, I know." The whisper barely reached Jamison's ears. "We shouldn't be seen by too many people. Come over here where we can talk in privacy."

The strip club owner walked up the alley and put out his hand. "Since no one's around, we don't have to pretend we don't know each other." He shivered. "What an evening I've had. I need . . ."

The blow to his chest hit so hard it cut off his breathing. He saw, as from far away, a knife blade coated in black rise and fall twice more. It seemed to be hitting his body, but, strangely, he felt no pain. Then Robert Jamison felt nothing. Not even the final plunge of the knife with a piece of paper stuck through it.

CHAPTER EIGHTEEN

Vincent Anderson made a quick check of the man he now knew as Gin McFain. He'd seen the blind man begging on the street corners in the area from time to time. McFain had sustained multiple wounds, but none seemed severe. On the surface, it looked as if he'd bled profusely. But the tiny gashes weren't deep; he'd live.

"McFain, I have to check on someone else just around the corner. I'm not leaving you, so don't worry. An ambulance has been called. You're going to be okay."

"I . . . I'm not gonna die?" Panic tinged McFain's voice.

Detective Anderson normally rated pretty low in the reassuring department, but he gave it his best shot. "I'll be straight with you," he said. "You'll probably spend a few nights in the hospital. You may have to have several of those lacerations stitched."

A low moan came from the man on the ground.

"They'll give you pain medication. You'll never feel the needle."

"Needle?" McFain squeaked. "They're gonna put a needle in me?"

The detective sighed. He certainly hadn't helped the situation any. On the other hand, with a guy like Gin McFain, he doubted if Maria could have done much better. Vince decided to quit before he made the man faint. He backed away, said, "I'll be right back," and darted around the corner to see if Jamison and the preacher had renewed their fighting.

No fighters greeted him. But two things caught his eyes, blood splattered on the alley walls and Robert Jamison lying on the rough stones. No echoing footsteps of someone fleeing. No witness to identify the killer.

When he saw the paper under the knife sticking out of Jamison's chest, Anderson gritted his teeth in frustration. Not another one! He bent down and felt for a pulse. Nothing. Jamison's eyes were wide open, as if in disbelief. Anderson leaned over until he could just see the words on the underside of the paper: *Use profanity and you will DIE!* So, the killer had struck again. And, Henry Watchman had again been in the vicinity.

As if he'd heard the detective's thoughts, Henry Watchman came around the corner and entered the alley. When he saw the body and blood, he stopped as if he'd run into an invisible wall. "What . . . what happened?" he asked.

"Pastor Watchman, where have you been for the past few minutes?" Anderson snapped. "I thought you were going to stay with me."

Henry Watchman took several deep breaths as he forced himself to look carefully at the remains of what had been Robert Jamison. Then he said, "I was trying to help. When I saw the man hurt, I ran back to the car and had Jenna call 911. I explained the situation to the operator, then ran back to the fire. You weren't there so I went looking. I came past the alley and saw you."

Vincent Anderson's face wore a mask of fury. He pulled his revolver and said, "Turn around, place your hands on the wall and spread your legs."

"Be reasonable, detective. I didn't . . . "

"Shut up!" Vincent ordered. "I'm trying to remember that

you're respected by a lot of people in this community. But you'll do as I say right now."

When the pastor had complied, Vincent called in to Shirl. "You're going to have to bother the chief again. We have a homicide in the alley behind the LadyZ-N-Waiting. Robert Jamison, stabbed to death." He could hear sirens in the distance, police and ambulance. "Yeah, Shirl. They should be here any minute." *But they're too late for Jamison.* Anderson kept the bitter thought bottled up as he glared at Henry Watchman.

———

Soft dinner music accompanied the amiable din of conversation throughout the restaurant. Chief Jinx Monroe sat down once more at the table with his two friends. A proposed tax increase for more law enforcement personnel should have been the main topic of the evening. Instead, the two city councilmen had watched Monroe jump up and down throughout the meal. Now, they sat in front of largely empty plates while the chief began only his third bite.

"Why don't you send that back and let them heat it up some," one of the men suggested.

The chief shook his head while he chewed. In a moment, he answered, "The way my phone's been ringing this evening, if I have to send the steak back, it will never get eaten!"

The other two men chuckled. "I'm telling you, chief, I thought my constituents kept me busy. But you." One of them shook his head. "I wouldn't have your job. No rest."

As if on cue, Chief Monroe's phone rang again. He moaned. "Since you two have finished eating, I'll take this call at the table, if you don't mind." The two councilmen nodded. .

"Shirl, this better be important," Jinx Monroe said as he checked the caller I.D. Then the easy smile left his face. "What? Where did it happen? Do we know the victim?" The blood drained from his face. "Do we have any clue as to who did it?

Okay, still wide open." He put another bite of steak in his mouth and spoke through the bites. "I'm on my way over there, Shirl. It's about three blocks from where I am right now." He grimaced. "Yeah, I know it'll take me at least fifteen minutes in this traffic. But it's as soon as I can get there. Bye."

Monroe stuffed some twice-baked potato in with the bite of steak. "Sorry, men, I've got to go. There's been a murder." He shook his head to show he couldn't give details. After several more quick bites and a hastily gulped glass of water, he headed for the door.

The two councilmen looked at each other. "Let's stay in politics," one said. "That's the kind of job that can kill you."

"Yeah," the other responded. "But notice who didn't have to pay for his meal."

———

A small crowd had gathered outside the LadyZ-N-Waiting. Several dancers could be seen weeping as the coroner took the body of Robert Jamison away. Gawkers in cars slowed traffic to a crawl, preventing the ambulance with Gin McFain in it from leaving. The detective's spirits rose a bit when he heard the police siren and saw Hank Thompson get out of the patrol car. At least one sane person was on the scene.

"Sergeant, good to see you," he said. "Get out there and direct that traffic, please." He pointed at his companion. "I'll wait here with Pastor Watchman until the chief arrives."

Watchman still looked shaken. Vincent hadn't cuffed him – yet.

A police car pulled up and parked where it blocked the alleyway. The bulky figure of Jinx Monroe emerged, looked around and then headed for the pair. "Another note?" he asked without preamble.

Vincent cut his eyes at Pastor Watchman, then responded. "Yes sir. Same as before."

The chief grunted. "Tell me what happened."

The detective gave him a quick rundown of the evening, leaving nothing out. When he finished, he turned to Henry Watchman. "By the way, pastor, why on earth did you leave to call 911? You had to know I'd planned to do the same thing – and quicker than you would have been able to."

"I know that now," Watchman admitted. "At the time, I couldn't read your mind. It looked as if you needed to help that Gin McFain. I thought while you were attending to him, I could get an ambulance on the way."

Vincent shook his head in disgust. "It also gave you time to slip into the alley and kill Jamison."

Watchman put up a hand in protest. "Wait a minute. I couldn't have had time to do something like that, talk to my wife and to the operator and then get back to you."

"Yes, you did have time." Detective Anderson pulled out his cuffs. "I'm arresting you as a suspect in the murder of Robert Jamison."

Pastor Watchman took a step back. "Hold on. What about *you*? When I entered the alley, I saw *you* kneeling over the body. You had more time than anyone to kill the club owner!"

The words froze Vincent. "But I'm a detective. It's my job to be in situations like that."

Pastor Watchman refused to give in. "Perhaps, but it's not your job to cause those situations."

Anger flew over Vincent and he thrust the cuffs forward.

"That's enough, Detective Anderson." Jinx Monroe's voice cut through Vincent's red haze of anger. "Pastor Watchman, you do have some explaining to do . . . but I'm going to let you go for now."

"Chief, I don't think . . ."

"Detective Anderson, I don't care what you think." The chief turned to face Pastor Watchman. "I know where you live. I'm assuming you'll not leave Hidden Beach without talking to me first?" The pastor nodded reluctantly. "Tomorrow, I'll expect a phone call from you as to when you can come down to the police station and have a chat with detectives Anderson and Da Silva . . . and with me."

Henry Watchman let a bushel of air out of his lungs. "You're letting me go?" The chief nodded. "Good. I've still got some people who need my help this evening."

As Watchman moved toward his car, Vincent hit his thigh in frustration. "I'm telling you, chief, we're letting a murderer go free."

Monroe swiveled to look at his young detective. "And your evidence?" he asked softly. "We can still take him down later. But you'd better do your homework first. For example, maybe that Gin McFain guy heard something. Check on him first thing tomorrow." The chief started toward his vehicle. "For now, leave Watchman alone. Do what I'm going to do. Go home and get some sleep."

Sgt. Thompson came to the entrance of the alley and stopped. "Okay if I join you guys?"

The chief wearily waved an arm. "Come on, Hank. We're all about to go home anyway."

"Uh, chief?"

Monroe looked a little more alert. He knew that tone, coming from Thompson, meant something. "What is it?"

"It's probably nothin'. But after Shirl radioed me to come, Eric Batts called to say that he'd take the job. I told him I could be there in five minutes, but he insisted he was just around the corner and could do it."

Anderson stepped forward. "Then why did you end up here anyway?"

"Well," the sergeant looked embarrassed. "I'd already gotten in trouble with the chief once this week. I figured following orders was the best way to stay on his – excuse me, Jinx . . . I mean, chief . . . I mean, you – your good side." Hank slapped himself on the forehead. "You idiot."

The chief stayed calm. "Don't worry, Thompson. And, you

did the right thing." He flipped open his cell phone and hit the number 2. After a moment, he spoke into it. "Shirl? Chief Monroe. Look at the duty roster. Is Batts on the evening rotation?" He waited while Shirl checked. "Okay, thanks. No, I'm going home. Which is where you should be, as well."

He turned to look at Vincent, holding his gaze for a minute. "Eric Batts is still on day shift. I can think of no good reason for him to be in this vicinity in his squad car at this hour. I wonder why he decided to show up?" The chief began walking toward his car at the end of the alley but threw one parting comment back over his shoulder. "Rushing a situation can often lead to the arrest of the wrong person, Detective Anderson. Remember that."

CHAPTER NINETEEN

Darkness covered the ocean. Henry Watchman stood on the wet sand, listening to the roar of the surf crashing itself into nothingness as the unseen ocean bed robbed it of its power. A brisk wind pushed at his face and he inhaled deeply. This environment normally gave him strength and a sense of balance. Tonight, however, everything seemed turned upside down. He felt as if some terrible tide of evil were rushing upon him, coming from an implacable enemy that hid in the night. Two murders that made no sense; a detective who hated him for who knows why. If he could only discover his foe, then he could fight it. Henry grimaced. Yes, fighting was something he could do very well. He'd hoped to put it behind him forever. This evening's events had taught him how wrong that assumption had been.

Beside him, the demon stared with a hungry intensity. Henry Watchman's spiritual fatigue had acted like a beacon in the night. Shi'intor had followed that signal from the alleyway of the strip club, all the way to the ocean's edge. A murder was a good start to the night, but it wasn't enough. The preacher's doubts had created an opening he might be able to exploit.

Toldin appeared on the other side of the preacher, but after a quick glance, Shi'intor knew he had nothing to fear. The angel looked washed out from his encounter with the concentration of filth and evil at the strip club. Toldin's brief burst of strength from the Christians' prayers was now expended. In the presence of doubt and depression, the angel could only look on as Shi'intor prepared to take the next step in Henry Watchman's downfall. "I hope you enjoy what's about to happen!" he gloated. "You might as well leave, angel. You have no power here."

The foul creature sank his claws into his own chest and pulled from deep within a murky, ink-like cloak woven, not from silk or wool, but from depression and hopelessness. The demon shook out the cloak and let it billow before him in the ocean breeze. Like a magnet to metal, the cloak strained toward the human. It positioned itself above Watchman's shoulders, awaiting the demon's command. A moment more, and the preacher would be covered from head to toe as the cloak sapped him of any desire to continue.

Henry Watchman looked once more out over the water. Past the surf, past the dim lights of distant boats, as far as the eye could see, there existed darkness. "Father," he prayed, "I need your help. I can't see what to do or where to turn. But I do believe You love me. And I know I love You. In Jesus' name, I ask for Your strength right now."

Toldin gave a mighty leap. The beating of wings, a flash of silver, and Shi'intor felt fire in his arms as a sword slashed from above. It shredded the cloak into nothingness, then angled up toward the demon's throat. Satan's servant managed to block it with a talon, but the blade sheared through the claw like paper. The demon screeched in anguish and leaped far back into the ocean, sinking beneath the waves.

On the shore, the angel hovered above Henry Watchman. As they had done for Henry's wife, Toldin's wings arched to form a divine cloak of protection. "The Father hears and answers His children's prayers," the angel shouted toward the foul creature. "You are not welcome here." Eyes of silver gazed down protectively on the beleaguered pastor. "He has asked for God's help."

Beneath the waves, moaning in agony, the demon raged with anger. How he hated prayer! He had come so close to succeeding. *I can wait, he thought.* "*The human will eventually come to me*. He allowed the undertow – a demon undertow, the creature thought bitterly – to pull him far out to sea, distancing himself from angel and believer. *I can wait*. The words sank, like the demon himself, into the vast darkness of the waters.

"In God I have put my trust; I will not be afraid. What can man do to me?"

The words of Psalm 56:11 seemed to float above the pounding surf. Henry had memorized the verse several months ago. Now, the beleaguered pastor bowed his head as he tried to apply the truths of the verse to his own life. The psalmist who penned those words thousands of years before had just reminded him that God, the unseen bedrock in his life, could stop the power of any enemy coming against him.

Peace welled up in his soul. A full decade ago, Henry Watchman had placed his trust – and control of his life — in God. But he sometimes needed a divine nudge to keep God at the center of everything he did. "Thank you, Lord," he said, before turning his back on the vast, black ocean and returning to his car.

Flying above him, sword at the ready to protect God's child, the angel smiled as he also thanked God for the victory.

CHAPTER TWENTY

"I think I should be going, Mrs. Watchman."

"Wanda, enough of that nonsense. And, please call me Jenna."

The two women sat at the kitchen table, a cup of coffee in front of each of them. Wanda Lemming had refused any offer of food – until Jenna had pulled some cold chicken out of the refrigerator. "I've changed my mind," she'd said, her face glowing. "I'd love some chicken. And don't heat it," Wanda had added hastily. "As a little girl, I used to *love* cold fried chicken." Jenna had placed a glass of iced tea with a mint leaf in it beside the plate.

As Wanda ate, Jenna had begun brewing the coffee. The real thing, not decaf. She had a feeling the evening was far from over.

"This is a nice house," Wanda had observed at one point, in between bites. "It looks, I think, so *welcoming*. The rooms seem to enjoy your presence." She had blushed as if she'd shared more with Jenna than she'd meant to. After the meal, however, Wanda had gone suddenly shy.

"Okay . . . Jenna," she continued. "I appreciate all you've done for me. But I also know what I am and what you are. My presence here won't help you with the people in your church.

The rumors will start flying, your husband will be mad that I'm still here and the two of you could end up in a huge fight." She shook her head. "I've hurt enough people and ruined all the marriages I want to ruin. I want a new beginning."

Jenna took that as an opening. "Wanda, on the surface, what you've said is admirable. But if you really want a new beginning, you'll have to change your pattern of running when the going gets tough."

Wanda sat up straighter, startled. "How . . . how did you know I do that?" A suspicious look crossed her face. "Have you been checking up on me?"

"No!" Jenna laughed gently. "I just know human nature, and I've been around long enough to have talked to lots of people who find themselves in difficult situations.

"Now, let's take your objections one at a time." She ticked them off her fingers. "First, something you didn't mention, but which is very important. You no longer have a place to stay; we can help you with that. I know several women who would love to have you sharing their house with them for awhile. Second, you're going to be surprised by the people in our church. Sure, there are some stinkers; you'll find those in every organization. But for the most part, our people know that you, I and all of them are in the same boat. None of us deserves God's love; all of us desperately need His grace and forgiveness. They also believe that the church is not a place for perfect people, but a hospital for spiritually sick people who want to get well." She nodded encouragingly at her guest. "Most of these people will welcome you with open arms and wish the best for your new life."

Wanda shook her head in disagreement. "I'm sorry, but a place like that sounds too good to be true. I've been around, and it seems to me most people are looking out for themselves and seeing how they can gouge you."

"Is that the way you are?" Jenna asked gently.

The question rocked the other woman back. "I used to be like that," she said slowly. "But something's been happening to me over the last few months, particularly the last couple of weeks. I . . . I don't want to hurt anyone else."

Jenna leaned forward. "If you feel like that, why can't you believe there are others just like you?"

Wanda held on. "Like I said, I've been in a lot of places, and those people you spoke of just don't exist."

"Maybe you just haven't been looking in the right places," Jenna responded firmly. "Now, the last objection. My husband won't be mad that you're here. He's spent his life . . ."

The back door opened and Henry Watchman came through the door. He leaned over Jenna and gave her a kiss. "Tough night. I'm glad to be home." Then he looked at Wanda Lemming. "I hope my wife hasn't stuffed you too much! She believes food and friendship can heal just about anything." Jenna cut her eyes at an empty chair. Henry understood.

"You're having coffee and I could use a cup right now. I don't want to intrude, but would you mind too much if I join you ladies?" When both women nodded, the pastor pulled out a chair and sat down at the table.

Wanda blushed as she murmured, "I'm no lady."

Watchman waited as Jenna poured everyone a fresh cup. Then he said, "Let's think about that statement about your not being a lady for a moment." Jenna sat down on the other side of Wanda as Henry continued. "If I understand the situation this evening correctly, Jamison not only had *not* fired you, he wanted to keep you from quitting, right?" Wanda nodded. "You must have been pretty valuable to him. He'd decided to beat you in an attempt to force you into keeping your job . . . right?"

Watchman took a sip of coffee. Again, Wanda nodded.

"But in spite of the money you were going to be out, and in spite of the beating, you held firm and quit because you didn't want to hurt anyone else." He raised an eyebrow at Wanda. She nodded a third time.

Watchman slapped the table for emphasis. "Then it's settled. If that doesn't make you a lady, I don't know what does!"

Wanda smiled, a little surprised by the turn of conversation.

"Maybe it's time for you to begin thinking about yourself in a new way," Henry continued. "Don't let the chains of the past hold you prisoner anymore."

Wanda cradled her head in her hands for a moment. When she spoke, the words sounded muffled. "No one's ever called me a lady before." Then she got enough courage to raise her head and look at her would-be benefactors. "Listen," she said, "I appreciate what both of you are trying to do for me. But the truth is, Mr. Jamison will never let me go. He'll just keep on harassing me until I'm forced back to the LadyZ-N-Waiting."

"You haven't heard the news yet?" Henry asked, startled.

Jenna shot a look at her husband. "What news?"

Henry waited until both women were looking at him. "Detective Anderson found Robert Jamison stabbed to death a couple of minutes after we left him in the alley. I don't condone murder. And, I'm sorry Jamison died. But at the same time, I also have to admit it's a relief to know you'll never have to worry about him bothering you again, Wanda."

Wanda's eyes grew round. "You killed him?"

"Of course not." Henry brushed the suggestion away. "I'd never do anything like that. God has called me to save lives, not take them. However," and he paused to look at his wife, "that detective wanted to arrest me on suspicion of murder this evening. The chief wouldn't let him, but I have to go down to the station tomorrow and let them question me."

Jenna got up and came around to Henry. She leaned over him from behind and placed her cheek next to his. "We'll face this together, dear. It will be okay."

Watchman nodded in agreement. "Thanks, Jenna. That's something the Lord confirmed for me on the beach this evening. Together, with God, we can face anything."

Wanda's doubt, however, still had to be dealt with. And at the moment, it seemed doubt had the upper hand. "I'm sorry I've caused you all these problems, Pastor Watchman," she said, seemingly on the verge of tears. "If it hadn't been for me, you would have never gone into that alley. If it hadn't been for me, Billy and Cherie's marriage wouldn't be breaking up." She began to quietly cry, tears falling unnoticed on her blouse.

This time, Jenna moved to comfort Wanda. "There, there," she said in a soothing voice, "you're blaming yourself for far too much."

"My wife is right, you know," Watchman said. "Wanda, you're free. Jamison won't bother you anymore; you don't have an apartment you have to go back to. In short, the future's wide open for you! As for my problems, you might as well begin your spiritual education right now." He pulled a small Bible from his pocket and opened it to Romans 8:28. Jenna motioned for Wanda to move her chair closer, where she could follow along as Pastor Watchman read: "*And we know that all things work together for good to those who love God, to those who are called according to His purpose.*"

He asked Wanda, "Do you know what that means?" When she simply shook her head and looked puzzled, he explained. "Not everything that happens in the world is good. You know that from experience."

"You can say that again," Wanda said with a trace of bitterness.

"God is sovereign. That means He rules over everyone and everything. But in His sovereignty, God created humankind to be free. In other words, He allows us to say no to His love and to His will. When people do that, a lot of innocent people get hurt – even Christians. But the Lord has not only promised to be with us during these times of difficulty, He also says that if we will give Him the situation and the hurt, God will actually use them for His good! Every tear, every scar, every bad event in your life can become useful for the Lord, when they are yielded to Him."

"That's pretty hard for me to believe," Wanda said.

Pastor Watchman nodded. "It is hard. But, let's do an experiment. You, Wanda, are in it from the beginning. I don't know what's going to happen with all this, but I believe God will bring good out of evil. As you watch this story unfold, I'm going to ask you to reserve judgment until these events have been wrapped up. Then you can decide if the Bible is true or not."

Wanda looked confused. "I'm not sure I understand what you're talking about," she said.

"There's been an attack on me; from where, I'm not sure. Three options are open to me: I can get angry, I can get bitter, or I can get closer to God. I've chosen the third alternative. You're in the front row, Wanda, a perfect seat to see what happens."

"But that means you have to stick around," Jenna interjected, placing a hand on Wanda's arm.

"And if you really want to help make a difference for good, we could use you to help put Billy's marriage back together," Pastor Watchman finished.

"How in the world can I help anyone with their marriage?" Wanda asked.

Henry chuckled. "All you have to do is tell Billy what the dancers say about the men and what you're thinking about when you dance."

A grin began to spread across Wanda's face. "I can see how that might give him an attitude adjustment."

Jenna raised her hand to get their attention. "Right now, we've got more urgent things to do. Let's find a place for Wanda to spend a few days. Then, we need to set up some time when the three of us can talk."

"You don't need to . . . ."

"Hush, Wanda," Jenna interrupted. "Let people give you something because they want to. We're asking for nothing in return, only that you give us a chance to help you."

Wanda thought about it for a few minutes. Then she looked directly at Jenna. "Okay, but I am asking for one more favor. If I talk, I talk only with you." She wouldn't look at Pastor Watchman. "Nothing against your husband, but my experience with men isn't very good. Almost none of them have ever proved to be helpful in the long run. They always want to use me in some way."

Jenna nodded. "I understand. And I'll respect that. However, I hope my husband – as well as some other men you'll meet at the church – will be able to change your mind in that area." She poured another cup of coffee for them all, then straightened as Henry motioned for her to come into the next room.

"Wanda," she said, "please excuse me for a moment." A small grin flickered around the edges of her mouth. "While I'm gone, feel free to eat some more of that cold chicken. And, speaking of cold, there's some chocolate ice cream in the freezer." Henry, almost into the other room, stopped so suddenly it looked like he'd run into a wall. He looked expectantly at his wife. "The ice cream," Jenna said in a firm voice, "is *all* for our guest."

———

Mary Connors had not been sleeping well. So when the phone rang, she was instantly awake.

"Hello . . . . Jenna, is that you?" Mary fumbled for the lamp beside the bed. A glance at the alarm clock showed the numbers 1:15 shining on its digital face. Why would the pastor's wife be calling her so late at night?

"What's wrong, Jenna?" Mary could hear a sense of urgency in Jenna's voice. "You need for me to let someone stay here for a couple of days? Sure, I'd be glad to have someone else here. The house is big and one more person certainly won't tax it."

But Jenna was saying something else, as well. Mary pressed her ear closer to the receiver. She must have heard wrong. "I'm sorry, Jenna," she said, laughing. "For a moment, I thought you said this woman was a stripper." Then the blood drained from her face. "That is what you said?" The widow took a deep breath, then said, "Could you hold on for just a moment, please?"

What am I getting myself into? she thought, putting the phone on the bed. *Have Jenna and Pastor Watchman gone completely mad?*

She raised her eyes in frustration, looking at the ceiling. For some reason, it reminded her of her prayer earlier that evening. She sighed. *Okay, God, this may be your way of answering my prayer,* she said silently. *I didn't think You would answer me quite so quickly . . . and especially not in this way!*

Mary put the phone to her ear once more. "Jenna, what is this woman's name? . . . . . Great, you and Henry bring Wanda over. I'm sure we'll have a great time getting to know each other . . . . Okay, see you in a few minutes."

After hanging up, she actually chuckled. How long had it been since she'd done that! "Lord," she prayed, "I'm beginning to believe you have a great sense of humor." Then she walked down the hall to the linen closet. Fresh sheets and pillowcases needed to be put on one of the guest beds quickly. As she mounted the stairs and entered a long-unused bedroom, the house seemed friendlier and not as big as before. She squared her shoulders. After making the bed, every light in the house was coming on!

––––––––––

The muted lights and soft music concealed identities and conversation in the upscale lounge at one of Hidden Beach's five star hotels. Seated alone at the bar, Jinx Monroe had to admit he didn't really care for the place. He preferred something a little less formal and more like his old neighborhood bar. He shook his head. That bar was gone. Most of his friends had moved away, died, or they'd turned to grandchildren and gardens. Jinx Monroe found himself at this point in his life to be in an unusual position: respected by nearly everyone – but lonely. The rest of the world, it seemed, had passed him by.

"Want another one, Jinx?"

The chief look up and nodded. "Sure Jerry, maybe one more wouldn't hurt me too bad." The bartender was the only reason Monroe had begun frequenting this place. Jerry had tended bar for years at "Bobbie's Place," the neighborhood bar in Jinx's part of town. When it closed, Jerry had found a job at the hotel bar. Most of the regulars at "Bobbie's" had found other places to go. Jinx, instead, followed Jerry. Anyone who could call him "Jinx" and get away with it deserved a little loyalty.

"You're risking a lot tonight, Jinx. You usually ask for decaf, not the 'leaded' stuff." Jerry's eyes had permanent laugh lines, and for a good reason. "You sure you can drive with all that caffeine in you?"

The chief smiled in spite of his melancholy mood. "Yeah, go ahead and laugh at me, Jerry," he said. "But I can't drink anything stronger, at least in public." He tilted the cup so the bartender could pour the coffee without spilling it. "As I've said to you before, I take my job and my reputation seriously."

"At the risk of repeating myself, Jinx, just how much has that attitude brought you happiness?"

"Look," the chief shot back quietly, "I'm already dealing with one preacher right now. I don't need an old friend preaching at me, as well."

Jerry put his hand on Monroe's shoulder. "I'm not trying to preach, Jinx. I'm just trying to get someone I've known a long time to relax a little bit. I don't know what's been going on in your life for the last several months, but it's changed you . . . and not for the better."

Monroe motioned for him to sit down. Jerry looked around to see if anyone else needed him. Everyone else seemed to be deep in their own conversations, so he eased onto the stool beside his old friend. "What's eating at you, Jinx?" he asked.

Monroe stared at his coffee for a long time, stirring it idly with his spoon. Then, without looking up, he said, "Actually, I don't think it's any one thing." He raised his head and looked around carefully. A cop's reflex. "I just know that I feel as if life is flying past and leaving me behind. Things are changing, the town's both growing and deteriorating at the same time, and people are putting up with all sorts of stuff we used to think of as wrong." He continued to stir his coffee absently. "Even on the force, now I've got a hotshot young police officer who thinks he's a whole lot better than he is. His attitude is either gonna get him killed, or he'll make chief before I'm ready." Monroe grimaced. "Then I'll really be alone."

He took a sip of his coffee, surprised to find it cold. But then, just about everything surprised him these days. "That police force is my only family, Jerry." The bartender nodded. He'd known the truth of that for years. "I know retirement is on the horizon. But it seems to be rushing at me faster than I'd ever imagined it would."

"You really need a hobby," Jerry said.

"You've been saying that for years," the chief retorted.

"It's still true," came the soft response. Jerry stood up as he saw another customer enter the bar. "This time, take me seriously, Jinx. You're a great guy who has a lot of responsibility. When that job load is gone, you're going to have to have something to take its place."

"Yeah, Jerry, I know." Jinx waved him away. "Go take care of your paying customers." He finally looked his old friend in the eyes. "I promise, I heard you. I'll try to follow your advice." He picked up his coffee and drained the rest of it, put the empty cup on the bar and walked out slowly, his head down.

Jerry watched him go and felt helpless. *This isn't going to end well*, he thought.

CHAPTER TWENTY-ONE

The normal level of noise in the precinct hit Vincent Anderson as he stepped through the door. It felt comfortable, familiar. This place was about as close as he'd ever gotten to having a home in his teenage and adult life. A few heads turned toward him, curious. One or two edged away from his path. Maria sat at a desk, her ear to a telephone, nodding as she listened. When she saw Vincent, the big detective raised a warning eyebrow and glanced across the room at Eric Batts and the group surrounding him. Vincent understood. The rumor mill had begun churning again, and Batts probably held the churn handle.

"Anderson!" Batts called out.

Vincent nodded in his direction. "Hello, Eric."

Batts sneered openly. "I didn't think you'd have the courage to show up this morning. After all, you have to be counted a prime suspect in – how many is it now? – two killings and a car bomb."

The men and women around Batts scattered, and the station grew quiet.

Vincent didn't even bother to stop, but continued straight on to his desk. "I had to come in." He sat down and picked up a sheaf of reports meant for him. "An investigation seems to be in order concerning why several people who had no business being in the vicinity of last night's crime scene were there." At this, he raised his head and looked directly at Batts. "I had a reason for being there, Eric. It was my assignment." His eyes bored straight into Batts'. "What was your reason?"

Batts stiffened. Snickers from those around him didn't help matters. Vincent could see the patrolman trying to work up the courage to charge him. He got his feet out from under the chair and prepared to stand. Instead, Chief Monroe's door opened and in a pleasant voice the chief said, "Good morning, everyone! It's good to see you arriving on time." His head swung around, taking in the room. "Da Silva, Batts, Anderson. Please come into my office for some instructions."

Jinx Monroe popped back into his office, taking with him most of the tension in the room.

Vincent walked past Maria's desk on his way to the office. "What's this about?" he whispered. She shrugged her shoulders slightly. Both of them had to take a step back when Batts jumped in front of them to get into the office first. Vincent held back and said to Maria, "A gentleman always lets a lady enter first."

Maria smiled, but they could both see Batts turn red. In the chief's presence, however, he held his tongue.

"All of you sit down."

Chief Monroe was being polite. That kind of attitude from the chief always worried Vincent. He kept quiet and decided to watch and try not to react to anything said.

"I've not yet heard the news, Batts," the chief began, "but it looks like congratulations are in order for you."

Batts looked pleased, then confused. "Sir? Congratulations?"

Chief Monroe's smile became even warmer. "Sure, Batts. You must have recently had a promotion. Isn't that right?"

Confusion now ran rampant over Batts' face. "I . . . I'm not sure I follow."

The chief still looked pleasant. "Sure you do. Evidently,

you've been promoted to detective and chief of this place, all in a couple of days." The smile disappeared. "Is that right, Batts?"

"No . . . no sir. I really don't know what you're talking about." Sweat begin dripping off the patrolman's chin, in spite of the near arctic conditions in the chief's office.

"Sure you do." Monroe never raised his voice, but somehow menace flowed from the chief to Batts. "You've been telling your peers that one of my detectives is guilty of multiple murders. You try to horn in on a crime scene when you've not been invited." Chief Monroe leaned forward until his face almost touched Eric Batts. "And, you become judge and jury of one of our finest officers without a shred of evidence."

Monroe got up from his chair and stepped around the desk. "Your powers of deduction are amazing, far better than mine. So, here, this must be your chair. Come sit in it."

Eric Batts wanted to be anywhere other than in that office. He tried to swallow a couple of times, but his mouth found nothing to swallow. "Sir, I . . . I don't belong there. That's your chair."

The chief nodded pleasantly. "And, it's also my police station. I decide what happens here, not you . . . unless you think I should step aside and let you take command." He motioned one more time at his chair. "Do you want to take over my job?"

"No sir, I don't." Batts looked at the floor, the ceiling, the walls, anywhere but at the other three people in the office.

"So, when you walk out of here, I'm assuming you're going to keep your mouth shut and just do the job assigned to you. Is that right?" The chief waited until Batts looked at him and nodded. "Fine, you're dismissed."

Batts went out, shutting the door quietly. They could see him head straight for the patrol cars, shaking his head at everyone who tried to stop him.

"Now, Detective Anderson."

Vincent tried to put a neutral expression on his face. "Yes sir?"

"Pull off of the preacher until about 10:00 each evening. The murders have happened late at night, so I think we're wasting our time if we pursue any other time. In addition, if he doesn't see your car or Detective Da Silva's, he may get careless – if he's the murderer. If nothing's happened after three or four days, I'll get some additional personnel to relieve you. And, Detective Anderson?"

"Yes sir."

"That speech I gave Batts is one I don't want to have to give to anyone else. You understand?"

Vincent simply nodded.

"Okay, go back to work."

Vincent stood and waited for Maria to get up, as well. But the chief waved him out. "You go ahead. I need to discuss a few things with Detective Da Silva."

After Vince had left, the chief said, "Maria, this is for you alone."

Maria raised her eyebrow again, but merely said, "Okay, chief."

"I want you to begin quietly checking Eric Batts' whereabouts during the times of the last two murders. And . . . I want you to check out Vincent, as well."

Maria gawked at him, incredulous. "Sir, you don't actually think . . ."

Monroe grimaced. "I don't know what to think or who to trust. But I do want us, at the very least, to begin narrowing the field of suspects."

"What about me, sir?" Maria asked. "How do you know I'm not the guilty one, at least for the first murder?"

"Because you were with your mother during that time." He grinned at her astonishment. "Yes, I cleared you personally. Now, you get to work clearing my other personnel."

Jinx Monroe never failed to amaze her. "You can count on me," she said as she got up to leave.

CHAPTER TWENTY-TWO

The afternoon sun, just beginning its slow descent, still had the power to drive all but the hardiest – or most foolish – indoors. Eyes closed, Wanda Lemming sat in a swing on the shaded porch and sighed contentedly. A breeze washed over her from above, thanks to the four swirling fans placed along the length of the porch's ceiling. She took another sip of lemonade from the tall glass and sighed once more.

A chuckle from the swing opposite Wanda caused her to open her eyes. Mary Connors, owner of the porch, the house and all the gardens surrounding them, regarded Wanda. Her clear green eyes missed nothing. "You seem to have adapted well to your new schedule."

Wanda smiled back. She still found it hard to believe people could care without demanding anything in return. But her cynicism had started to crack a little. "I know this can't last forever, but the solitude and the" – she tried to find the right word to explain how she felt – "the *respect* are so wonderful." She looked at the sun-dappled flowers and the burgeoning green plants just off the porch. "I think my spirit has been thirsty for years, but I never realized it until I came here."

Both women turned their heads as tires crunched on the

gravel driveway. Birds drinking from a fountain flew away as Jenna Watchman got out of the car and started for the porch. Mary got up quickly, despite her age. Tall, white-haired, her lean body stooped slightly, a result of osteoporosis. Wanda, on the other hand, stood with difficulty. A groan escaped her lips and she placed a hand on her lower back.

"Gardening getting to you?" Jenna asked.

Wanda groaned again. "You wouldn't believe it! I figured all the exercise my body got dancing had kept me in shape. But the last couple of days have taught me I have muscles in places I never knew." She rubbed her back slowly. "And all those places hurt!"

"Don't let her fool you," Mary laughed. "I tried to make her quit several times, but she wouldn't leave the flowers alone. Jenna, I think we've unleashed a flower maniac."

Jenna sat down next to Wanda as Mary put a glass of lemonade in her hand. The birds, sovereign in their territory once more, glided down to drink and bathe. Jenna noted the visible changes in Wanda. A floppy shirt and loose, comfortable shorts adorned her. No makeup, and she still looked fresh and actually younger. The tension had, for the most part, left her face.

"Seriously," Jenna asked, "how are you doing?"

Wanda studied the flowers and greenery. "I can dig in the dirt and make a difference in something's life immediately. I can recognize the dangers to the flowers and pull up weeds. The plants don't try to paw at me, lie to me or put a guilt trip on me if I don't sleep with them." She looked sideways at Jenna. "Does that make sense?"

"Sure it does," Jenna said. "Near-immediate results for your labor; simple rules you can work within; true beauty as a result of your efforts. What could be better?"

Mary stood up and moved into the house for a moment. When she returned, the aroma of fresh chocolate chip cookies accompanied her, along with a plate piled high with the objects giving off the aroma. She passed the plate around and everyone took several, at her insistence.

"I don't need even one of these," Jenna moaned. "Henry eats, and I gain weight!"

"Come out here and work with me in the garden for a couple of hours," Wanda said. "You'll have earned the right to eat that whole plate if you want."

Mary lowered herself once more into the swing. "Wanda has also learned the joy of hard work," she observed. "The rest, afterwards, is wonderful because it's been earned. There's a peace that comes from useful effort that can't be explained. It has to be experienced."

Wanda nodded in agreement.

"So," Jenna asked, "how would you rate your experience Sunday at church?"

"I don't know how to rate it," Wanda responded. "It certainly wasn't what I'd expected."

Jenna nodded. "You mean, we didn't bite the heads off chickens, yell and scream?"

Wanda blushed fiercely but said, "That's about right. Instead, I found the music more up-to-date than I would have imagined. And," she aimed a sly look at Jenna, "I actually listened to your husband's sermon . . . most of the time."

"Did anyone give you a hard time?" Jenna asked.

"No, not really. But you kept me so busy meeting people, I guess the ones who didn't want me there stayed away from the crowd."

Jenna nodded once more. "Like I said, there's a few whiners and complainers in every group. But the majority of our folk welcome anyone who wants to turn their life around." She looked out over the porch. Shadows had begun to lengthen under several willow trees. "Wanda, would you mind taking a walk with me for a minute?" she asked. "We'll stay in the shade."

"Sure," Wanda said. She groaned once more as stiff muscles

protested being used. "If I don't get up now, I may have to sleep here tonight."

Mary chuckled and got up as well. "I'll go inside and start supper. Jenna, come tell me bye before you leave."

The two women stepped off the porch and into the hot Florida sun. "Let's reach that shade before we begin talking," Jenna suggested. Even then, however, she noticed Wanda couldn't help but stop several times to prop up a plant or pull out a recalcitrant weed.

Once in the shadows of the willows, Jenna spoke. Her quiet tone reflected the surroundings. "Are you up to helping Henry and me with Billy and Cherie's marriage? They're coming to our house tonight, and we'd love for you to be there." She shook her head ruefully as she added, "Henry thinks Billy is so into the macho thing he won't listen to any suggestion that isn't presented in the strongest way possible."

Wanda looked once more at the flowers. "I'm just realizing how much more life can be." Her voice had grown so soft Jenna had to lean forward to catch the words. "The other night, I vowed to not cause anyone any more pain if at all possible." She swiveled her head to look at Jenna. "If you and Pastor Watchman think I can undo some of the hurt I've caused Cherie, I'm willing to do it."

———————

Detective Maria Da Silva pursed her lips as she thought. The past few days had brought her little success in tracing Vincent's movements. The man played everything close to the chest. He confided in no one and called no one a close friend. She rubbed her eyes, thinking back over this whole case. It had started with their questioning the motel owner about the dead body and then . . . . How could she have forgotten *that*!

"Shirl, come in, please." Maria couldn't remember if the dispatcher was due to work today.

"Go ahead, Detective Da Silva."

Maria paused to get her question framed right. "Shirl, why did Detective Anderson decide to go to church the other day?"

"Because I invited him." Shirl's voice crackled through the cruiser. "I've been attending Pastor Watchman's church for several months. He's a great speaker and the people seem to care about each other. Detective Anderson doesn't have a lot of friends, so I thought he might enjoy being a part of Hidden Beach Community Church."

Maria couldn't believe Vince would enjoy going to church. "How did he react to the service, Shirl?" she asked.

"It's funny, he wasn't too excited about attending with me at first. But when Pastor Watchman got up to speak, Vincent – I mean, Detective Anderson – seemed to hang on every word. His eyes never left the preacher the whole time. And afterwards, on our way out, he asked all sorts of questions about Pastor Watchman. I told him that I'd only been going there a couple of months, so I didn't know much about the pastor's past."

Maria frowned in the car. "Shirl, remember when Vincent and I investigated the murder of the man on the beach? Where did he go right after that?"

Maria could hear the papers shuffling, then, "I think it's on the computer. Hold on a second." About two minutes later, Shirl came back on. "After he left you, I called him for a report and Detective Anderson said he had to go to the library and check something out."

"Thanks, Shirl." Maria hung up the microphone and put the car in gear. A moment later, she thumbed the mike once more. "By the way, Shirl, keep this to yourself. I'm acting on orders of the chief." She hung up once more and hit the accelerator. The library contained information on lots of things. She hoped it could shed some light on this crazy case.

CHAPTER TWENTY-THREE

"The library is certainly becoming popular with law enforcement personnel." Mrs. Jakoba Danforth kept her voice just above a whisper. The librarian sported two long hairs growing from her chin. Maria could hardly keep her eyes off of them, but it didn't matter. Mrs. Danforth noticed only the books on her desk. A short, plump woman with graying hair, she continued to speak even as she glanced over the due dates of returned objects. An ancient pair of half-frame glasses hung from a chain. Maria guessed that they'd been bought from one of the racks that also hold sunglasses in convenience stores. This woman cared for little besides the volumes filling the shelves around her.

"The policeman who was here last asked for information on newspapers from about ten years ago. I showed where he could find them online, and he stayed here about thirty minutes looking at old articles." Mrs. Danforth finally glanced up and seemed surprised to find Maria still actually there. "I can bring up those newspapers for you, if you wish."

Maria smiled encouragingly. "Please, that would help me a lot."

A few minutes later the detective found herself peering at newspaper images from *The New York Times* on an ancient monitor. *What were you trying to find, Vince?* she thought. This could take days, and she didn't even know what she was searching for. Maria decided to look at just the front page of each edition. After all, Vince had only stayed a few minutes. Either he had found something quickly, or he'd given up.

Nine editions later, a headline caught her attention. She read it in its entirety, then went back and read it more slowly, trying to digest everything.

"Mrs. Danforth," she called. "Would it be possible to get several copies of this article?"

The librarian looked displeased with the request, but she came over and turned on the printer. After a moment, when the paper came sliding out, shiny with fresh ink, she said, "It seems to me you law enforcement people should already have enough copies of this article. Just how many do you need?"

Maria gave her a hard look. "Isn't that what you're here for? Or is the job getting too difficult for you?"

Mrs. Danforth took a step back even as she handed the muscular detective the copies. Maria nodded politely at her and started out of the library and toward the car. Nausea threatened to make her lose her lunch. She didn't want to show the chief the article, but her duty lay before her clearly. However, she knew the information in the article could rightly be termed explosive. It had the power to hurt quite a few lives – and one of those lives happened to be close to her.

———

Vina didn't pause for even a moment when she heard the front door open. Five small cups sat on the counter, waiting to be filled with the sweet, seductively strong liquid known as "Cuban coffee." She'd invited several friends over for the afternoon. By the time the ladies had finished the coffee and their versions of the latest events, Vina would know everything happening in Hidden Beach that she cared to know about.

"Come on back to the kitchen," she called out, still concentrating on the coffee bubbling in the pot.

"Mama, could you add another cup for me?"

She looked up to see Maria standing in the entranceway. Shoulders, normally straight back and proud, slumped; her eyes seemed dull and almost lifeless. Vina quickly pulled another cup down from the cabinet. Something bad had happened, and her daughter needed her!

"Sit down, Mi Hita." She filled the new cup with the thick brew and handed it to Maria.

Her usually calm, strong daughter took the cup with shaking hands. After a cautious sip to judge the temperature of the coffee, she took an even larger swallow. Vina waited. She knew Maria would get to the subject when she was ready. With quick, efficient motions Vina poured herself a cup of coffee. She took a drink and sighed in appreciation.

Maria smiled briefly. "You're right, mi alma. It is good." Her mouth turned down in a grimace. "But what I've got to do in about an hour is not only distasteful, it's probably going to turn Vincent against me." She glanced at her mother. "Of course, I'm the only one who has the information that's so damaging to him. I'm thinking that I could just keep it to myself."

Vina was already shaking her head. "Is what you have the truth?"

Maria nodded. "But, Mama, it's also potentially devastating, and . . ."

Vina stopped her with a raised hand. "Did the police chief ask you to get this information for him?"

Maria looked at her in amazement. "How did you know that?" she asked.

"Just a guess." She waved away her shrewd observation. "Does it involve Detective Anderson's becoming a suspect in the murders we've been reading about in the papers?"

This time, Maria goggled at her mother. "What . . . how . . ."

"Mi Hita," Vina said. "Why else would the police chief,

himself, have you looking for information about Vincent? It just makes sense."

Her daughter finished up the cup of coffee and stood up. "Mama, if the chief ever retires, you should put in your application to take his place." She shook her head. "But that still doesn't help me with what I should do next."

"Sure it does." Vina caught her daughter's eyes. "I've raised you to never be afraid of the truth. The moment you begin holding secrets, you start down a path that will hurt someone – maybe even an old woman who leaves her door unlocked during the day."

Maria looked startled. "Why do you say that?"

"Think about it," Vina continued. "If Vincent is really the murderer, and if he finds out you know something that could damage him, but you're still keeping it private, won't he kill again? And, don't you think he'd also kill anyone close to you that could have learned about the information?"

Mara looked down at the floor for a long moment; then she nodded. "You're right – for a change." She smiled, taking the sting out of the words. "I'll give the truth to the chief. What he does with it is his business."

They both heard the door open, and a flock of voices talking excitedly. "Here come the A.P., the U.P.I., and the Pony Express," Maria quipped. "I'll leave you to the news gathering." She leaned over and gave her mother a quick peck on the forehead. "Thank you, once more," she said softly. Then she stepped aside so the women could enter the kitchen, waved a goodbye to her mom and to the group, and headed for the door.

———

The wooden floors glowed warmly in the afternoon sun. Henry Watchman, passing through the auditorium on his way to his study, stopped to admire the work his custodian had done. "They look beautiful, Raymond. You've done a good job," he called out to the old man.

"Thanks, pastor."

The response came slower than it should have. Henry looked closer at Raymond. Leaning on his mop, the custodian finally raised his head enough so that Henry could get a good look at him. What the pastor saw shocked him.

"Raymond, you feeling all right? Would you like to sit down for a minute?"

The custodian's face looked gray. Tired eyes stared blankly at the pastor for a few seconds. Then Henry saw recognition dawn.

"Don't mind if I do, pastor." Raymond looked around as he eased down on a pew. "The building's the same size it's always been, but it seems to be getting bigger every time I clean it." He leaned back and rested his head against the cushion. A sigh escaped his lips and he closed his eyes. "Reverend Watchman," he said, eyes still closed. "You given any thought to an associate or even a replacement for me?"

Henry wanted to say, "How would I have had time? Two murders, a police investigation against me and a passel of counseling problems have taken up just a tad of my days!" He *wanted* to say that, but he didn't. Instead, Henry placed a comforting hand on Raymond's shoulder and said, "I've got a couple of ideas on how to get you help. But it will take a few more weeks and several visits. Do you think you can hold on a little longer?"

Raymond smiled. The color slowly returned to his face. "Not too much more than that, pastor. I love this place. Cleaning it has been my ministry for the Lord. But now it's time for someone else to have that privilege." He sat up and looked squarely at Henry Watchman. "Find them soon, Reverend Watchman."

CHAPTER TWENTY-FOUR

The precinct headquarters seemed to produce a low hum throughout the premises. Phones rang, pens scratched on reports, keyboards clacked. Few on the police force looked up to take notice of the somber detective as she entered the building and marched straight to her goal.

Maria took a deep breath, squared her shoulders and knocked on the chief's office door. In her hands she carried what might well be Vincent Anderson's destruction. She counted herself a friend of his, but duty was duty and the law was the law.

"Come in, if it's *really* important."

Impatient as ever, she thought. *Get ready, chief, I'm going to get your attention in about one minute.* The big detective opened the door, stepped inside and even sat down without an invitation. Jinx raised an eyebrow. Maria never presumed on the chief or showed bad manners.

"What's up?" he asked.

In response, Maria shoved the pages of the photocopied article toward him. "I got these from the library about twenty minutes ago," she said. "Shirl confirmed Vince went there after our questioning of the motel manager. Mrs. Danforth, the librarian, also confirmed that I was not the first law enforcement personnel to come and ask for the New York headlines from about fifteen years ago. I asked her to pull up what Vince had been reading, and after about ten minutes, I found this." She pointed at the article.

Maria stopped talking as Jinx Monroe read the article. His lips pressed together and a slow flush started in his neck, moving steadily upward until his whole face resembled a beet. When he finally looked up, it startled Maria to see a little moisture in the chief's eyes.

"Well," he said absently. "This changes everything." His eyes focused on the corner of the ceiling for a moment, then he nodded his head. "Get Detective Anderson in here right now."

Maria opened the door, only to find Vincent standing there, hand raised to knock. "What are you trying to do to me, Maria?" he hissed. "I thought you were my friend. Now I find you sneaking around, trying to stab me in the back." He clenched and unclenched his hands several times, trying to control himself. "You, of all people," he said.

"That's enough, Anderson." The chief's voice shot out of the office and had the same effect as a slap in the face. "Both of you get in here . . . and bring Shirl with you."

By the time Shirl joined Maria and Vince, Chief Monroe had arranged three chairs across from his desk. Maria could see Shirl shaking like a leaf. She'd never, *ever* been called into Monroe's office that Maria could remember.

"First, what is said in here will stay in here." The chief's voice sounded colder than the refrigerated air pouring into the room from the vent right above them. "Shirl, you seem to have a problem keeping what you know to yourself."

Vince spoke up. "Chief, it's my fault. I . . ."

"Shut up, Anderson." Jinx Monroe's eyes never left Shirl.

Vincent shut up.

"You told Detective Anderson about an official investigation I'd asked one of my personnel to conduct." He shook his head in disgust. "You let that soft spot in your heart that is reserved for him cloud your judgment. That calls for firing you." He paused while Shirl's face turned pale. "But you're getting off with a warning this time. I'll write up the reprimand and you'll sign and date it." Monroe waited until Shirl looked him in the eyes. "If this happens again – if you tell anyone but me about information you've received – you're out of here. Do you understand?"

Shirl nodded once.

"Do you agree to what I've just said?"

Shirl nodded again, this time accompanying it with a hard swallow.

"Now, get back to work." The chief dismissed her with a wave. Shirl rose with difficulty and, with a swift glance at Vincent, opened the door and exited.

When only the three of them remained, the chief looked hard at Anderson and said simply, "Why didn't you tell me?"

The detective managed to muster an impassive countenance as he stared at his boss. "It's something I just discovered a few days ago. And, I didn't know for sure until I saw the article. After all, I was young when it happened. The . . . the emotions it all brought back overwhelmed me." Maria could hear strain in the voice as Vince tried to maintain his calm. "To tell you the truth, I didn't know what to do. I've been self-sufficient for so long – and now . . . now . . ." He stopped and said nothing else for a moment. "I'm innocent, chief. I swear it," he finally added, staring into Monroe's eyes.

Monroe drummed his fingers on the desk. He fiddled with the article and rubbed absently at his face. Finally he returned Vincent's gaze. "You screwed up major time, you realize."

"Yes sir, I realize that."

"You're still a suspect because of all of this and I'm pulling you off the case immediately."

Vince jumped up in protest. "But Chief, I . . ."

"DO YOU UNDERSTAND HOW MUCH TROUBLE YOU'RE IN?" The chief's roar rattled the walls. Even people outside the office turned to see what had caused the commotion.

"You are off the case. There is no objectivity that you can possibly show toward Pastor Watchman or these murders." He threw up his hands in disgust. "I'm doing you a great favor by moving you as far as *possible* from any more *possible* involvement with something that could ruin your career. The least you can do is cooperate with me a little."

"He's right, Vince." Maria's quiet voice still reached the ears of her partner. "And, for what it's worth, I didn't try to stab you in the back. I was just following my chief's orders to try to clear you of all suspicion."

Vince slumped in his chair. To his credit, he continued to look Monroe in the eye. His voice did shake ever so slightly as he spoke. "Maria, I'm sorry. I completely overreacted. Chief, I really didn't mean to do wrong. I've tried so hard to do what's right for years. I just wasn't ready for . . . for the past to rush back into my life so suddenly." He looked from one to the other as he added, "I'll cooperate in whatever way you suggest."

Jinx Monroe nodded brusquely. "Good. Now, let's decide how to best handle this new evidence we have."

CHAPTER TWENTY-FIVE

"Stay out here, Wanda, for just a few minutes." Jenna and Wanda stood by Titus' fence. They had parked on the back side of the church, where no one in the house would see them arriving. Billy and Cherie's old car sat next to the flower bed. "Give Henry and me time to talk to Billy. You can hear us from the back door. When I think it's the right moment for you to intervene, I'll come get you." Jenna grinned at Wanda. "Then you can come on in and give Billy an 'attitude adjustment'."

Wanda smiled and nodded at Jenna to go on in.

Sudden silence came with the back door closing and Jenna leaving. The silence made Wanda acutely aware of how uncomfortable she really was with the situation into which she was about to insert herself. She could feel a heavy weight of nervousness settle on her shoulders. Because of her background, she hated seeing people getting mad – especially if they were mad at her.

How could she walk in that house and face Billy's wife? Though Wanda hadn't meant to, she knew her choice of lifestyle had nearly broken up their marriage. What would Cherie say? The nervousness spread from her shoulders into her chest. Her heart seemed to beat harder and faster. She just couldn't do what Pastor Watchman and Jenna wanted of her.

A soft whine right behind her caused Wanda to jump. Just inches away, Titus sat with his nose pressed up against the fence, his tail wagging slowly. She wondered if the dog sensed her fear. Something clicked in her mind as she and Titus looked at each other. Wanda hesitated, then opened the gate, used her body to block the entrance to keep Titus from escaping, and went into the back yard, carefully closing the gate behind her. Titus, for his part, surprised her. Instead of jumping up on Wanda and trying to lick her to death, the dog slowly walked over and lay down beside her feet, keeping his eyes on hers. Looking down on the overgrown puppy, emotions she had suppressed for a long time suddenly resurfaced – as did the memories . . .

"You old sot, don't you dare hit me this time!"

Carefully hidden in the bushes underneath the kitchen window, twelve-year old Wanda shivered and held her knees. Her grandfather had come home drunk and angry again. She knew the big man would hit anyone in his path, and words or arguments couldn't persuade him otherwise.

When her mother started yelling at the old man, Wanda knew the attention had moved away from her for a brief moment. That was her signal to disappear as fast as possible. Her mom and grandfather couldn't hit what they couldn't see.

Angry voices rose in volume. The sound of a slap startled Wanda. Her mom must have landed the first blow. Though she'd learned to make herself scarce during her grandfather's drunken tirades, Wanda's mother, on the other hand, always stayed and fought with him. Sometimes her mom held her own and gave as much as she got. Tonight, though, Wanda could hear heavy blows finally beginning to land on her mom. Wanda couldn't tell who she heard crying, her mom or herself. A lamp crashed and broke.

Suddenly a wet nose pressed itself against the young girl's arm Wanda jumped, her heart in her throat, knowing she'd been found and that another beating awaited her. Instead, she turned to see Sam, her mongrel dog, trying to work his way into her arms. Relief flooded her, replacing the recent panic. Wanda pulled the dog into her lap and cradled Sam like a baby. He lay still, as if knowing she needed the closeness. After a long time, the lonely girl buried her face in Sam's soft fur. The dog whined, Wanda sobbed, and more shouts filled the night.

Wanda hugged the dog tightly once more. At least here was someone who loved her.

———

Jenna stepped through the back door by the kitchen, looked at the three individuals and said, "What in the world happened here?" Henry and the Lawrence couple, Billy and Cherie, sat around the small table, laughing about something as they sipped iced tea. Billy's hair stuck out in all directions and the tight t-shirt he liked to wear showed dirt and grass stains. Cherie's face sported two bright spots of red high on her cheeks, and her eyes sparkled. As for Jenna's husband, he looked happy, but embarrassed.

"Honey, I really didn't want the discussion to begin like this, but . . . ." He stopped, not sure how to continue.

Billy spoke up. "It's actually my fault, Mrs. Watchman. If I hadn't been so stupid, it wouldn't have happened."

"Hush, both of you," Cherie interrupted, then blushed even brighter as she realized she'd just told the pastor to be quiet. "Men!" she said, shaking her head.

"Go ahead, Cherie," Jenna said. "Tell me what my husband's been up to while I've been gone."

Henry looked properly abashed.

"It's like this, Jenna," Cherie continued. "We got here about thirty minutes ago. We were a little early, but I figured if Billy wanted to come talk to the preacher, I'd better strike while the iron was hot, so to speak." She looked at Billy for confirmation as she spoke. He nodded for her to continue.

"When Pastor Watchman let us in, Billy immediately began to make a stink."

"I did not!" Billy yelped. "I was just . . . just . . ."

"He made a fool of himself." Cherie went on as if there'd been no interruption. "Billy told the pastor that he couldn't listen to a 'reverend' who didn't know what it took to live 'out there in the real world.' He said preachers only became preachers because they couldn't take the toughness of regular work."

Henry snorted and shook his head.

"Pastor Watchman pointed out that his workout sessions were about as tough as anyone's at the gym, and his hours of work every week amounted to far more than fifty hours, but that meant nothing to Billy. My brilliant husband said only a 'real man' would understand why he needed to go to a strip club. When Pastor Watchman asked Billy what he considered a 'real man,' he came back with, 'someone who can hold his own in a fight.' Billy said until proved otherwise, the pastor wasn't tough enough to earn his respect so Billy could listen to him."

"Uh-oh," Jenna mumbled.

"So, Pastor Watchman kind of sighed, stood up and invited Billy into the back yard. He said he didn't believe in fighting, so he wouldn't hit Billy. But, he invited Billy to swing at him as much as he wanted. When Billy sneered that . . ."

"I didn't sneer!"

"Yes you did." Cherie quieted her husband with a glance. "When he sneered that the fight shouldn't take long, Pastor Watchman smiled and agreed. He just sort of stood in front of Billy with his arms by his sides and waited. Billy put up his hands and feinted twice at the pastor's head. Reverend Watchman never moved. So, Billy threw a right – but the pastor just ducked. Then he stood still again. Billy got mad, and started swinging as hard as he could. Nothing landed. When he stopped, Pastor Watchman still stood there in front of him, his hands at his sides."

Billy broke in. "I'll take over now," he said. "Mrs. Watchman, your husband told me he could have hit me at any time." Billy grinned at the memory. "But he said fighting was a last resort, and he wouldn't hurt me because he loved me and my wife. It made me so mad that I took one last swing at him. I swung so hard – missed, of course, just like the other times -- that I fell on the ground.

"Then the dog jumped on me and wanted to play. That's where all the dirt and grass stains came from."

Jenna just shook her head. "I'll say it this time: Men!"

"Anyway," Henry broke in hurriedly, "Billy's ready to listen now." He turned serious for a moment as he looked at his wife. "I didn't hit him, Jenna. And, I couldn't figure out a way to get him to listen to me otherwise."

Cherie placed her hand lightly on Billy's arm. "There's still a problem, though, isn't there, Billy?"

Her husband ducked his head and nodded.

"What's the matter?" Henry asked.

Billy remained silent. After a moment, Cherie said, "He's still crazy about the stripper, Wanda Wonder. He thinks none of us can understand, because we've not been in his shoes."

Billy finally found his tongue. "You don't know what a rush it is to have a woman like that care for you, desire you. It should be plain to anyone that she really wants a relationship with me. But none of you have seen her looking at me. None of you can understand."

"I understand, Billy."

The two couples turned to look at the newcomer. Wanda Lemming had quietly slipped in through the back door to hear the last part of the discussion. Billy flushed a deep red. Cherie did too, but for a different reason. She seemed not even to have realized she'd stood up and started toward the woman.

"Easy, Cherie." Jenna grabbed her shoulder firmly. "I brought Wanda here to explain a few things to you and Billy."

"Her?" The scorn in Cherie's voice was unmistakable. "She's

the one who ruined my marriage. I don't need any more 'help' from the likes of her."

Jenna tugged on Cherie to swing her around, where they were facing each other. "First, the problem is with your husband, not Wanda. Second, you might want to ask yourself why I allowed Wanda here this evening."

Cherie took a deep breath; then she took a second. Sinking slowly back into her chair, she cut her eyes at the former stripper and muttered, "Sorry. I'm just fighting for my marriage."

Wanda seemed untouched by the emotion in the room. She turned slowly toward Billy and advanced on him until they were only a few feet apart. "Do you want me, Billy?" she asked in a flat voice.

Billy didn't know what to do. He looked from his wife to the woman he'd thought held the answer to all his dreams. "I . . . I'm not sure what's going on here."

"Let me help you make up your mind," Wanda said. "Let me tell you what I and all the other women think about when we're up on the stage stripping." Her eyes remained locked on Billy. "We think about money. Period. We laugh at all the stupid men who leave their families and are naive enough to believe we actually care for them. The truth is, we *loathe* all of you. We can't stand your touching us or looking at us. If it weren't for the money, we wouldn't be there at all."

Billy broke in. "I don't believe it. The way you looked at me can't be faked."

Wanda threw her head back and laughed. "Watch this," she said. Turning to Cherie, she began to move her body ever closer to Billy's wife. Her face took on a seductive air. Everything about her seemed to glisten and she began caressing the lush curves that now undulated only inches from her target. The other three could see Cherie was the most important person in the world to Wanda Wonder at that moment. The air in the room seemed to grow hot and heavy. No one spoke. The stripper writhed ever more seductively, her eyes dilated . . . then she stopped. Wanda backed up, allowed her body and face to relax, and it seemed another woman – an ordinary woman – had suddenly taken the siren's place.

In a flat, unemotional voice, she continued what she'd been saying. "What I did for you, Billy – what I did for Cherie – I do for all the men and women who watch me. I'm an actress, a sales person. I make you believe I want you, and I sell my interest and attention to the person who gives me the most money."

"Did you know I quit stripping, Billy?" The unexpected question took Billy by surprise. He shook his head.

"The reason I quit was because of your wife." She glanced at Cherie. "The other night when she came in and embarrassed herself and you, I knew how much pride it must have cost her to do what she did. I thought to myself, here's the kind of love I've always wanted – someone who would fight for me and humiliate himself because of his tremendous love for me." She sat down where her face was on the same level as Billy's. "You have what I've been looking for. It's real love. And you're throwing it away for something fake, something that's only built on how much money you can throw a stripper's way."

The former exotic dancer nodded at the Watchmans. "Pastor Watchman and Jenna are beginning to make me believe I can have a different life. I don't know what the future holds, but I do know I'm done with stripping forever." She smiled at Cherie. "I envy you your marriage, flawed though it may be right now. I want a job where I can like what I'm doing, not dance for an audience I despise."

Then she turned and walked out toward the backyard and Titus.

Billy looked stunned. Jenna imagined the reality check he'd just received would take some getting used to.

"The problem with sin," Henry explained, "is that it presents such a beautiful face. Sin looks good, tastes good and feels wonderful. But wait awhile and it turns bitter. Look beneath the surface, and it's all sham." He punched Billy's shoulder to get his attention. "You've just been given an honest look beneath the surface. What are you going to do about it?"

Jenna spoke quietly. "Don't you find it a little ironic that you wanted what you thought Wanda desired to offer you, and all the time she wanted the type of marriage you're trying to throw away?"

Billy didn't say anything immediately. He looked at his wife as if seeing her for the first time. His hand went to her face as he traced the outline of her cheek. Then he flushed and dropped his gaze. "You must think I'm a fool," he said to Cherie.

"Yes, I do," she responded. "But you're a fool that I love. And you don't have to keep acting stupid. Admit you've made a mistake and come back to me." Cherie put her arm around Billy's shoulders. "We can make it through this . . . together."

"Actually," Pastor Watchman said, "this will make your marriage even stronger than before, if you'll let it turn you to God and to His family."

Billy squared his shoulders, stood up and pulled Cherie with him. He took her hand and turned the two of them toward Henry and Jenna Watchman. "What time is church this Sunday, pastor?" he asked. "I'm not sure what all to do as a husband, but Cherie deserves more than I've been giving her." He nodded to himself, as if coming to a decision. "This isn't going to be easy," he looked at the door where Wanda had exited, "but I'm willing to begin learning how to live without being controlled by . . . other things."

Henry smiled and stuck out his hand, while Jenna and Cherie embraced. "You're not alone," he said. "Between Lamar and his wife, Jenna and me, and the power of Christ, you two will have a team to rally around you."

CHAPTER TWENTY-SIX

"Watch out for sharks!" The young mother's words battled with the roar of the ocean for the attention of her over-eager children. Two boys, 8 and 10, rushed across the beach and toward the incoming tide as fast as little legs could run in the sand. "Wait for your father. He doesn't want an undertow to pull you out to sea."

That last comment slowed down the two budding swimmers. "And jellyfish can brush up against you and sting you all over," the mother added.

"Honey, do you want to scare them away from the ocean forever?" the father asked. He lined up the boys and his wife for a picture, the foam-flecked waves providing the backdrop.

They needn't have worried about sharks or jellyfish. The predators somehow instinctively knew a creature far more dangerous had claimed that area of the beach and ocean for its own.

A thick, dark, greasy stain rose from the water's depths and floated toward shore, invisible to swimmers and sunbathers alike. Satan's servant had stayed hidden far beneath the waves after its defeat at the hands of the angel, waiting for its wounds to heal. Much time had passed, time the demon had used to plot new strategies.

It oozed out of the ocean and assumed its natural shape. Leathery wings unfolded and catapulted the demon into the air, where it oriented itself and then flew for the center of Dollar Town. Evil knew where to find reinforcements. Let the angel try to stop him this time!

———

Patrolman Eric Batts wrinkled his nose at the smell in the room. Urine, dust, mold and who knows what else made it almost impossible to breathe. He looked about him in disgust. The boarded-up store, empty for more than a year, now had a different kind of "customer." Three people lay on dirty blankets. One of them, a young woman about 20, pushed weakly at a strand of greasy, unwashed hair, trying to get it out of her eyes. She and one of the men stared vacantly at Batts. The other scrambled to his feet.

"Stay right where you are," Batts snapped. The drug dealer, whipcord thin, looked at the overweight, rumpled policeman, then glanced at the rear door. "Don't try it. I'll beat you to a pulp if you run," Batts warned.

A sneer crossed the dealer's face. "You and who else will stop me, fat man?" He threw a used needle at the policeman and wheeled around fast. Batts sighed, then pounced before the man could take three steps. He grabbed the dealer by his shoulder and flung him viciously to the ground, then kicked him hard several times. The man curled up into a fetal position, gagging.

"You scum never learn," Batts said. "I hate doing this, because there's nothing good here for me. If I go to the trouble of arresting you, your bail will be paid and you'll be out on the streets again by tonight."

The dealer held his stomach where Batts' shoe had landed. He struggled to sit up, the sneer back on his face, and gestured toward the two addicts. "They're not going to cause you any problem. Leave me alone, and I'll slip out of here while you book them. After all," he added, contempt in his voice, "no one will bother to bail *them* out."

A dark stain began to spread over the already filthy wall. Hot, steaming liquid dripped from the stain onto the floor beside the addicts. Neither they nor Eric Batts could see the growing pools of black slime. The stain deepened in color, grew wetter. The pools of filth stretched toward one another, changing their shape until eventually they formed a charcoal-stained rectangle that resembled a door in the floor. The liquid hardened, then lurched upward, opening.

"I hate having to hide from the angel," a voice rasped, filled with bitterness. "Being limited to the dark places makes travel harder, slower," it said. "But very soon, things will be different. Starting . . . NOW!"

A dingy, mottled form rose from the depths. Once Shi'intor oriented himself, the demon scuttled sideways into the room, a giant beetle intent on consuming its prey.

"My problem goes way beyond who I do or don't arrest." Menace filled the policeman's voice as Batts continued talking to the dealer. "See, the real issue here is that I don't make any money off you people. If there are any bribes, they're going somewhere else. Not only that, you scare off the johns from the very area where I'm making some serious inroads with prostitutes who pay me for protection." He pulled out his gun. "What do I do with you?"

The dealer's face lost all its color. "You're not going to shoot me in the middle of Dollar Town in broad daylight! Even as a cop, you'll never get away with it." He looked at the two addicts. "And what about those two? Three people with bullets in them has to make the news. That will scare away the prostitutes faster than anything."

The demon loomed over the policeman. He could sense no barriers whatsoever in the human's mind. A long history of moral shortcuts and living only for self had opened Batts to anything that brought him pleasure. Possession should be easy. Slowly, steadily, the demon began sinking into him, merging with the human's body until finally only Shi'intor's head remained visible, grinning above the policeman like an evil jack-o-lantern.

Eric Batts considered the problem and reholstered his gun. Possibilities he'd never considered before roared through him. This could work out to his benefit after all! He watched as the dealer let out a lungful of air he'd been holding.

"What's your name?" Batts asked.

"Jerome. Jerome Landis." The dealer swallowed hard. "Let me go, and I swear I'll never work this area again."

"Kill them all."

Where did that come from? Batts almost looked around to see if someone else was in the room. Suddenly, he felt powerful, invulnerable.

Then he had it.

"How do I make sure you'll keep your word?" he asked Landis. "For all I know, you'll be back tomorrow, selling the same drugs to the same people."

"Kill them all."

Batts got out his phone and pulled up the camera app. He pointed at a needle lying beside the woman. "Is that loaded?"

Landis nodded, unsure what was taking place.

"Start injecting that into your arm. I'm going to take a couple of photos of you shooting up; then I'll take some of all three of you together." He held up the camera. "I'll keep these private. But if I ever find you in this area again, the pics will go public and I'll make sure you do prison time."

He could tell the dealer didn't like it, so Batts pulled out his revolver and pointed it at him. "Your choice. Get high or get killed."

"Kill them all!"

Batts shook his head, trying to think clearly. "Quick. Make your choice."

Landis picked up the needle, found the vein and began

shooting up. "Normally, I don't like doing this. I have to keep a clear head if I'm going to expand my business."

Batts raised the camera and pretended to take pictures. "I understand. I won't hold this one time against you." He snickered at his own humor. "Now, scoot over beside the others." The two addicts never noticed as Landis moved a blanket to a spot next to the girl. His head began to loll as the drug took over.

"Now, kill them all."

The policeman shook his head again. All in good time. He waited another ten minutes, then put on some gloves and began searching through the dealer's jacket. An inside pocket held more drugs.

The outside window rattled as someone pounded loudly on the glass. The demon turned his head to take a look. Only spiritual hands could get through the boards to the glass beneath. Sure enough, Toldin, the angel, stood just outside, sword drawn.

"Hey, angel!" Shi'intor called out. "Come on in and fight me!" He laughed as the angel continued to beat on the window. "Oh, that's right," the demon mocked. "You can't come into the presence of absolute evil, can you? I guess you'll just have to watch some souls as they prepare to go to Hell!"

"Don't do this," Toldin pleaded. "Leave them alone. There may yet be hope for every one of these people."

"No, it's just the opposite," the demon replied. "For them, time has run out!"

Batts filled the syringes and bent over the three unconscious victims. Slowly, he injected as much as he could into their veins. Then he forced the syringes into the dealer's hand, leaving Landis' fingerprints on them. Verdict: drug overdose administered by a junkie/dealer. He knew no one would look twice at the "accident" scene.

They would die soon. He felt better than he had in a long time.

"There will be more."

Batts didn't know where the voice came from . . . and he didn't care anymore.

The demon turned to look once more at Toldin. Heaven's angel had a look of utter sadness on his face. "Such waste," the angel moaned. "All for nothing."

"Now there, you're wrong," the demon cackled. "I'm so much stronger than you now, and I'm nowhere close to being finished."

Shi'intor rose up out of the patrolman, expanding until his dark presence entirely filled the squalid room. He lunged for Toldin, grabbed the angel by his shoulder before Toldin could react, and pulled him into the dilapidated store. With a swiftness he'd not displayed before, the demon unsheathed his sword and swung the blade at Toldin's neck. The angel barely blocked the blow in time, but the force of the evil-infused attack threw him across the room. He stumbled and fell beside the dying addicts. His ankle touched the drug dealer, and Toldin cried out in pain. The sin and despair in the man seemed to reach out and try to pull goodness from the angel.

Toldin jumped aside and put his great sword in front of him, ready for battle. "I will never give up," he panted, exhaustion threatening to overwhelm him.

Shi'intor merely laughed. "Your defeat is closer than you realize," he said. "Evil is growing, and I with it. You cannot win. Give up on this town; go back to heaven and forget about these people." The demon swept his hand toward the outside of the building. "Look around. These people don't care about anyone but themselves. Hidden Beach certainly doesn't want a relationship with God."

"But God wants a relationship with them," Toldin said quietly. "So, I will not give up and return to heaven. I will stay and fight, because you, the other demons, and your master will ultimately be defeated. You know the Final Battle is coming soon."

Shi'intor screamed, "Don't talk about that!" With blinding

speed, he sent his sword whistling through the space between them. Toldin managed somehow to block the attack once more, though it sent him to his knees.

The demon sneered at him. "Look at you. You're so weak you can't stand. Beside you are three souls on their way to Hell. And you talk of my defeat! This town is a well of evil, and I'm drinking from it all the time." He sheathed his sword. "I'm getting stronger. You're getting weaker. Give it up."

Toldin used his sword to push himself off the floor and to his feet. He swayed slightly, but his voice was firm. "I will never give in to any type of sin. My job, given me by God, is to remain faithful to Him, no matter what. But you wouldn't know about that, would you?" His eyes, blazing silver light, seemed to pierce the demon.

Shi'intor snarled at the reminder and unfurled his wings. "Enough of meaningless talk. You and I," he said, pointing a claw at the angel, "will soon have a final reckoning. I repeat, you cannot win here." And with an explosion of sooty wings, he was gone.

CHAPTER TWENTY-SEVEN

"Councilman Godfrey's office, Marsha Schweppman speaking. How can I help you?"

The too-sweet voice grated on Chief Monroe. He swallowed his irritation and tried to be pleasant, as well. He knew it was just politics. "Ms. Schweppman, it's Chief Monroe. I need to talk to Jim, please."

"I'm sorry, chief, but he's not here." Her voice dropped to a whisper. "If it's an emergency, you can reach him on the golf course."

Monroe gave one of his famous sighs. Didn't anyone ever work anymore? "Nah, no emergency. Tell Godfrey I need to talk to him about how the city's revenues are doing this year. I'm working on the budget for next year and need to know how much, if any, I can expand the services of the department." He paused, feeling his blood pressure start to rise. "And . . . and tell him he can call me any time, because *I don't play golf during business hours!*" He hung up, berating himself. He shouldn't have thrown in that last dig. Staying polite would encourage Marsha to keep being open with him. But, honestly, he felt more and more like a relic these days. What had happened to respect, honor and taking pride in your work?

"I'm not sayin' a word 'till I talk to the head of this place!"

The words, spoken right outside his door, accompanied a slap. Bodies thudded against the office wall. Monroe heard Hank Thompson's voice rise in anger, which was amazing in itself. Hank never got angry. "You'll do no such thing. If you're not careful, I'll charge you with battery of an officer!"

Another slap could be heard. "I'll do this all day, you big idiot, until I see the number one guy."

Monroe shook his head and started for the door. Sometimes being chief was *so* much fun.

He stepped out quietly and surveyed the situation. Six women milled about, waiting to be processed into jail. Their skimpy outfits told Monroe the latest sting had netted a number of prostitutes. Loud, shrill voices shouted each person's innocence. For the most part, the other police officers ignored them and continued filling out the paper work for their arrest. They'd heard the stories hundreds of times.

The woman with Hank Thompson, however, stood apart from the rest. Petite, wiry, a cheap blond wig askew, she had managed to drag a man easily twice as big as her all the way to his office door. Thompson's face, red from anger, embarrassment, or both, looked ready to explode. Two pale hand prints on each cheek showed clearly the slaps had been intended for him. At the moment, neither Sergeant Thompson nor the woman faced him. She was yelling at the six other women. "Don't say a word about nothin' to no one 'till I tell you." She raised one of her hands and Thompson grabbed it quickly, before it could do more damage. This just made her angrier. "Listen, buddy," she snarled, "you put me back in cuffs, and I'll make you eat them."

Thompson's face, incredibly, got even redder. He looked like a volcano about to erupt any moment. Monroe decided to intervene. Hank Thompson was a good man, and the chief didn't want him to do something he'd be sorry for later.

"You wanted to see me. Here I am," he said. "It had better be important."

Both the prostitute and the sergeant whipped around, startled.

Thompson began first. "Chief, I'm so sorry she bothered you. Don't worry, I'm getting a handle on all this and . . ."

"You shut your face," the woman spat out. She turned to look at the chief. "If you're the guy in charge, we need to talk." She gestured at the officers in the process of booking the other women. "Those bozos are making an already stupid act much worse by what they're doing."

Monroe sized up the situation. It would get worse if he didn't do something. He wasn't sure what was going on, but it had *definitely* raised his curiosity.

"Come on in," he said, nodding toward his office. Thompson moved to accompany the prostitute, but the chief shook his head. "Just give me what you've already got on her, and I'll take it from here."

Thompson's startled look said it all. "But chief, you don't know what this woman's like! Don't you want me in there for added protection?"

Monroe smiled grimly. He spoke to his sergeant, but looked at the prostitute the whole time. "Wrong, Thompson. I know *exactly* what this woman's like. Don't forget, I wasn't always a police chief. I've dealt with people like this all my career." His eyes narrowed. "She won't be a problem at all."

The prostitute paled, but she kept her eyes squarely on the chief as they entered the office. This was going to be interesting.

By the time they were seated, the chief behind his desk and the prostitute slouched in a chair behind the door, Monroe noticed that somehow the blond wig now sat perfectly, hiding the mousy, brown hair. He took a moment to look over the arrest papers. Thompson was a careful typist; Monroe could find no typos. "What's your name?" he asked the woman.

"My name's Fancy," she said. "And if you'd like to discover why I'm called that, we could . . ."

"Let's get a couple of things straight right now," the chief interrupted. "First, your name is Lavenia Waters, not Fancy." Lavenia pouted but said nothing. "Second, I'm not interested in anything you're peddling." His tone sharpened. "Let's get to the point. Why did you want to speak to me?" The coy look disappeared from Lavenia's face. Monroe suddenly found himself facing a cold, calculating woman. Now, he thought, he saw the true "Fancy."

"Okay," she said. "Here's the straight dope. Your boys in the other room were never supposed to arrest us. We had an arrangement with Jamison and you that we'd be protected. We're paying good money not to be bothered, and now you go and screw up the deal." She looked Monroe square in the eyes. "What gives?"

Batts, you idiot. You just couldn't leave well enough alone. Monroe kept looking at the woman, pinning her to her chair with his glare. While he stared, his mind raced through a number of solutions, none of them good. Then . . .

"Ms. Waters, three things. One, answer all my questions and I'll make sure neither you nor your girls are arrested." Fancy started to speak, but he shot her another warning glance. "Two, your chance of living until tomorrow isn't worth a plug nickel. If I don't help you, you'll be dead before you know it." The woman seemed to shrink at this, her face going slack jawed. "Three, you'll never talk to anyone – *ever* – about the arrangement you think you had with this department. As long as you're silent, I'll protect you. Spill anything to anyone, get drunk and brag about it to one of the other girls, try to blackmail me or my people, and you're on your own; my hand of protection will be removed, which means you're dead within 24 hours of saying it." He paused for a moment to let the words sink in. "You got that?"

The sudden glint in her eyes was the only warning Monroe got. Fancy flew out of her chair straight for the chief. She curled her fingers and aimed long, sharpened nails at his eyes. Monroe ducked beneath the prostitute's arms and brought one hand up quickly. He grabbed her by the throat and, still holding her, stood up.

Fancy choked as she flailed at the hand cutting off her air supply. Her feet swung helplessly in the air. Monroe squeezed even tighter, pulling her ear up close to his mouth.

"Now, listen carefully. It's time you learned the rules. They're my rules and there is no discussion. No more games, no more fighting, and above all, no lies. I'm going to either kill you right here in my office and make it look like self defense, or you're going to obey me exactly. I'm not nice like most of those cops out there." Her eyes flicked rapidly from his face to the door, looking in vain for someone to help her. She was close to passing out, and she knew it. "If I let you down, you only get one chance. If you agree, close your left eye."

Fancy winked with her left eye immediately, and Monroe let go of her. She fell to the floor and sobbed as she dragged in as much air as she could. After a minute, she managed to climb back into the chair. She straightened her wig and dabbed at the tears in her eyes. Saliva flecked the corners of her mouth and she looked around for a tissue. Monroe pushed a box across the desk and gestured for her to take one.

"I like to treat a woman as gently as possible," the chief said. "But if she insists on acting another way, I'll deal with her on that level, even if it makes me uncomfortable." He sat forward and put his arms on the desk, leaning toward his guest. "Do you understand?"

Fancy gave a convulsive swallow and nodded.

"One more thing," Monroe said. "What you *think* you know about this arrangement is false." He held up his hand and pointed two thick, gnarled fingers. "First, Jamison is dead, so he sure can't help you now. Second, you had no agreement with me. I haven't made a cent off of you and your friends selling your bodies, and I wouldn't take anything if you tried to give it to me." Monroe went to the window and pulled the blinds apart.

He looked out briefly, nodded his head, and turned back to his now- terrified subject.

"Someone used my name. I want to know who, and I want to know if he's on my force."

Fancy trembled violently. She'd been beaten before, and if she lived, she knew someone, somewhere, would probably try to do so again. But until coming into Monroe's office, she'd never known someone who was both willing and able to kill her. She felt as if her life were about to end. Nevertheless, she had to say something.

"Look, mister . . . Chief. I'm just a simple working girl." Monroe grunted at this, but she ignored him. "These two men came to me and made me an offer of protection and quality clients if I'd pay them money. Jamison was one. The other, I didn't know his name. But he was fat and looked like he'd slept in his uniform." She shuddered. "Jamison wasn't interested in any of us. Said he had a 'supply' at his own place. But that other guy. He wanted money and . . . more. The girls took turns with him, 'cause no one wanted to be with him more than once." A sneer came on her face. "He's one of those guys who likes to hurt people. Makes him feel big and powerful."

"Did the other girls know about the arrangement you thought you had with the police department?" Monroe asked.

Fancy shook her head violently. "I wouldn't dare let them know that. Those kinds of deals don't usually last long when you start spreading secrets to others. No, it was just me." She kept her eyes on the floor as she spoke. "And you don't have to worry. The secret will stay with me. I ain't *that* crazy."

She flinched when Monroe rose from his chair, but he went past her and opened the door. "Sergeant Thompson," he called out. "Come in here a minute."

Hank edged through the doorway and moved to the wall, as far away from Fancy as he could get. Chief Monroe shook his head in disgust. "Do two things for me. First, dismiss all charges against those women." He saw the shock on Thompson's face.

"Second, let them know that if they're ever picked up again, I'll figure out a way to make sure they don't see the outside of a jail cell for a long, long time." He swiveled his head to look at Fancy. "It's your job to convince them I mean what I say."

Fancy nodded once. A hard look had returned to her eyes.

"Oh, one more thing," Monroe said. "Before you go, Ms. Waters, I think you owe Sergeant Thompson an apology for the way you acted toward him. Someone not as nice might have slapped you from here to Miami." He smiled at her pleasantly. "Isn't that right, ma'am?"

"I got the message," Fancy muttered. She turned to look at the big policeman. "Please forgive me, Sergeant. I leaped to the wrong conclusion, and if I hurt you, I'm sorry."

Thompson just stared at her. What had happened in here while he'd been outside?

The chief waved them both away. "Get 'em out of here, sergeant."

Strolling through the precinct, the demon Shi'intor laughed and raised his fists in victory. And the best (or, the worst for that hated angel) was yet to come.

The seedy buildings, paint peeling off the facades, announced to Jinx Monroe he had entered Dollar Town. The denizens of Dollar Town looked even seedier than the buildings around them. More prostitutes had already taken the place of those his officers had picked up. Monroe couldn't see it, but he knew a few feet down one of the many alleys in the area drugs were being exchanged for money. His battered, scratched, ancient car attracted no curious eyes as he moved slowly through the area. The chief had kept the car around for years, only using it for moments like these when he wanted to be as invisible as possible. As he drove, Monroe concentrated on the parking lots outside the strip clubs. It took time to drive the length of each one, but he knew time wasn't an issue. When he found what he was looking for, there would probably be a wait of a couple of hours before his prey came out.

He hit pay dirt on the fourth club. The lime green car sat at the back of the lot, hard by the back door where the girls entered. If he'd not known where to look, Monroe would have never seen it. *I'll give it to him, he's smart in some ways*, the chief thought. He parked his car on the upper side of the building. Anyone coming out the back door wouldn't see it until rounding the corner of the club. By then, Monroe would have made his identification. He settled down in the seat, opened up a canned drink and a sandwich, and sat back to wait.

Ninety minutes later, with the window down so he could hear, the scrape of metal on concrete reached Monroe's ears. He straightened. Batts rounded the corner and headed for his car. He never even looked in the chief's direction.

Monroe stuck his head out the window. "Batts," he called out.

The man reacted faster than Monroe would have expected of a man of that size. He took note of it and filed it away in his memory. Small incidents like that could make or break a person.

When Batts saw who had called to him, he relaxed a bit. Coming around to the open window, he said, "What's up, Chief?"

"Get in the car with me for a minute. We need to talk."

Monroe waited until Batts closed the door, then he picked up the nightstick beside him and hit the policeman in the side of the throat. Batts, stunned by the sudden attack, put his hands up to avoid another blow, but it proved too late. The chief turned the club and punched the end of it just underneath Batts' jaw. Then he leaned on the club. A little more pressure, and the jaw would break.

Intense pain flooded Batts. He tried to move toward the safety of the door, but the chief proved far too difficult to get away from.

"Move another inch, Eric, and I'll shatter your jaw. Got that?"

Batts froze in place.

The nightstick eased back a fraction; so did the pain. "Eric, and I'm calling you that because you're not worthy to be called Officer Batts, you don't seem to have believed the warnings I've given you these past few weeks. So now we've moved things up a notch." He pushed harder once again. Batts groaned. "Do you think you might be able to follow my instructions from now on?"

Batts managed to whisper, "Yes."

"If I put this club away, will I still have your attention?"

"Yes," Batts repeated.

The chief pulled the nightstick away completely and put it down beside his leg. Batts, for his part, rubbed his throat and jaw, trying to get circulation to the area once again.

Monroe got straight to the point. "I know about Fancy, you and Jamison. After I'd warned you, the 'deal' still continued. Tonight, I ended it. Period."

"Now Chief," Batts began, "you don't really believe . . ."

The nightstick reappeared in Monroe's hand. He feinted at Batts' head. When the patrolman reacted, raising his hands, Monroe lowered the club and punched him hard in the stomach. Batts bent double.

"Open the door," Monroe ordered. "You mess up my car, and I'll flay you alive."

Batts just managed to get the door opened before spilling the contents of his stomach onto the pavement of the parking lot. Monroe gave him a minute to recover, then pulled the man back into the car.

"No more games, Eric," he said. "These are the new rules. You understand?"

Batts nodded, his eyes round with fear.

"I know this is difficult," Monroe said. "You're thinking, what happened to good ole Jinx, the chief everyone makes fun of when he's not around? Right?"

Batts started to shake his head. The nightstick came up once more and Batts changed his mind. "Sir, that's exactly what I was thinking. I never saw this side of you."

Monroe nodded. "You saw what I wanted you and everyone else in the department to see. I don't like to use force. I want the people under me to do the right thing because they're committed to it, not because I'm forcing them to act that way." He put the nightstick down. "But when my police force is threatened by *anyone*, Batts, I'll do whatever necessary to protect it. Do you understand that?"

"Yessir."

"Now, back to Fancy. For you and her, the deal's off. If you try to harm her or one of the other girls, I've got the necessary evidence to not only throw you off the force, but I'll also make sure you end up in jail. Try to come at me, and the evidence I've put with a certain lawyer will come to light, even after I'm dead." Monroe watched Batts carefully. Wonder of wonders, it looked like he was finally getting through to the thick-headed man.

"I'm not going to fire you over this, if you behave from now on. And on the day you retire, if you make it that long, I'll destroy the evidence we have against you."

"Can I ask something, Chief?" When Monroe nodded, Batts continued. "If you know all this, and you attacked me like this, why are you lettin' me off the hook?"

"Good question, Eric. It's simply this way. Bringing something like this out into the public would hurt our reputation. We need to be seen as a strong law enforcement agency." Monroe pointed out the window at the area around them. "If the scum out there ever thought they could compromise our integrity, we'd be done as an effective defense for this city."

He turned to face Batts squarely. The patrolman scooted back closer to the door. He wanted no more of the nightstick. "Now, Eric about your future with this force. From the moment you get out of this car, you will stay away from this area for as long as you're a police officer. You'll not be seen in a strip club. You will leave the prostitutes and the strippers alone. I want you so clean your momma would finally be proud of you.”

Batts opened his mouth to protest, then clamped it shut.

“Good, Eric, you *can* learn something new,” Monroe said. He reached out and patted Batts’ shoulder. “Now, you can do me and the force a favor. Unknown to anyone else in the department, you and I will begin a very quiet investigation. I need to know if anyone else knew about this agreement you, Jamison and Fancy had. If you find out anything, you bring it to me immediately. Then, we’ll deal with it as privately as possible.”

“Thanks, Chief, for the confidence. After all this, I’m surprised you’re lettin’ me do anything.”

“Officer Batts.” Monroe could see the man’s shoulders square a bit in pride when he said this. “Officer Batts, everyone makes mistakes. Don’t make another one, and we just might get this police force back on track.” He gestured toward the door. “Now, go home and get ready for tomorrow.”

“Yessir,” Batts blubbered. “Thank you sir.”

The chief watched him get out and wobble towards his lime green car. *Something’s going to have to be done with that one*, he thought.

CHAPTER TWENTY-EIGHT

Ms. Jakoba Danforth believed in rules. Following them brought comfort and stability to her life and her work. In a world gone change-crazy, the environment of her library remained stable, predictable. Take this evening. At 9:50, as usual, she pressed the intercom button on her desk phone and announced, albeit softly, "The library will be closing in ten minutes. Please return all books and magazines to their proper places." Ten minutes later, as usual, the last patron exited the building. Ms. Danforth bustled through the stacks, looking for stragglers or mischief makers. As usual, she found no one lingering.

"You can go home," she said to her crew of volunteers. They thanked her, nodding their gratefulness. Most of them appreciated Ms. Danforth's willingness to work later than anyone else. Everyone could see in her behavior a love of books and the accumulation of knowledge. They didn't mind her officiousness because they saw the bright mind behind the rules enforcer.

She began shutting down the library. Some lights had to be left on for security purposes, but she turned off all unnecessary electricity-consuming devices. And she always turned them off in the same order. It ensured she'd remember to leave nothing out. It also meant one more level of stability in her life.

Until tonight.

Books on the subject "Religion" lined the shelves closest to the front. They made up an eclectic collection. Everything from Christianity to Hinduism, from positive thinking to believing nothing sat next to each other, filed alphabetically according to the author's last name. One of those books, a best seller written by a militant atheist, proclaimed to readers everywhere how Satan and Hell could not possibly exist.

"What a great book!" The demon of Hidden Beach slid from between its pages, laughing. "A deluded man who can delude others!" Shi'intor shook his head in derision, slithered down the side of the shelves, then looked around. Beside him, the head librarian went about her work. "Don't mind me," the demon said, his voice filling with menace. "I'm just here to watch the fun."

As Ms. Danforth made her way down one of the aisles in the stacks, she found herself again having to turn sideways. Her increasing bulk made the already narrow space between shelves seem even narrower. "I've got to lose weight," she muttered once more. Though she wouldn't realize it, she said the same thing every night about this time.

"I think you look just fine, Ms. Danforth."

The voice took her by surprise. At the far end of the aisle, a figure stepped from around the corner and started toward her. She felt no fear, only curiosity and a mild annoyance. "What are you doing her at this hour?" she asked. "You've had all day to find what you want. It's late, and I'm going home."

"I had to wait until now," the figure apologized. "It's the only time I could kill you."

"Kill me? What a ridiculous thing to . . ."

Ms. Jakoba Danforth felt not another emotion. She said not another word. And her routine world changed forever as a pressure grew and grew in her chest until she thought it would burst.

Which it did.

Gin McFain writhed in pain. The cuts, in and of themselves, hadn't proved too severe. But put together, their sheer magnitude made him feel like nothing but a mass of wounds. He should have been out of the hospital by now, but a nasty staph infection, coupled with cellulites, kept him hospitalized, on antibiotics and uncomfortable no matter how he tried to turn. He had to admit, however, that even with the pain medication administered to him, his mind felt clearer than it had in years. His body missed the gin, no question about it. But he had begun remembering what life used to be like. He'd been strong; his mind had loved mechanical problems, the tougher to solve, the better.

He bent his mind to solving the problem of his pain. It seemed obvious that diverting his attention to something else would help alleviate how he felt. Gin turned his mind back to the night of the accident. His memory still had holes in it. He could only remember a terrible explosion, followed by shards of glass embedding themselves in his body . . . . No — something had happened before the explosion. He ground his teeth in frustration, trying to force his brain to remember. Then, a deep breath. He calmed himself, saying, "Slow down. You still have time to get it right."

Gin froze. Those words. He'd heard them before. And the voice — it had been so *familiar*. Who did it belong to? And, why was it so important? An image hung just beyond the edge of his consciousness, refusing to come any closer. Gin yawned. It would come later, he knew. In any case, the thinking had done its job. Fatigue swallowed him and he let himself be drawn down into the soft pillow of sleep.

CHAPTER TWENTY-NINE

Henry and Jenna arrived at the police station five minutes ahead of their 10:00 appointment. A winding route had taken them down quite a few side streets. But they'd avoided the tourist traffic on the main drag and had managed to make a quick stop along the way to see how Billy and Cherie were doing after the previous evening. The couple, all smiles, affirmed they had talked almost the entire night. Things seemed to be improving steadily.

In the lobby of the police station, Jenna saw Maria and waved to her. Maria nodded, but seemed cold. "Something's up," Henry whispered to his wife.

An office door opened, and Chief Jinx Monroe stuck his head out and motioned for the Watchmans to come in. Maria followed them, bringing several extra chairs. Inside, another surprise. Detective Vincent Anderson rose from his seat to greet them, shaking hands with Jenna, but pointedly turning away as Henry put out his hand.

Jenna made a decision.

"Chief Monroe, we're leaving," she stated.

The chief gawked at her. "You just got here! Let's at least talk a few minutes."

Henry's wife shook her head. "I don't like the atmosphere in this room. You saw the childish way your Detective Anderson just acted. And after we bent over backwards for Ms. Da Silva, she repays us by a barely civil attitude. I won't be a party to insults to my husband, and I certainly won't stand for a lynching before all the facts are in." She whirled around. "Come on, Henry, let's go."

"Hold on just a moment." Chief Monroe held up a placating hand. "I admit my two *employees*" – and the chief emphasized the word as he took in both detectives with a hard stare – "have gotten too emotionally involved in this for their own good. However, perhaps when you've heard everything we know, then you'll make allowances." He gestured toward the chairs. "Give me five minutes."

Henry eased Jenna toward one of the chairs. "Come on, honey. We have to do this some time. Let's get it out of the way now."

Jenna hesitated, but allowed herself to be directed toward a chair by Henry. The couple sat down and turned toward Jinx Monroe. "Okay, let's get this over with," Jenna stated.

"Thank you, Pastor and Mrs. Watchman," the chief said. He reached into a desk drawer and pulled out a bright red folder marked "Profanity case."

"Profanity case?" Henry said. "That's an unusual crime."

"You don't know the half of it," Jinx Monroe muttered. Then, taking a deep breath, he shoved a photocopy of an old newspaper article in front of Henry. "You know anything about this?"

Jenna trembled as the words swam up from the paper and threatened to drown everything she and Henry had tried so hard to create.

"*Kid Dynamite Kills Opponent in Third Round.*"

Henry looked up from the headline and took his wife's hand. "What do you want to know about this?" he asked. "It's old news and I was charged with no crime."

Vincent Anderson made a lunge for the preacher. The chief simply reached out his arm, grabbed Anderson by the back of the collar and pulled him back into his seat. "None of that, son," he commanded. "Remember what I said earlier. I'll handle all of this."

Jinx Monroe turned to the couple. "You admit you fought under the name Kid Dynamite?"

Henry responded with a nod.

"And you admit you killed a man in the ring, like the story says?"

At this, Henry Watchman shook his head. "Not at all. The papers didn't cover the story correctly. When the true facts finally came out, the reporters had moved on to the next new scandal, ignoring that they'd missed the truth."

Chief Monroe turned to Vincent Anderson. "Now," he said.

The detective leaned forward. In a strangled voice he asked, "Remember the man you killed?"

Pastor Watchman frowned. "He fought under the name Randy Savage. I never knew if that was his real name or not."

"It's a shame you never bothered to find out more about the man you killed," Anderson continued. "Randy Savage boxed. But when he came home, he went by his real name . . . Randy Anderson. He was my dad."

Silence filled the room.

"Pastor, you killed my father."

Henry Watchman cleared his throat. He eyes focused on some distant point as his mind focused on what he considered a shameful part of his past. "The fight had been scheduled as simply a pre-championship tune up," he began. "My manager had two or three more fights for me to win, and he knew we'd have a shot at the middle-weight title. Your dad, Detective Anderson, had been struggling the last couple of years. He'd been a good fighter, but by the time we fought, he'd aged and his reflexes weren't what they should have been."

"That didn't stop you from beating him to death!"

Maria put a restraining hand on her partner. "Easy, Vince."

The pastor rubbed his eyes. "For what it's worth, that fight turned out to be the last one for me. When your dad collapsed in the ring, they took him to the hospital. He died two days later without regaining consciousness. I vowed never to fight again, even though it wasn't my fault your dad died."

"How can you say that?" Vince demanded. "You murdered him in a fit of anger and got away with it because it happened in a boxing ring. You killed him, and you've started killing again in my town."

"Detective Anderson!" Chief Monroe's roar stopped everyone. In a quieter voice, he went on, "Let's watch the allegations. And, remember, it's my town, not yours."

Henry Watchman looked at the chief. "May I continue?"

"Yeah, I want to get to the bottom of this," Monroe said.

"The boxing commission did some investigation after the fight. They discovered Randy had not been cleared to fight by his regular doctor. He'd sustained several concussions in previous fights, and his physician knew it would be dangerous for him to ever get in the ring again. So, Randy went to a different doc who didn't know his history. That physician cleared him to fight."

"You're lying and . . ."

"I'm trying to be patient, Detective Anderson." Jinx Monroe's voice came through quietly. "I know you're emotional about this, so I'm cutting you some slack. But if you disobey me one more time, you're out of here." He held Anderson's gaze with his own. "You understand?"

"Yes sir."

Jinx Monroe nodded. "I know it's hard," he said. "But you're expected to do the hard stuff." He gestured for the preacher to continue.

"Randy Anderson died of a brain hemorrhage. My manager and I talked to the boxing commission and asked them to only release the clean bill of health from the last physician. We did it so that Randy's wife and son would be able to get the insurance money." Henry Watchman glanced briefly at his wife. "I walked away from the ring the day after Randy's death. I found God and a new calling.

"Detective Anderson, I'm sorry about your Dad's death. I don't blame you for hating me. But I didn't kill your dad in a fit of anger. For a normal boxer, my blows wouldn't have caused the lethal hit that killed him. In fact, I wasn't even mad at your dad. We had talked a little before the fight, and he told me how happy his family had made him."

Maria Da Silva finally spoke up. "Can you prove any of this, Pastor Watchman?"

"Yes, we can." Jenna Watchman opened her purse. "Here is the key to our safety deposit box. If you want to go with us, we'll show you a copy of the official report from the New York Boxing Commission."

"If you're so honest, then why have you been hiding out here in Florida?" Anderson asked. "Why have you kept all this a secret from everyone?"

Henry Watchman spoke carefully. "I didn't want the notoriety that comes from everyone knowing their pastor is a former prize fighter. But Jenna and I knew we had to have some accountability. So, when the church talked to us about becoming their pastor, we took the board of elders aside before they ever hired us and told them the whole story. The chairman of the board of elders called and talked to someone in the boxing commission, who verified our account." He looked around the room. "The elders agreed to keep the whole thing quiet, and I've been able to have a good ministry in the years since then."

"I have no power over any of you," he added. "But if it's possible, I'd still like for this to stay quiet."

Vincent Anderson's head jerked up. "We can't guarantee anything like that . . . ."

"We'll talk about that at a later date," Chief Monroe interrupted. "It all depends on if you're innocent or not."

Jenna stared at the chief. "Innocent? Of what? You have no proof my husband has done anything wrong. We've just explained fully and totally what happened in New York. Not only should all your questions be answered, the death of Randy Savage and the murders here in Hidden Beach have nothing in common with each other! Why don't you leave us alone and find the real culprit?"

The chief shook his head as he listened. "Believe me, Mrs. Watchman, we're not trying to single your husband out for anything. Do you think we like targeting a respected member of this community?"

"Then why the continued doubt?"

Henry smiled behind his hands as he listened to his wife. The normally placid Jenna would go to the gates of Hell to defend her husband from perceived wrong.

"Mrs. Watchman," Jinx Monroe chose his words carefully, "while we appreciate your husband's account of what happened in New York, we still have to check it out ourselves."

"You don't believe my husband!"

Henry reached over and put his arm around Jenna. "Honey, we do the same thing when we're counseling. You know most people try to put themselves in the best light possible. We've had to do investigating ourselves to get to the real story in some marriages." He smiled at his wife. "Let's let the police do the same thing. After all, we know our account of these events is truthful. So, the more information they gather, the better we'll look."

Jenna took a deep breath and sat back in her chair. "Okay." Then, to the chief, "What else is causing you doubts?"

"You were wrong in something you said a minute ago, Mrs. Watchman," Chief Monroe replied. "There is a common denominator in both sets of events. Even though they're separated by both miles and years, Vincent Anderson and your husband are involved – and it's hard for me to believe it's just a coincidence."

Henry Watchman looked around at the group in the office. "I'm innocent. You're going to discover that fact sooner or later. When you do, you'll realize I'm also being set up. Who would benefit from something like that? Who would be willing to kill just to get back at me?" He stood up and prepared to leave. "Those are the key questions you should be asking."

"You're accusing me!" Vincent Anderson looked incredulous. "I don't hate anyone enough to break the law!"

"I'm not accusing anyone," Pastor Watchman said. "I'm just suggesting some questions that should be asked if these killings are to be stopped."

Chief Monroe nodded to the pastor. "We'll check things out and get back to you . . . one way or another." He stood as well and put out his hand. "Thanks for coming in and clearing some of this up for us."

Pastor Watchman took the hand and shook it. "Keep looking for the killer, Chief," he said. "And, I'm around if you need more information."

———

The dog's tongue hung out of its mouth. The tail wagged furiously as Titus dodged from side to side in the back yard. Pursuing the dog, Henry Watchman wiped the sweat from his face. This game of tag was good for both of them. It relieved the dog of his boredom, but it also wiped away the tension from a pastor sorely in need of some relaxation.

"Whoa!" Henry jumped aside at the last instant and Titus tumbled into the latest hole he'd dug in the formerly pristine backyard. "Jenna, we've got to get something that'll stop this monster from digging all the way to China." He peered into one of the holes. "You could hide a car in these things." He stooped to look closer. "I think I see miners at the bottom digging for coal."

Jenna choked back a laugh. "Let's see," she said. "Help me remember who had the bright idea of getting a dog."

"I know, I know," Henry gasped as he dodged the dog once

more. Just who was supposed to be chasing whom? "But you'll see, Titus is going to be a great watchdog one day."

"Hmph," Jenna snorted. "He'll lick them to death, maybe. But that's all."

Titus whirled from playing with Henry and ran to the gate, tail wagging delightedly. A few moments later, the Watchmans saw a familiar car pull into the driveway. Mary Connors got out of the car and approached the fence. Henry opened the gate and said, "Give us just a second, and we'll be right out."

"Henry, the dog!" Jenna yelled.

A bolt of golden lightening shot by Henry and out into the parking lot. "Titus, come back here!" Henry shouted. He could have been talking to the wind. The dog continued to lope toward the open side door of the church. Henry groaned. The custodian would kill him, if he didn't have a heart attack first.

The passenger door on Mary's car opened, and Wanda Lemming could be seen emerging quickly. She turned toward the fleeing dog and said in a soft voice, "Titus, what do you think you're doing?"

The dog stopped in his tracks. He wheeled around and sat on his haunches, looking at her across the parking lot.

"Come here, Titus," Wanda commanded.

The dog ran to her feet and lay down on his belly, head raised expectantly. Wanda stooped down and began to rub behind his ears and under his chin. "What a good dog you are," she crooned. "You're my champion. You must be the best pet in the world."

"Close your mouth, Henry," Jenna said. Her husband looked as if he'd been pole axed. The dog he and Jenna had worked so hard to control and contain – usually in vain – sat in front of Wanda like a lovesick puppy, ready to do fulfill her commands.

"How did she do that?" Henry wondered aloud.

Wanda straightened up and pointed toward the backyard enclosure. "Go back inside, Titus. You know that's the best place for you."

Her voice, so soft it could hardly be heard by the others, nevertheless had a direct effect on the dog. He got up and followed Wanda straight into the yard. Once inside, Wanda waited for Mary to come in, as well. During all this time, the dog made no attempt to flee. He sat contentedly beside Wanda and looked adoringly up into her face.

Henry Watchman shook his head. "You're a wonder," he said to the former stripper. Wanda's face darkened at the comment.

"Henry!" Jenna snapped.

Watchman's face turned red as what he'd said registered. "I'm sorry, Wanda," he said. "I didn't mean anything by it. The comment was meant as a compliment." He pointed at Titus. "You're the first person who's been able to corral that stubborn dog." He looked hard at Titus; the dog, for his part, simply wagged his tail excitedly. Partly to change the subject, and partly out of curiosity, the pastor asked Wanda, "How are you able to control him so well?"

Wanda shook her head. "I'm not sure." She looked at Jenna. "Remember the other night when you picked me up and brought me over here to talk with Billy and Cherie?"

Jenna nodded. "I asked you to wait outside a few minutes while I went in to check things out. I had planned to come out and get you at the right time, but I never got a chance to do that. You walked in before Billy and Cherie could walk out."

It was Wanda's turn to nod her head. "When you left me alone on the carport, it suddenly hit me how nervous I felt. I'd entertained plenty of men and women over the past several years, but trying to help put a marriage back together was something altogether new. I felt a lot of pressure on me to do the right thing . . . and I felt pretty unsure of myself." She looked fondly over at Titus. "Then I heard some whining coming from behind the fence. When I walked over to take a look, the sweetest, cutest dog I'd seen since my childhood days seemed to be saying he couldn't wait to become best friends with me."

Jenna couldn't be sure, but she thought Titus might be blushing.

"Growing up as a girl in Kentucky, I didn't have a lot of happiness. But my dog gave me companionship and a level of love that got me through some hard times." Wanda smiled down at the dog and petted him some more. "Titus made me remember all those great times, and before I knew it, I'd slipped inside the fence and wrapped my arms around him."

"Titus never lets me hold him," Henry said. "He's always wiggling, trying to get away."

"But that's because he knows you're the one he plays with. He loves you, but in his mind your role is to romp and run with him."

Wanda knelt down and put her arms around Titus' neck. The dog snuggled closer. "I used to talk for hours to my dog. So, I began talking that night to Titus. I told him how scared I was and how grateful I felt for all you two and Mary have done for me. Before I knew it, the fear had crept away and a quiet peace had taken its place. That's when I came inside." She stood once more. "I told Titus he'd helped me, and I think he understood how much I needed him that night." She shrugged her shoulders. "We've got a bond, now."

Henry shook his once more. "God uses all His creatures to accomplish His will. If he can use a stubborn mule like me, he can certainly use a dog."

"I agree completely with the 'stubborn mule' part."

Henry turned to look at Jenna. She grinned and kissed him soundly. "Lucky for you I like mules."

CHAPTER THIRTY

The call came into the police station mid-morning. Whatever it contained, the message had an immediate effect on Jinx Monroe. He stepped to his door and looked around until he saw Maria. "Detective Da Silva, I need you in my office right now!" His voice, quiet and calm, could barely be heard in the room. Deceptively calm, Maria decided. She entered the chief's domain, treading carefully.

"Detective, do you recall interviewing a woman named Jakoba Danforth?" The words seemed to float lazily in the air. Not for an instant was Maria fooled. A thrill of fear shot through her. Surely not another . . .

"Yes sir. I talked to her yesterday. What's the problem?"

"She's dead. When the library didn't open at the regular time, one of the volunteers used his key to open the door. He found Ms. Danforth stabbed to death in the stacks." The chief leaned in close to Maria. "What's going on, detective?"

Maria shook her head. "Sir, don't start that with me." She held up a hand as Jinx's face began to redden. "I'm not challenging you, sir. But just because you're frustrated with this case, you don't need to lash out at me. I want to find the killer as much as you do."

The chief took several deep breaths. The color began to fade, draining from his face and neck. "You're right." He nodded once. "I am frustrated." He shuffled some papers in front of him for a moment, then looked back up at her. "Take Sgt. Thompson and bring me back a report as soon as possible."

"What do I tell Detective Anderson if he asks about what's going on?"

"Tell him nothing. And also tell him I said to stay as far away from your work as possible . . . for his own safety."

Maria stood up. "I'll get on this right away."

The chief grunted and waved her out.

———

Stanley Greenberg knew that when nervousness took control of him, his Adam's apple bobbed up and down. It had to be bobbing furiously right now. The detective interviewing him *seemed* nice enough. But the current situation and all the law enforcement personnel in the library intimidated him. Stanley swallowed convulsively and tried to quell the rising panic. A grad student getting his master's degree in Library Science, the part time library worker knew books and magazines, not grisly murders.

"Mr. Greenberg." Maria Da Silva but on her best smile. This young man had to be calmed down. His thin frame trembled even while sitting. "Tell me from the beginning what happened." She tried to sound encouraging. "Take your time and give me as many details as possible."

Stanley shifted in the chair. "Detective, never in my wildest imagination – well, maybe in my *wildest* imagination – but never in any kind of rational thought would I ever have believed I'd be mixed up in something like this."

Maria damped down her impatience and nodded at him to continue.

"Ms. Danforth never wanted us here very early. She liked to

get the library ready herself. Anyone else trying to help just slowed her down, she always said."

Stanley looked at his watch. "I got here about 10:00, only to find the doors locked and some angry customers milling around outside. Ms. Danforth had given me keys several months ago so that I could close up on the nights she got off early. I unlocked the doors long enough to get inside. Then I told the people outside I'd get the library ready for them, relocked the doors and began turning on lights and checking the stacks."

Stanley shuddered and his face paled.

"Would you like some water to drink?" Maria asked.

"No thanks. Ms. Danforth doesn't – didn't – allow anyone to drink in the library. Anyway, I saw what I thought was rust on one of the shelves and went to investigate. Ms. Danforth normally wouldn't let something like that get out of hand. But when I got closer and could see around the corner, I got a glimpse of someone's legs sprawled on the floor. I stuck my head around the corner, and saw her . . . I mean, it . . . I mean, the body. Blood had spattered on the books, shelves and some of the chairs. I didn't even stop to check and see if she might be alive." Tears gathered in the corner of his eyes. "All I could think about was that the killer might still be in the library. So, I rushed back to the front doors where everyone could see me and used my cell phone to call you guys." He sighed and looked down. "I'm sorry I didn't do more for Ms. Jakoba."

"You couldn't have done anything for her, Mr. Greenberg," Maria said gently. "She'd been dead a number of hours when you found her."

Behind Stanley, Maria could see Sgt. Thompson motion for her. "Mr. Greenberg," she said, "We have your address and phone number. You can go now. If something else occurs to you, please call us." She stood up at the same time as Stanley and shook hands with him.

"What about the library?" he asked. "Someone has to stay here until everyone's finished."

Maria nodded. "You're right. However, you may as well know that this place will have to stay closed for several days until we've finished with the crime scene. I suppose you'll have to keep the people out and lock up once we're done." She watched the young man straighten his shoulders and march to the information desk. Good. Having a task had given him a sense of purpose.

Hank moved to her side. "I want you to look at something," he whispered. They ducked underneath yellow tape and made their way through the stacks to the murder scene. The body had been face down on the floor. Now, however, the late Ms. Jakoba Danforth lay on her back, eyes staring sightlessly at the bright lights in the ceiling.

"I see it," Maria said in a tight voice. She put on gloves, bent down and carefully examined the knife embedded in the corpse's chest. Without reading the piece of paper made dirty by contact with the floor, she knew what it would say. *I'm beginning to hate profanity, myself,* she thought sourly. The bulky detective didn't look forward to the report she'd have to make to the chief.

CHAPTER THIRTY-ONE

The chief surprised Maria. When she reported the details of Ms. Jakoba Danforth's murder, no temper tantrums or shouts resulted. Monroe only looked out his window absently for a minute, then slapped the desk and stood up.

"I've been an idiot. Detective Da Silva, we've got one witness left. This murderer, whoever he is, always seems to be one step ahead of us. I'm going to assign an around-the-clock watch outside the door of McFain. It's an outside chance that he knows anything, but if the one responsible for these three previous stabbings is even a little bit worried, that man's life is in danger." He turned to the intercom and thumbed it. "Shirl, get me Danning in here as quick as possible."

Monroe dismissed Maria, and by the time she had made her way to the door, Luther Danning stood just outside, waiting to come in. The lieutenant's gray hair lay close against his head in tight curls. His black skin showed a few wrinkles, but Luther Danning's erect carriage still gave evidence of discipline and energy. A few years from retirement, Danning found himself enjoying his new position. After he'd been pulled off the streets, the lieutenant had displayed, much to his surprise, a gift for administration. Chief Monroe had decided to put that gift to work in a new area.

"Lieutenant Danning, I've got a job for you. There's a patient by the name of Gin McFain in the hospital. I have every reason to believe his life is in danger. I'll give you two hours to come up with a 24-hour watch for him." Monroe paused. Danning's eyes stayed squarely on Monroe. The lieutenant nodded as if getting the necessary manpower were no problem at all. "Remember, in two hours I want a guard on McFain's door," the chief emphasized.

"The guard will be there, sir." Danning swiveled and left the office. Monroe could see him moving straight to his computer and phone. The chief allowed himself a small smile. It always helped to see someone he could count on in difficulty.

———

The killer moves, unseen, into the hospital stairwell. A well-used, blood-stained knife lies close against his chest, hidden from view, yet ready to fulfill its master's orders. He remembers Gin McFain's room number. It will be quite a climb, but the stairs offer more privacy than the elevators. Soon, blood will be spilled in places other than the operating and emergency rooms. He feels pleasure at the thought. The first ones had been done out of necessity. Now, however, he feels excitement at the thought of the knife's plunge and another life snuffed out. His rapid progress in this new area of experience has both amazed and pleased him.

He reaches McFain's floor and looks through the small glass opening. No one around. Easing into the corridor, the killer moves carefully until he reaches the right room. Time for Gin McFain to die. Behind him, watching with anticipation, the demon of Hidden Beach urges the killer forward. He eases the door open a crack . . . .

———

"Reverend Watchman, what are *you* doing here?"

The pastor whirled around from his seat beside Gin McFain, putting a finger to his lips to silence the new arrival. In his bed, McFain jerked awake and looked startled to see the two visitors. "What are you guys doing in my room?" he demanded.

"I was just asking the pastor the same thing," said the new arrival.

Watchman relaxed a little in his chair. "You must not know much about what pastors do. I'm at the hospitals at least two days every week. Checking up on Mr. McFain seemed like the polite, nice thing to do." Watchman's eyes narrowed. "Now, I can ask you the same question. What are you doing here, Detective Anderson?"

Vince started to answer when someone knocked on the door. Lieutenant Danning entered and looked in astonishment at both men. "You're not supposed to be in here. This room is off limits to all non-essential personnel as of this moment." He jerked his head toward the door, showing them he expected immediate compliance.

Out in the hall, a policeman unknown to Watchman motioned excitedly to Vincent Anderson. "Come here, sir. Look what I just found."

Anderson and the policeman slipped into the stairwell. In the corner, underneath a piece of newspaper, lay a blood-stained knife and a piece of paper that said, *"Use profanity and you will DIE!"*

"The killer must have been waiting right here, sir."

As Vincent bent down to examine the evidence, he heard someone say, "And so were both of you!"

Anderson turned to see Lieutenant Danning pointing an accusing finger at the pastor and him. Vincent stood up and marched past the three men. "Report it, Danning," he said bitterly, moving toward the elevators at the end of the corridor. "Someone's trying to set me up, and it seems to be working."

The elevator door opened; Vincent entered and savagely punched the button for the first floor. Before the door could shut, however, Henry Watchman jumped in beside him. Vincent turned to face him squarely. "Want to murder me right here in the elevator?" he taunted. "Of course, your knife has been confiscated, so you'll have to use your fists . . . but you're good at that."

Pastor Watchman ignored the vitriol. "Detective, I've been wrong. We've been going at this from the wrong direction. What if both of us is innocent?" He cocked his head to the side, waiting for a response. When none came, he continued. "Maybe someone else is looking for a scapegoat and is using your hatred for me to ruin both or either of us. If that's so, then your continued anger may well destroy your career – or even your life."

The elevator door opened. The pastor stepped out and turned around to face Vincent once more. "Detective Anderson, I'm not even asking you to give up on me as a suspect. Just widen your vision and imagination a bit. It might save both of us."

Vince watched the pastor walk away. He never even noticed that he'd stayed in the elevator. The door closed and as the elevator began ascending again, Watchman's words floated before his eyes.

CHAPTER THIRTY-TWO

Sunday dawned . . . at least, Jenna Watchman *thought* it had dawned. She'd not seen the sun all morning. Standing on the carport, she watched as thick, gray clouds lumbered inland from the ocean, laden with a heavy burden of moisture they seemed anxious to drop on the community of Hidden Beach. Towering waves crashed onto the nearby beach with more vehemence than usual. On most days the sound of the ocean soothed her. This morning, the roar reminded her more of an angry beast that wanted to clear the land of its human invaders.

"We may have more people at church than we normally do," Henry called out from the kitchen.

Jenna ducked back into the house as tablespoon-sized raindrops began hitting the backyard. "I'd think it would be just the opposite. People tend to stay home when bad weather moves in."

"That's true." Henry took another healthy swig of coffee and closed his Bible. The top page of his sermon notes had a coffee stain on it. "However, our people can't surf, swim, sail or lay out today. Some of them are bound to come to church — out of boredom, if nothing else!"

Jenna shook her head and laughed. She picked up the page with the stain on it, intending to wipe it off. But when she lifted it, Jenna saw other pages equally stained. "What am I going to do with you?" she sighed. "It's a good thing your people love you, because you're not the neatest individual to come along."

"That's my secret, honey. I make everyone else feel so much neater just be being around me." Henry stood up and placed his empty mug and plate in the dishwasher. "I'd better run go finish getting ready. Bible study will be starting in . . . . Who's that?"

Mary Connors' car pulled into their driveway. They could see Wanda Lemming get out and run for the carport, trying to stay as dry as possible. Mary pulled away and drove to a parking spot next to the side entrance of the church.

Jenna opened the door before Wanda could ring the doorbell. "Come on in," she said, already moving to pour a cup of coffee for their guest.

Wanda sat down and gratefully accepted the hot beverage. She took a sip and then raised her eyes to Pastor Watchman. "Mary thought I should come see you," she began. "Now that I'm here, I'm not so sure it's the right thing to do."

Jenna moved beside the young woman and gave her arm a reassuring pat. "Why don't you tell us and let us make that decision?"

"That might be best," Wanda said. She turned to face the pastor once more. "Mary got a phone call this morning warning her not to bring me to church. The caller said I was an 'evil influence on our impressionable children.'"

She took another sip of coffee, her eyes fixed on the back yard where Titus cowered in his doghouse. "I really enjoy church, Pastor Watchman. These past weeks have been wonderful. And, the people I've met – for the most part, every one of them has encouraged and welcomed me." Her eyes swiveled to take in the couple. "I don't want to make trouble . . . but I don't want to quit coming to church, either. Mary thought it would be a good idea to let you decide what I should do."

Henry's fingers had turned white. He gripped his Bible so hard Jenna raised an involuntary hand to her throat, thankful that the Bible wasn't a person's neck. "It's an easy decision. In fact, it's so easy my wife and I don't have to discuss it. Tell her, Jenna."

Jenna could hear the edge in her husband's voice. She tried to clear her throat so that her own anger wouldn't show *too* much.

"My husband and I both think no one in the church is perfect. As he said the first night we met, the church is a place for sick people who want to get better."

"And, we're all in need of healing," Henry broke in.

Jenna nodded in agreement. "God welcomes anyone who seeks to do better; so should we. We're going to church today, and we'll worship the God who loves us. You stick close with me. I'll keep you surrounded by people who love you and want only the best for you."

"Okay, Jenna." Wanda relaxed a bit. "I'll try to stay out of the way as much as possible. Maybe we could go in late to avoid attention."

"We'll do no such thing," Jenna said firmly. "That would be admitting the rightness of the caller's accusations. We'll both attend Bible study and church, and we'll enjoy the whole time."

Henry moved toward the back of the house to finish getting ready. "By the way," he called back over his shoulder, "does Mary know who the caller might have been?"

"She said the voice had been muffled by a cloth or something. They didn't want us to know their identity."

Jenna sat down beside Wanda. "While you're finishing that coffee, tell me how the plants are coming along. They should be flourishing under your care."

Pastor Watchman saw the informal committee waiting for him outside his office and knew one of the three men had to have been the caller to Mary Connors. "Good morning, gentlemen," he called out. Better to be what he called "warmly aggressive" with these men. Any show of weakness toward them would act like blood to a group of sharks. "I'm glad to see you here early, wanting to get a good seat in your Bible study class."

His attempt at humor fell flat. It was just as well, he thought. Ralph Johnson, Owen Stiller and David Jones would take the fun out of any situation.

Ralph normally wouldn't prove to be a problem by himself. But if he got with the wrong crowd, he could be led into doing or saying the wrong thing. As for David Jones, Pastor Watchman felt only pity; the man always seemed to pick the wrong side. Again, David wouldn't be leading this group. He followed, usually staying in the background as much as possible.

Pastor Watchman swung his gaze toward a small, extremely well-dressed man who stood a few steps in front of the others. Owen Stiller exuded neatness. His pencil-thin mustache gleamed, matching the ebony, thick, swept-back head of hair. Here is where the trouble would come from. Behind the group, Ralph's wife, Owen's wife and several other women hovered to see what would happen.

"What can I do for you men?"

Owen tried to push past Pastor Watchman into the office. "We shouldn't discuss these delicate matters in public," he said. His disapproving glance at the pastor showed he didn't think much of Henry Watchman's judgment in talking out in the hallway.

The pastor never moved.

"I think we'll talk about this in public, Owen. Our other members have the right to know when prospective members are being blackballed."

A gasp went up from the women, and David snorted.

Owen acted as if Henry hadn't spoken at all. "Like I said, let's go in, pastor."

"You've not been here for the past several weeks, have you, Owen?" Henry stood in front of the office door, unyielding. No one in that corridor would get by him. "How are you able to make a decision about someone you've never met?"

A line of silver appeared above the pastor's head. Heaven's servant stepped through the divine portal and placed his hands protectively on the pastor. Toldin's wings filled the entire hallway and his head brushed the ceiling, so massive was he in this house of prayer. Through his angelic hands came a silver glow that grew until it encompassed Henry Watchman entirely. Invisible to everyone else in the hallway, the glow nevertheless formed a divine barrier of protection no evil would penetrate in this place of assembled believers. The demon might be growing more powerful with each passing night, but here, surrounded by prayers in a place where God's Holy Spirit moved and worked, Toldin felt energized.

Owen, knowing nothing of this, sighed as if he hated to embarrass the pastor in front of everyone. He looked around at his audience as he spoke, giving the impression everyone agreed with him. "You've got an immoral woman trying to infiltrate our church. I haven't been here, but I know she's a danger. And if you're the man of God you claim to be, you'll protect our children by getting rid of her."

"Is that what we're here for, Owen? If so, I gotta tell you, you're out of line!"

Startled eyes swiveled to focus on Ralph Johnson. His face looked pasty in the neon light of the corridor, but his words certainly got everyone's attention. He was the last man Henry would have expected to speak up.

Owen dismissed him with a glance. "Now, Ralph, you don't understand everything going on here."

"I know you didn't tell me the truth about why we were coming to talk to Reverend Watchman," Ralph answered, still speaking in a soft tone. "I don't believe in railroading anybody." He pointed a finger at Owen. "Without going into anything here, you, of all people, shouldn't be throwing stones at immoral women."

Owen's face turned an ugly red. "What do you mean by that? After all, you and David have got your own problems, don't cha!"

Ralph startled Henry, and probably everyone else. The man who always backed down in a confrontation simply shook his head with a sad smile. "Yes, Owen, I do. That's why I'm here at church today; I want to change." He started walking down the hallway. "I don't know about you, David, but I need some Bible study." And with that, he turned into a classroom and disappeared from sight.

Good for Ralph, thought Pastor Watchman. *Something is getting through to the man.*

"Okay, Watchman," Owen snapped. "Gloves off. Get rid of the prostitute or you may be out of here as pastor."

"Owen, for one thing, you don't represent the majority of this church. Most of the membership have been very accepting of this woman. Second, she's not a prostitute." Henry Watchman tried to keep his temper, but it was getting harder. "But even if she were, it would be okay for her to be here if she wants Christ to change her life."

The angel smiled broadly. He'd thought about a fist pump when Ralph Thompson had made the decision to put Christ and the Bible above anything else, but that might have been a little undignified. Heaven's messenger continued, however, to smile as his eyes swept the group, waiting for the next part in the drama. Sure enough, looking through the outside door, the angel saw some new additions coming that made his face grow serious. "Owen, judgment time for you," Toldin stated. "May you make the right decision."

Owen Stiller wasn't one to give up easily. He continued to argue with the pastor. "Now preacher, I really don't know what kind of person this woman is. All we have is your word . . ."

"Now, Slick. You know what I am, if you'll just stop and think about it."

The words, floating on the air from behind the group, had a galvanizing effect on Owen Stiller. He blanched and put out his hand on the wall for support. The women moved aside for Wanda and Jenna to approach the group. Two bright spots of red showed high on Wanda's face.

"Slick," she repeated, "I didn't know you lived in this town. And I'm surprised to find out you go to church."

Owen moved away from her, but when he came up against his wife, he flinched at the contact and jumped forward as if he'd been burned.

"My name is Owen Stiller, not Slick. And, I've never seen you before in my life." Sweat broke out on the man's forehead and he hastily wiped it away.

A thin, gray-haired woman in a dark purple suit eased her way around Owen. "My name is Connie," she said in a somewhat hesitant voice. "I'm Owen's wife. Are you telling us you know this man?"

Wanda looked at her and nodded somberly. "I'm sorry, but yes, I do. He comes into the LadyZ-N-Waiting strip club almost every week. He always told us he lived in Miami and had no wife. Of course, we could see the pale circle on his ring finger where he usually wore a wedding band."

"That's a lie!" Owen shrieked. Several others nodded in agreement. They didn't want to believe Wanda. One of their own being accused was just too much. "Preacher, get this woman out of this church right now, or . . ."

"Mrs. Stiller, Slick came into our club every Thursday night." Wanda continued to look at Owen's wife. "Where did he tell you he was during those times?"

The energy drained from Connie Stiller and she slumped against Pastor Watchman. "He told me he bowled in a league on Thursday evening," she said softly. "He's been bowling there, I thought, for years."

The women began edging away from Owen, as if he might contaminate them – or even worse, he might contaminate their marriages.

Owen Stiller knew he stood on the edge of ruin. A haunted

expression now marred his good looks and the sweat began to drop from his nose. "Honest, Connie, none of what she said is true. This is exactly what I tried to warn you and the pastor about. She's poison, a liar and this stripper doesn't care who she ruins."

Connie shook her head. In a faraway voice, she said, "I could call the captain of your team, but he'd lie for you. I don't know who to believe . . . but I'm going to do some checking."

"Okay." Wanda took a deep breath. "I didn't want to do this, but you won't be sure any other way." She moved closer to Owen. "Do any of you wonder why the dancers call him Slick? It's because of this." Wanda reached out and, before Owen could stop her, pulled off his beautiful thick hair.

"A toupee!" someone said. "I never knew!"

Owen tried to cover his bald pate, but it proved useless.

"Slick loved for the strippers to kiss him on top of his bald spot and leave lipstick prints, just like Jamison sported on his face," Wanda continued. "Then he'd give a big tip, show everyone at the bar what he'd received and sit down for another show. He loved to have as many kisses on his head as possible before he'd call it an evening."

Owen started to protest – but then he saw his wife. Tears ran down her cheeks as she stared at him in horror. "You always told me I was the only one who did that for you. You said you allowed it because you love me." She started to sway. "Everything you've said to me about your love and faithfulness has been a cheap lie." Owen tried to reach out for her, but she jerked back from his touch and fell into the arms of the two women behind her.

"I hope you change, Owen," Wanda said softly. "I'm trying with all my might to leave my past behind. I want what this church represents. Maybe you need to start listening to what's being taught here instead of living a lie."

David Jones turned to the pastor. "I'm sorry I ever got involved in this," he said. His head hung so far down it made him look several inches shorter. "Ralph's already invited me to his class for Bible study. I think I'll take him up on it." And with that, he and his wife abandoned Owen. They stopped for a moment to whisper in Connie's ear before continuing down the hallway.

His work done for the moment, the angel moved down the hallway toward another, larger room. In a short while, believers would gather here and begin singing praises to God. Prayers from several men and women already kneeling at the front of the room ascended to the Father, as members prayed for their pastor before the service. They knew Henry Watchman would read, talk about and apply the holy scriptures, and they asked for God to guide him, giving Pastor Watchman divine wisdom as he spoke. In other words, worship, already begun, was getting ready to take place on an even greater scale. Toldin loved watching God's Spirit fill believers as they came together in Christ's name. The angel thought of it as food for his very being. "You've not won yet, Shi'intor," he said softly as he entered the worship center.

———

"Mary, you make even a rainy day beautiful."

Henry helped the three women dry off chairs and arrange them around the small table on the long front porch. He and Jenna had accepted an invitation to have lunch with their host and Wanda after church. Considering what had happened earlier, it seemed like a good idea.

The rain had eased a good bit by the time they were ready to eat. Drops of water fell softly on the roof and surrounding gardens, creating a silver curtain between the four diners and the yard. Mary spread a starched, white tablecloth and set out paper plates and plastic ware. A variety of sandwiches, sour and sweet pickles, deviled eggs and baked beans adorned a smaller table by the door. Wanda busied herself pouring tea for everyone, while Jenna placed napkins by each place.

"It's not fancy, but it's filling," Mary said. "I've decided it'll be easier for everyone if we do this buffet style. Fill your plate and then pick a chair." She looked at Henry. "Pastor Watchman, will you say grace, please?"

After the blessing, Henry made Jenna lead the way to the food while he waited until everyone had been served. "I know what you're doing, Henry," Jenna said as she sat down with her barely filled plate. "You can put as much on your plate as you want because no one is behind you to take more."

Wanda and Mary laughed as their pastor looked guiltily at his plate heaped high with what looked like enough for three people. "I really am praying to have your metabolism in heaven," his wife said, shaking her head in mock sorrow.

Henry somehow managed to engineer sitting down without spilling anything. He took a sip of tea, sighed contentedly, then turned toward Mary's house guest. "So, Wanda, in light of every-thing that happened today, how did church go for you?"

The young woman looked over at Mary and raised her eyebrows, asking an unspoken question. Mary nodded, telling her to be honest. "I felt really sorry for that Owen Stiller." She shook her head. "No, I actually felt sorry for Connie. Owen's choices aren't her fault."

"That's the problem with sin," Henry said. "So often it hurts innocent people."

Wanda nodded. "This is new for me, pastor. I'm not used to having people care about me. And it's certainly different for me to be caring about others. It's . . ." she struggled to find the right words. "It's difficult, but wonderful. And, church was good. The people, except for that man in the corridor by your office, have been so accepting." She grinned. "I even found myself enjoying your sermon."

"That truly is amazing," Jenna said with a straight face.

Henry picked up the pitcher of tea. "Honey, how would you like this to cool your lap off?"

"Behave, you two!" Mary said. "Honestly, I can't take my pastor and his wife anywhere!" It did her good to see Wanda laughing and smiling. She'd worried that the phone call and confrontation might sour Wanda on the church, but it seemed as if the young woman had decided to stand strong.

"What will happen to Owen and Connie?" Mary asked. She began gathering the plates and dirty napkins to throw them away. "Wait, don't answer that until I get back." She headed into the house. "Wanda, would you pour everyone some coffee while I get dessert?"

When Mary reappeared a few minutes later, Henry's eyes lit up. "Is that butterscotch pie?" he asked.

"I figured you two might be joining us for dinner today, so I made your favorite." She placed a huge piece in front of the pastor.

"Make it a much smaller piece for me," Jenna said. "Well, maybe not too small!"

They dug into their slices of pie, and for a few minutes, no one spoke. But after downing several sips of coffee, Henry returned to Mary's question. "I'm not sure what the Stillers will do. I talked to Connie during the Bible study hour, but she isn't ready to speak with Owen. As for him, he'd already called his wife on her cell phone and left a message saying he would be trying to find a hotel room to stay in for the next several days. Connie said it had better be several weeks, not days."

"Do you think their marriage will survive?" Wanda asked. Husbands and wives staying together had become more important for her than ever. She twisted the coffee cup in her hands as she thought about "Slick" and his lies.

"Frankly, I think there will have to be a major change in Owen's life for Connie to be willing to continue in the marriage." Henry shook his head. "But maybe, just maybe, this has given him enough of a shock that he'll finally become the man God – and Connie – want him to be."

"Wanda's doing well, don't you think?" Jenna glanced back at the house they'd just left.

Henry, full and mellow, nodded in agreement. "Mary may be doing better than Wanda. They're certainly good for each other. I haven't seen Mary this energized since her husband died. The way they get along, you'd think those two women had been friends for ages."

"Now that we're alone," Jenna said, "I thought I'd tell you about a conversation I had with David Jones' wife after church."

Henry moaned. "Don't tell me he is complaining again!"

"No, it's just the opposite. She said that after Bible study, David took her aside and confessed he had been with Owen twice in the strip club. He apologized and begged her for another chance. He even admitted his temper was out of control." Jenna watched for oncoming traffic as Henry eased the car onto Highway A1A. "She believes it's a watershed moment in their marriage, and he's promised to start going to a marriage counselor with her."

A few hundred yards away, on the other side of the road, the ocean could be seen continuing its flirtation with the shore. The ocean seemed incapable of a commitment. It came, but never stayed. A steady breeze had swept nearly all the clouds from the sky. That same breeze created a vacuum effect, drawing swimmers, sunbathers, sandcastle builders and children galore to the beach.

"I never get tired of looking at it," Henry murmured.

Jenna smiled. She and her husband loved the beach as much as anyone. "It's great to be able to live and work for God in a place you can appreciate, honey. God has certainly been good to us." She thought back to Mary. "It's also great to see God work small miracles in ways we would never have imagined."

Henry nodded in agreement. "Another miracle is that God answered our prayer about David Jones' marriage and family. Let's just continue to pray that David will follow through with his promises." He parked the car in the driveway and got out slowly, seeming unsure of what to do next.

"What's the matter, Henry?" Jenna asked.

He grinned. "I'm a little embarrassed to admit it, but I'm thinking about an afternoon nap, instead of going to the office like I usually do."

"You need that nap today," Jenna replied. "It's been a good day, but it's also been very emotional. That will take a toll on anyone." She put out her hand to Henry. "Come on, it won't hurt you relax on the day of rest!"

Hand in hand, they entered the house as the sun began moving toward the western horizon.

CHAPTER THIRTY-THREE

Vincent Anderson moved closer to the sheltering darkness of the seawall. Cramped muscles begged to be stretched, but he ignored them. Henry Watchman could appear at any moment, and the detective didn't want the pastor to see him . . . if Watchman came at all. He'd taken a chance that Watchman would keep to his regular habit of running on the beach late Sunday night, and the detective had arrived at 10:00 p.m., ready to follow his dad's killer.

He frowned at that last thought. He no longer felt as sure that the man he'd hated and searched for most of his life had meant to kill his father. He saw Watchman as eccentric, to say the least. But he couldn't deny the minister's compassion. And his refusal to get angry didn't fit with a murderer's profile. Besides . . . his body tensed as Watchman appeared.

The preacher stood looking out over the ocean a good ten minutes. *What's he doing?* the detective wondered. Watchman's face raised gradually toward the starlit sky and he lifted his hands toward the heavens. Anderson felt a little embarrassed when he realized the preacher was praying. Hard after that, however, came the thought, *What if he's some kind of sicko who's praying for success in his next killing?* The detective hardened himself. This was life, and he'd seen some strange things in his brief career. He couldn't let emotions get in the way again.

Fangs dripping, the demon rose out of the ocean and waded ashore. Scales snapped in the breeze as he came alongside the detective. *"Tonight,"* he whispered in Anderson's ear, *"the preacher will be destroyed."* Dark, livid eyes glinted in the moonlight. *"And do I have a surprise for you!"*

Vincent Anderson felt uneasy for some reason. He knew something had to happen soon. Watchman had finished praying and now moved through some stretching exercises. Finally, he turned and began a steady lope down the beach. Anderson felt in his gut there would be a murder attempt tonight. He wanted either to rule out Watchman or catch him in the act.

He gave the preacher a couple hundred yards head-start, then quietly stood and began following. They'd run about a half-mile, with Anderson staying far enough behind that if his suspect turned around, Watchman wouldn't be able to I D him. The detective needn't have worried. Watchman never looked back. As far as Anderson could tell, the man still kept to the same pace. Anderson began to breathe a little harder. He prided himself on being in good shape, but running in the sand, some of which tended to be a little soft, made the short distance they'd covered seem longer.

The roar of the surf covered his heavy breathing, but . . . a shuffling in the sand behind Vincent caused him to turn his head. Before he could see anything, a powerful blow to the side of his head knocked him into the surf. He twisted violently and managed to avoid the worst of a kick aimed at his groin, catching it in his ribs. He felt at least one snap.

"Hey!"

He managed to yell only one word before a fist slammed into his face.

"Kill him!" the demon screamed. *"Make him pay!"*

Vincent saw two images swim before his eyes as darkness began closing in – a knife coated in a black substance descending, and Henry Watchman running toward him from down the beach. Then . . . nothing.

————

"Vince, wake up."

The voice seemed to come from far away.

"Vince, Jenna and I are going to have to take you to the hospital. Please wake up."

After great effort, the detective managed to get one swollen eye open a bit. Above him, two concerned faces peered at what had to be a face that had seen better days. "You've never called me Vince before, Henry," he managed to croak.

Pastor Watchman grinned in relief. "I figured saving your life put us on a first name basis."

Saved my life? Vincent thought. The recent events came surging up out of his memory and he sat up . . . only to groan and quickly fall back on the Watchmans' couch.

"I have to get to the station. Someone tried to kill me." The last words came out in a whisper as the pain forced him to gasp for breath.

"You'll do no such thing," Jenna said firmly. "You're going to the hospital. I think a couple of ribs are broken, and who knows what else."

Vince shook his head weakly. "Not yet. We have to talk, first."

"Oh no, mister stubborn detective," Jenna said.

Henry laid a hand gently on his wife's arm. "Hold on. Vince is right. Let's take a few more minutes to see if we can figure out who we're facing." He held up his hand to forestall any more protests. "Then, I promise it's off to the hospital. But I don't want to deliver the only witness that can prove I'm not the killer into the wrong hands and let him become another victim."

"I've told you all about my past, Vince. Now, it's time to let me in on just what's going on."

Vincent turned on his good side, and the pastor moved around to sit beside him. "It all began with the strangest note attached to a body," Vincent began slowly. "We got a call from a motel owner just down the beach from where you usually begin your run. He'd discovered a common criminal by the name of Terrence Duggan stabbed to death. Detective Maria Gonzalez and I investigated. An old tarp had been thrown over the body to hide it, so nearly fourteen hours had passed since the murder." He paused for a moment to get his breath.

"Here's some water." Jenna Watchman handed Vince a glass with ice in it.

He sipped painfully and winced as he swallowed. "For a jaw that's not broken, it sure does hurt," he muttered.

"Henry." He shifted around again. "What I'm getting ready to tell you is confidential. The police are holding the information to avoid a sensation." He caught the preacher's eyes and held them. "A knife had been stabbed into Terrence's chest. It held a piece of paper with an unusual message on it: *Use profanity and you will DIE!*"

"Wait a minute!" Henry Watchman exclaimed. "You and detective Da Silva came to question me the week after I preached the sermon on profanity! That can't be a coincidence."

Vincent nodded wearily. "Now you know why we locked in on you as a possible suspect. You preached about it on a Sunday morning. The next day, a body turned up with the note."

Jenna cleared her throat. "How in the world did you keep the motel owner from telling what was on the note?" she asked. "People love to spread that kind of news."

"We think the killer wanted to send a message to society," Vincent said. "He was so passionate about what he believed, he'd placed the message directly over the center of the con man's chest, where the words pressed down on his heart. I had to lie down on the ground and put my head right next to the knife to see them." He grinned at the memory. "The motel owner didn't want to get that close to a dead body." He looked up at Jenna. It was getting harder to talk, now. "That's why no one else knows about this. There have been three notes on three different bodies, all facing the heart." Vincent took another drink of water. "The police are stumped and the chief is furious. It's getting toward the height of tourist season and the last thing he needs is a scandal like this. We don't . . . what's wrong?"

Henry Watchman's expression had changed dramatically. Jenna recognized the look. It revealed the prize fighter who could have been a champion; the pastor who'd turned a sleepy, complacent church around. She leaned over and rubbed the back of his neck.

Vincent didn't know the pastor nearly as well. "You mad at me?" he asked, a belligerent tone creeping into his voice. "I couldn't tell you any of this earlier."

Henry shook his head. "I'm mad, but not at you. This is a horrible situation, and we have to stop these killings. Now that I know who the murderer is, we must move quickly."

The words had a galvanizing effect on Vincent. "What?" he shouted . . . then groaned with the effort.

Henry sat down again beside the detective. "I don't have the whole thing worked out, but I'll tell you this. The Bible talks about the evils of jealousy and envy. For someone to kill innocents simply because they . . . ." He paused. "I don't know how, but we have to fix this." He turned to Vincent and smiled. "I hate to bother you more, but I need the rest of the story."

The detective still looked at the preacher, stunned. "What did you figure out in five minutes that's escaped the whole police force? Come on, spill it."

Henry shook his head. "No, not yet. Not until I'm sure. I have to protect you, Vincent. You confided in me. You're beginning to forgive me – whether you realize it or not – and, you've come to my church. I have a responsibility; I'm not going to blow it by exposing you or having your career ruined." He put out his hand to shake with Vincent. "I promise, I'll let you know within a day. But right now, I need to know about the others killed."

Vincent hesitated, then took the pastor's hand and shook it. "Okay," he conceded with reluctance. "But as soon as you know something for sure, I need to be aware of it." When Henry nodded, the detective recounted the rest of the events. Over the next fifteen minutes, he went over everything he could think of. Watchman asked a couple of questions, then sat back with a faraway look in his eyes.

"Could you get Shirl on the phone for me, Vince?" he asked.

"Sure. She's off right now, I think." He picked up the phone and dialed a number. Shirl answered on the third ring. "Shirl, it's Vince."

"Vince, what's wrong with your voice? You sound terrible!"

The detective sighed. "Too long a story. You'll get all the details later. Listen, Pastor Watchman just saved my life. He's a good guy."

"Saved your life? What happened, Vince? If you need . . ."

"Shirl, hush." Vincent sighed once more. It was getting hard to talk. "The pastor needs to ask you a couple of questions. Answer them as best you can." He handed the phone to Henry and sank back onto the couch.

Watchman greeted Shirl, then walked toward the back of the house, saying, "I need to know the duty roster of everyone for the night of . . ." His voice faded as he rounded the corner.

In the sudden quiet, Vincent began to relax. He felt someone – probably Jenna – put a cool washcloth on his forehead. She was certainly being nice after the way he'd treated her and her husband. He wanted to thank her, but his voice didn't seem inclined to cooperate. A dull pain began to tighten around Vincent's chest. The room darkened and, from far away, he thought he could hear Jenna yelling to her husband, trying to get his attention. Strange, she seemed to be alarmed about something. Maybe he could help her . . . He started to get up, but couldn't because of hands holding him down in . . . a van? When had he left the pastor's house?

Vincent could see several nurses reaching in to pick him up and put him on a stretcher. Behind them the anxious face of Hank Thompson peered at him. It finally dawned on Vincent that he was at some kind of hospital – and in friendly company. He lay back and relaxed. Somehow, he trusted Henry Watchman to take care of things. Events seemed to swirl around the man without knocking him off his feet. *That's the kind of friend I'd like to have.* The words floated across his mind and he smiled absently. Then, blessed darkness.

CHAPTER THIRTY-FOUR

"Believe me, Hank, the chief has no idea what's going on in his own department."

The addressed Hank Thompson was sweating bullets. He and Pastor Henry Watchman stood before the door to Gin McFain's hospital room, and the sergeant had to make an important decision. If the preacher spoke the truth, it could be a life-saving decision. But it could also get Thompson busted or even fired. The good sergeant didn't like making decisions at the best of times. His personality leant itself to getting along with everyone, not making waves.

"Hank, sometimes you have to make someone else feel bad in order to save a life."

Where did that come from? Watchman seemed to be able to read his mind.

The pastor grinned. "No, I can't tell what you're thinking. But I do have a lot of experience reading emotions and watching people in tough situations." He turned serious. "McFain may very well die in this hospital room if we don't get him out *now*. If you want, I'll let you stay with him every second he's away from here. But the longer you wait, the higher his probability of being killed."

The sergeant looked from the pastor to the physician standing beside him. He made a decision. "Doc, if you'll release McFain, saying it's okay for him to leave the hospital, I'll accompany him until such time the man is able to make it on his own." Whew! A long speech, thought Thompson. But it felt good to make a decision – even that one.

The doctor nodded assent. Hank turned to the policeman on duty and said, "Let these men in the room. If anyone asks, I go on record as having given them permission."

————

Henry Watchman took a long look at the patient before speaking. This would be delicate, and he wanted to understand as much as possible about the patient as he could. Gin McFain's life hung in the balance; Watchman was sure of it. The good pastor could almost feel the evil hanging in the air, waiting to drop on and envelope this accidental witness.

From what he'd learned, McFain had been blinded as a child. Early on, a craving for alcohol had driven him, and he'd wound up a panhandler, albeit a gentle one, on the streets of Hidden Beach. Several weeks had passed since the car bombing, and McFain's cuts seemed to be healing well. But Watchman knew a powerful urge to drink had to be pushing at the patient from every direction right now. If they let McFain out, he'd try to bolt. How could they persuade him that life could be more than a drink and a temporary fog?

For some reason, Henry remembered the conversation his wife had initiated with Kathleen. She'd mentioned Joshua . . .

What is your name?

The words seemed to float in the air before Henry Watchman. A shiver of excitement covered him. *Is this from you, God?* He prayed. From time to time, the pastor would get a sense of destiny about someone. He'd had it when working with Wanda Lemming. Now, it seemed God had a plan for this man, as well.

Beside him, the angel glowed with power. His wings had covered the patient's bed protectively for some time. "Father," he said, "I have been faithful to my task of guarding this one who does not yet know you." The angel's eyes seemed to look through the ceiling, straight into heaven's throne room. "I sense this might be a moment of decision for this wounded, hurting man. Speak to him, please, Father."

A holy hush came over the entire group. The atmosphere seemed to vibrate with excitement. Then, God's Holy Spirit descended in power, filling the room with His presence. The angel bowed in worship and adoration. Henry Watchman, God's servant here, was getting ready to be part of more than he knew!

"Mr. McFain, get up. It's time to get on with your life."

Watchman's words provoked no response, other than a momentary opening of the man's eyelids.

The preacher tried again. "I said, get up. We need to leave."

Again, no motion from the patient, except for him to grimace and say, "Leave me alone, mister. At least in here, I get hot food and I stay sober." He closed his eyes again. "From where I'm lying, that's about all old Gin can expect."

So, he wants to stay sober! *There is some hope, after all,* Watchman thought.

"My name is Henry Watchman. I'm pastor of Hidden Beach Community Church." This brought a snort from the man in bed. "The policeman is Sergeant Hank Thompson. Dr. Ernest Cassidy has your release signed and is ready to be your personal physician until you get back on your feet. The sergeant has graciously consented to protect you when he's not on duty. We'll have another detective watching you during those hours."

No movement from the bed.

"You'll be dead within twenty-four hours if you don't get out of here *now!*" Henry said in a firm voice.

McFain finally raised up a bit. "I got no place to go. They kicked me out of my last place because I couldn't pay the rent." He shivered. "Besides, I'll just drink up whatever money I get."

The patient turned to the pastor. "You preacher-types don't know much about the underside of the world. There ain't much for a guy like me to look forward to, and . . . ."

"Cut the poor mouth stuff, McFain," Pastor Watchman interrupted. "You don't know what I've been through at all. My past might very well be as bad as yours. But I decided to quit moaning about how tough life is and God helped me get my life in order."

The patient's eyes narrowed. "That's fine and dandy for you, Mr. 'Preacher Man.' But God don't care about drunks and blind men."

Watchman shook his head. "Not true. When He was on earth, Jesus healed a blind man everyone else had given up on. If God did that, He can heal your inner wounds, at the very least, McFain."

"Call me 'Gin,' preacher. Everyone else does."

"I'm not going to do that. Every time you hear that name, it's a reminder of a failed past." He looked at McFain. "What's your real name?"

The man's eyes dropped. "I don't have any other name that I know of."

"What about on your Social Security card? What does it say?" the sergeant asked.

"Never had one," Gin explained. "I was raised by a couple of women in Georgia who were friends of my mother. I never knew my mom or my dad. Dad walked out sometime during my first year of life. Mom died when I was almost two years old. I called the women who raised me "Aunt Mollie" and "Aunt Bell." They taught me how to get around on my own, but I never went to school because they had this fear the state would take me away from them." He swung his legs over the side of the bed and sat up. "They both worked during the day, so I had a lot of time to myself. A neighbor of theirs gave me some watered-down gin to drink when I was a little kid. They say I lapped it up and begged for more." A resigned tone crept into his voice. "That's how I got my name and my future."

"Then you need a real name," the pastor said with a smile. "And I think we'll let God give it to you." He sat down in a chair across from the bed. "There's a story in the Bible about a loser named Jacob. He'd run from God and from society all his life. Finally backed into a corner, he faced the possibility of both him and his family being annihilated the next day."

"Sounds like the same fix I'm in," the blind man said. "What'd he do?"

"An angel came and wrestled with him all night. Even though he knew he'd probably lose, Jacob wouldn't give up. The angel knocked his hip out of socket, and the pain had to be horrendous, but Jacob hung in there and wouldn't let go. Finally, toward morning, the angel asked Jacob for his name." Watchman stopped to explain something. "Understand that in the Old Testament, a man's name also indicated his fate and his personality. 'Jacob' meant a sly, slick person. Someone who tricked others. For Jacob to tell his name to God's representative, he had to also admit to his bad character. In effect, Jacob gave up his pride and finally owned up to all his character flaws.

"Let me see if I can find a Bible." Pastor Watchman opened the top drawer in the night stand. Sure enough, a blue Bible rested inside, as if waiting for this moment. He opened it to Genesis and read, *"The man asked him, "What is your name?" "Jacob," he answered. Then the man said, "Your name will no longer be Jacob, but Israel, because you have struggled with God and with men and have overcome."*"

"With a new name came a new future," Watchman continued. "The next day, God worked a miracle for Israel and his family. They escaped being killed and eventually grew and prospered." He closed the Bible and looked straight at McFain. "You need a future like that – as well as a new name."

Pastor Henry Watchman stood up. He placed his right hand on Gin McFain's head.

The angel beside him glowed brighter and brighter. He put his hand on top of the pastor's hand. Together, they spoke. Earthly ears heard only Henry Watchman. But those around Heaven's throne heard two voices, joined as one, proclaim:

"Your name is no longer 'Gin.' That life is in the past. Your new name is 'Israel.' God is giving you the opportunity to be in a place where you can overcome and prosper." Henry Watchman looked down and spoke a command. "Israel, get up now and begin your new life."

To his own surprise, the newly named Israel did just that.

CHAPTER THIRTY-FIVE

Voices from the open area of the police station, even though lessened by Chief Monroe's closed door, could still be heard faintly. The muted, steady noise proved a comfort to Maria Da Silva as she sat across from the chief. The voices reminded her that life went on in its everyday manner even when difficult, radical events threatened to claim all your attention and energy. She sipped from a cup of coffee as she and the chief talked over the situation of Vincent Anderson one more time.

"He's changed in the last couple of weeks, Maria. That confidence – swagger, really – is just about gone. The up-and-coming, success-oriented young man has turned into an emotional wreck." Jinx thumped the table with a heavy fist. "We have to get this case solved and Anderson back on track."

Maria chose her words carefully. "Chief, remember everything that's happened to Vince. He's finally found the man who killed his father. All those memories and emotions he'd hidden away have come surging out. He has to be given some time to sort them out." She took another sip of coffee. "Give him some time. He'll be all right."

"Yeah, you may be right," Chief Monroe conceded. "And, I guess I'm harder on Vince than the others. But he's got so much potential that – who's there?" Someone had rapped timidly on the door.

Eric Batts stuck his head partway around the corner, as if afraid to come in too far. His flushed face betrayed a man upset and unsure of what to do.

"I said, come on in, Batts."

Maria could see the chief trying to squelch his impatience.

"Uh, sorry to bother you chief. I see you're busy. Maybe some other time I can . . . ."

"Spit it out, Batts. Da Silva can keep a secret." Jinx Monroe shook his head in disgust. "What's the matter?"

"Uh, well, I just came from the hospital, checking on that McFain fella."

Chief Monroe stood up suddenly. In the small office, he looked even larger and more imposing than usual. Eric Batts took a step back

"Who told you to do that, Batts? I don't remember giving such an order."

The patrolman began to sweat. The acrid smell filled the office. Maria wrinkled her nose. Nervous sweat seemed to have an aroma all its own. And the man must have been *very* nervous.

"Sir, I was just trying to get back in good with you. I thought if I helped guard McFain even when I was off, you might see me in a better light."

The chief waved off the reason. "So, what did you want to see me about?"

Batts hesitated a moment. Maria could tell the man didn't want to say what he had to say.

"Sir, McFain is gone."

"What!" Monroe roared. "Where is he? What did you do with him? If you put him in harm's way, Batts, so help me I'll . . . ."

Batts waved his hands as hard as he could. "No sir. Not me, sir. He'd already disappeared when I got there. The policeman on duty said a physician signed him out of the hospital." Batts pulled a dirty, sodden notepad out of his back pocket. He flipped through a few pages, then said, "I got the doctor's name: Dr. Ernest Cassidy. And, here's his pager number."

The chief snatched the notebook out of Batts' hands. "Let's call the good doctor and find out what's going on." He picked up the phone, but paused when the patrolman pointed to another name on the same page of the notebook.

"The policeman on duty said Pastor Henry Watchman accompanied Gin McFain out of the hospital. The doctor put him in a van driven by some old woman. Sergeant Hank Thompson was with them." Batts looked down at the floor, unwilling to meet his chief's eyes. "Do you want me to contact anybody for you?"

Monroe waved him out of the office. "I'll take care of this." He looked sharply at the patrolman. "You're still off-duty, aren't you?"

Eric Batts nodded.

"Then go home and do something relaxing. This isn't your affair."

"Yes sir," Batts mumbled as he closed the door once more.

As he left Jinx's office, Batts' mind whirled. In his present state of mind, he couldn't think of what to do next or where to go. He glanced toward Shirl, only to see her get up and start for the break room to get some water. With nothing better to do, the patrolman wandered over and began looking at the slips of paper haphazardly covering the surface of her desk. The messages told snippets of events, everything from flat tires to muggings to charity events. One in particular caught his eye: *"H.W. phoned @ 23:00 re: EB's shift schdle prev 3 wks."*

The words hit him in the stomach with the strength of a mule. He looked around. No one seemed interested in what he was doing. Batts palmed the note and walked out of the building.

Once in his car, he tried to force his mind to wake up. The "H.W." had to be Henry Watchman, just as "EB" had to be him, Eric Batts. Why would Watchman be interested in his whereabouts over the last three weeks? There could be only one answer.

The demon waited in the patrol car's back seat. He watched the human get into the driver's side. Waves of uncertainty roiled about the human, mixing with his acrid sweat and fear. The servant of evil inhaled deeply; the pungent smell was like perfume to anyone one who loved despair and failure.

Setbacks had occurred. Shi'intor had planned Anderson's death and Watchman's guilt carefully. No one could have anticipated the hated preacher doubling back to help an adversary. After all, who loved and gave aid to their enemies?

That's why the demon of Hidden Beach worked alone. Shi'intor grinned cruelly as he thought about his past. At first, smaller demons had been sent to help him in previous tasks. Every time, however, Shi'intor had eventually ended up fighting with them, losing his temper and then consuming them. It also seemed he grew stronger each time he tore a demon limb from limb and turned what was supposed to be a teammate into food. For some reason no one wanted to work with him anymore. "That's okay with me," Shi'intor hissed. "Teamwork is over-rated anyway." And this way, only he would get the glory of destroying both the angel and the preacher.

The demon shook with rage as he thought how close he'd been to success. Now, however, was not the time to give up; he would regroup. The night could still be won. The situation called for a few changes, but Watchman would still end up guilty or, even better, dead. The demon sank quickly into Batts' willing mind, making a few "suggestions."

In the darkness of his car, Batts pulled from underneath the back seat a gun the police had confiscated from a petty thief two years before. Batts had stolen it, wondering why at the time. Now he knew. It couldn't be traced back to him, and the thief had been released from prison four months ago. Eventually, any murder committed with it would lead back to a thief with a prison record.

Eric Batts smiled as he caressed the gun. Finally, he had a plan. The gun had killed before, and it would kill again. He put the car in gear and moved smoothly out of the parking lot. He had a preacher to find.

———

"Detective Da Silva, get me some details on this Doctor Cassidy. I'm not sure what's going on, but I don't like it."

A knock on the door interrupted the chief.

"What now?" Monroe sighed. "Come in; everyone else seems to want to tonight."

Shirl opened the door and stepped all the way into the office. Her body trembled from head to toe, but she made herself close the door and advance to the chief's desk. Monroe raised an eyebrow. This had to be important. He forced himself to calm down and tried to smile.

"Sit down, please," he said.

The dispatcher fell into the chair next to Maria and tried to speak. "Chief . . ." her voice squeaked and she tried again. "Chief, that pastor Henry Watchman called tonight and asked about the shift schedules of several police officers. He seemed especially interested in Eric Batts."

The chief tried to keep a pleasant expression on his face. Scaring Shirl would produce no new information. "Did you give him any information?" he asked in what he hoped sounded like a neutral voice.

Shirl nodded convulsively. "I had to. Detective Anderson told me it was a matter of life or death."

Monroe wanted to throw something at his harebrained dispatcher. Instead, he said, "Thank you, Shirl. We'll take it from here. Now if you'll . . . ."

"That's not all, sir – if you'll excuse me interrupting you." Shirl's voice shook, but she continued anyway. "I had written down the call on a piece of paper with a little information underneath it to remind me of what we talked about. The note was sitting on the lower left edge of my desk just a few minutes ago. I got up to get a bottle of water from the break room. When I came back, it was gone." She paused, trying to gauge her chief's anger status. He looked okay, so she went on. "I looked for it on the floor, but nothing had fallen off. When I asked one of the police officers at another desk, he said patrolman Eric Batts had stopped at my desk just before I returned."

Shirl faced her chief and raised her chin slightly, as if trying to get more courage. "What do you want me to do, sir?"

Chief Monroe looked at the ceiling for a moment, then sat down in his chair, took out his revolver and clipped it to his belt. "Shirl, keep this information to yourself." He looked at Maria. "Head to the hospital and find the doctor. Call me when you know something."

Maria stood, but didn't move. She didn't even know the chief *had* a gun in his office! "Sir, don't you think you'd better stay here and let us take care this?" she said.

Jinx Monroe shook his head. "Batts is more of an idiot than I thought." He moved toward the door. "I've got to stop him before someone else is murdered. The best way you can help me is to find the doctor – and the others – as fast as possible." The chief nodded to Shirl and to Maria Da Silva, then walked out of his office and the station.

The two women looked after him for only a moment. Maria put her hand on Shirl's shoulder and gave her a reassuring pat. "Let's get to work," she said, walking out, as well.

CHAPTER THIRTY-SIX

Henry Watchman moved quietly through the alleyway outside the LadyZ-N-Waiting strip club. A dead-end alley at night in Dollar Town, the seamy section of Hidden Beach, didn't rate high on the list of places the pastor wanted to visit. Something about the car explosion and subsequent murder, however, bothered him. The two couldn't simply be a string of coincidences, but how the murderer got from the burned car to the alley and then disappeared still mystified him. The cul-de-sac seemingly assured that the one who'd killed Robert Jamison had to have come either from the street or from the club – and no one had seen anyone but Watchman and Anderson enter from the street. Vincent had admitted the police couldn't find anyone from either the club or the photo supply shop across the alley who'd seen a man or woman leave through their doors.

At the far end of the alley, a garbage dumpster squatted against a faded brick wall. Henry looked inside the bin. Nothing there but a couple of banana peels and a red shoe with a broken heel. All seemed normal . . . for a garbage bin. Henry rubbed his eyes; he didn't have much time for this detour. Jenna needed another pair of hands to help her care for Vincent and Israel. A few things, however, still needed answering. The alleyway, Henry had felt, might hold the solution.

He looked once more at the dumpster and shook his head. Nothing unusual anywhere. The alleyway was a dead end in more than one way . . .

Something about the garbage bin didn't feel right. He walked back to the stage door. Bending down, he noticed scrapes and indentations, even on the hard surface. A large object had sat just across and down from the club for a long time. Could it have been the dumpster? From the look of the scrapes, the bin had been sitting not far from the stage door until recently. But why move it so far to the back of the alley? People wanting to get rid of their garbage would have a long walk. And with the dumpster's lid shut, odor wouldn't be that much of a problem.

Henry walked to the back of the alleyway once more and faced the bin. "Let's see if you're hiding something," he murmured. Moving behind the bin, concealed from anyone passing by on the street, he managed to wedge himself between the wall and the dumpster. He flicked on a flashlight and let the beam play over the wall. Sure enough, the faint outline of a door showed itself.

The preacher pushed against it with his shoulder and nearly lost his balance as the door swung inward easily. Hmm, he thought. Someone had recently oiled the hinges to make a quiet exit – or entrance. Moving farther into the darkness, he retraced the steps of the murderer . . for now, Watchman knew positively who had killed, and why.

____

Evil hungered. Some might question its existence. But evil flourished when ignored, working best in the shadows of amorality and the blackness of ignorance. A dark carnivore, it eternally lusted for blood. Like a deadly fog, this night the evil emerged from its lair and oozed across the community of Hidden Beach, ready to destroy.

The demon paused for a moment to touch a recovering alcoholic, whispering seductively that she could go to her favorite bar and have "just one drink" with her friends. He reached down into a home and filled a couple's minds with anger, pausing for a moment to watch the beginning fight, then moving on. For tonight, he hoped to see the plan to ruin Henry Watchman come to fruition. One tool waited, already honed and ready to use. Now evil took the second step, settling upon the soul of Eric Batts for one final time.

The night felt comfortable to Eric. It hid his sweat, his fear, his impending doom if Watchman couldn't be put away.

His wife, the demon whispered.

Of course! The patrolman smiled as he suddenly figured out the next step in his plan. But first, he had an "errand" to run. He grinned cruelly in the darkness, gripping and regripping the stolen revolver. This was going to be fun.

Evil moved on, seeping ever outward from Hidden Beach. It had two teeth sharpened for the trap. Now, one more act and all would be ready. The demon continued his search for the right bait.

*There! His target carefully selected, the demon dipped downward, invaded the artery of his third victim, nudged loose a piece of plaque and directed it toward a feeble heart. As a final touch, he reached out and squeezed **hard**.*

"Oh, dear Lord!" gasped Raymond.

The pain struck him right between his shoulder blades and drove him face down onto the carpet he'd been vacuuming around the pulpit. He couldn't seem to catch his breath. Everything began turning black.

"Dear God, not yet," he prayed. Fingers that didn't want to work fumbled for the cell phone his daughter had insisted he carry with him. He'd laughed when first presented with the notion he needed a way to get help at all times. Now, belatedly, he saw its wisdom. As unconsciousness tugged every harder at him, he hit the speed dial for the person who could act quickest under pressure.

Hang on a little longer, he told himself. Someone answered

the phone. Raymond managed to gasp out a few words. Then . . . he knew no more.

———

Eric Batts turned off the motor of his car and let it coast silently downhill and into a small grove of trees. The path got little use. It meandered behind the condos on either side of it, serving as a pickup point for the sanitation workers. Those living in the condominiums would take their garbage cans out through the gates in the back yards lining the path. In that way, when it came time to empty the cans, the workers could cover double the number of dwellings quickly and efficiently. Other than the once-a-week garbage pickup, the path got little use.

The car door opened quietly. Batts slipped out, holding duct tape, a truncheon and some plastic wire. A soft, warm breeze from the ocean caressed the branches overhead. The sweet smell of honeysuckle wafted through the grove. Eric Batts neither felt nor appreciated any of it. Tonight, he had work to do. Eric eased through one particular gate he knew well and made his way toward the back door of the condo. He knew Da Silva's door would be unlatched if Maria wasn't there.

The first hint Vina had that something wasn't quite right coincided with a heavy thump on her dresser, as if someone had bumped into it. She started to turn over in her bed to look toward the doorway when something slammed into her neck. Nearly unconscious, her head was pushed down into the bedding and she felt her arms forced behind her back and tied together. A hand pulled her face up slightly, and she saw a napkin coming toward her eyes. Then, in the darkness, she heard a ripping sound and it felt like tape placed across her face to hold the napkin in place.

"Please . . ." she started.

"Shut up," a voice whispered. The intruder pulled her up and then more tape went across her mouth. Whoever the person was, he was strong. She was picked up and moved into another room. He shoved her onto a chair and tied her to it.

"Don't move." She couldn't tell from the whisper who the intruder was. "You know, I really enjoy doing this. In fact," his breath, hot and fetid, assaulted her ear, "I've come to realize I want to do it a whole lot more."

Etelvina Da Silva didn't frighten easily. She had overcome a great deal during her years on earth. But now she felt beads of sweat pop out on her neck and chest. This man was sick – and his sickness enjoyed hurting people.

The sound of the refrigerator door opening helped Vina orient herself. She was probably sitting at the bar. She heard the man pour something, then drink it. It must have been ice water, because the sudden coldness of his lips on her ear made Vina jump, in spite of herself. "I have something else to do, but I'll be back later on tonight." He pulled back for a moment, then Vina jumped again as his glass shattered on the hard tile floor. "Didja hear that, old woman? That's what I'll be doing to you," he whispered with a chuckle. "Yeah, I'll be breaking you into a thousand pieces."

Vina heard the back door open and close. Then . . . silence.

———————

Maria walked out of the hospital knowing no more than when she went in. The officer had confirmed Hank Thompson, along with the reverend Henry Watchman, had taken Gin McFain away from the room and from the hospital. But no one seemed to know exactly where they'd gone. As she got in her car, the detective decided to try Watchman's house next. It amazed her how often criminals, when they escaped from prison, simply went home to hide out.

Even at this late hour, cars came and went on A1A. The T-shirt shops looked to be doing a brisk business. She turned the car toward the ocean, toward Hidden Beach Community

Church, and toward Pastor Henry Watchman's house. Maybe she'd finally get some answers as to Vincent's whereabouts. As she prepared to thumb the radio to let Shirl know her next move, Maria's phone rang. The caller ID showed her home number. That was strange. What was her mom doing up at midnight? She answered it.

"Mama, that you?"

A voice she almost didn't recognize said, "Maria, I think you're right. It may be time to put more locks on the door and start using them."

Blood began pounding in Maria's head. "What happened, Mama? Are you all right? Do I need to call 911 and get you to the hospital?"

"No, child. No. Except for a sore neck and a messy kitchen, I'm just fine." Vina breathed into the phone for a moment. "I'm leaving the kitchen alone until you can look at it for clues. But I can tell you one thing: whoever did this said they'd be back later on in the evening. They tied me up, but I managed to work my hands free enough to get the tape off my mouth and crawl to this phone." Vina's voice sounded stronger now. "Come on home. Let's prepare a surprise for Mr. Intruder."

Maria grinned in spite of herself. She knew where her spunkiness came from. "Lock the doors, if you haven't already. I'll be there within ten minutes." She thumbed the radio to bring Shirl up to date on what had happened to her mother. A quick glance in her mirror showed no one coming from behind. She whipped the car into a U-turn and sped toward home.

CHAPTER THIRTY-SEVEN

Jenna stood up from her post between the two hospital beds and stretched cramped muscles. To her left, Israel slept soundly. The conversation with Pastor Watchman and the hurried trip in the van had sapped the man of what little physical strength he had.

"Relax, Detective Anderson," she said, looking at the other bed. "Let the medicine the doctor gave you do its job." Vincent Anderson tossed restlessly in his bed, ignoring the advice. The pain meds he'd been given should have knocked him out. Instead, the detective kept trying to wake up enough to look around or ask Jenna what was happening. He simply couldn't relax. At the same time, the broken ribs and bruises kept him from being able to move off of the bed. He wanted to help protect Israel. Jenna could see the frustration on the detective's face at not being able to do his job.

The door from the waiting room opened quietly and Henry slipped in. He tiptoed up to his wife, gave her a quick kiss and nodded at the two men. "How are they doing?"

"Israel is sleeping like a baby," Jenna said, "and I wish our good detective would do the same."

Vincent rolled over, nodded to the preacher and tried to sit up. He groaned with pain. Jenna pushed his shoulder gently back onto the bed and fluffed the pillow underneath his head. "I haven't had a mother in a long time, and I don't need one now," the detective protested.

Being the motherly type, Jenna ignored him completely and held him down until Vincent finally gave up and relaxed into the mattress.

"How do you live with this woman, pastor?" he asked.

Henry grinned down at the detective. "It's easy. You just do what she says and everything will be fine." Jenna nodded at both men in complete agreement.

"What did you find out, Pastor Watchman?" Vincent's voice shook from fatigue, but he refused to give in to the pain and weakness.

Henry pulled up another chair and started to sit down. "I found a connection that may prove interesting. It shows . . . "

Henry Watchman jumped as his cell phone went off in the small room of the surgery center. Vincent weakly managed to raise his head as the preacher flipped open the cover and said hello. After listening for only a few seconds, Watchman's face went white.

"Raymond. Raymond!" he shouted. He punched savagely at the call button and dialed 911.

"What is it?" Vincent asked.

Watchman held up a hand to forestall any other questions. "This is Henry Watchman, pastor of Hidden Beach Community Church. I have reason to believe my custodian, Raymond Corley, has just suffered a heart attack at the church. He phoned me from there and gasped that he needed help."

He listened for a moment, then said, "Yes, he has a history of heart problems." Another moment passed, then . . . "Great. I'll meet you there."

Henry hung up and turned to the others. Wanda and Mary had come into the room when the phone rang. They eased between the two beds to stand beside Jenna.

"What happened to Raymond?" Jenna asked.

"I think he had a heart attack. He sounded pretty bad." Henry scooped his keys off the bedside table and started out the door. "Sergeant Thompson's right outside. I'll leave you in his care. I'm going to meet the ambulance at the church."

"Phone us when you know something," Jenna called out as the door closed.

———

The car whipped through the darkness. As the speedometer crept over seventy, Henry Watchman hoped on this night to attract a policeman. He could use an escort to the church.

"Dear Father, keep Raymond alive," Henry prayed. "Please, protect my wife and friends, as well."

The pastor felt as if something was trying to squeeze all the life out of him. The image of a boat knifing through an ocean of evil came to his mind and he shuddered. "Your strength, Father," the beleaguered pastor breathed. "Give me your strength."

You are not alone.

Pastor Watchman actually glanced around for a moment to see who had spoken. The words had come so strongly, it was as if someone – Henry laughed in spite of himself – or Someone had spoken them aloud. Whether from God, an angel, or his own subconscious, the thought was correct: Henry Watchman was not alone. The Hidden Beach Community Church family supported one another. He nodded to himself as he flipped open the phone. Time to engage more of God's warriors.

"Daryl," he said to the first person who responded, " thanks for all your help the other evening. Now, I need something else from you and Jocelyn."

"Sure, pastor," Daryl responded. "What can we do?"

"You haven't heard me talk like this before, but I'm pretty sure we're under attack from Satan in a major way. Raymond's at the church, fighting to survive a heart attack. Someone's tried to murder a patient in the hospital who is now under our care. And

I can just feel the pressure from God's enemy pressing down on us."

Daryl responded immediately. "Pastor, my wife and I will begin praying for you immediately. But I have a feeling there's something else you want us to do."

Henry smiled in the darkness of the car. He could always count on people like Daryl. "I'd like for you to begin calling as many members of the church as you can, and simply ask them to pray for God's strength and protection right now, for me and for everyone else involved in this who's under attack."

"I'll do it right now, pastor, just as soon as Jocelyn and I have finished praying for you ourselves."

Henry thanked him and hung up. Prayer support, he thought. It was good to have a team – a family – he could count on.

Back at Daryl's house, Jocelyn and her husband joined in prayer for Henry and his friends. Then each went to a separate phone and began enlisting more support from other brothers and sisters in Christ. Invisible to human eyes, nevertheless the skies above Hidden Beach began to turn silver as, with each new phone call made, more saints added their prayers to the growing river of intercession flowing straight to Heaven's throne.

In the darkness below, Henry Watchman's car sped on, as if on the wings of angels.

———

Another car, lime green, bearing no police logo or lights, stayed carefully within the speed limit as it negotiated back streets. Eric Batts wanted no attention drawn to himself. There were only so many places Watchman could have taken a sick person still hooked up to an IV. A systematic search would turn up their hiding place sooner or later. The plan to eliminate any witnesses that could ruin him was well on its way. He wiped his face in the humid air and turned the air conditioner even colder.

The old woman, Vina, had never known what hit her. Batts

had been careful to hide his face and camouflage his voice. He'd also made sure the tape and wire weren't too tight. Right about now, he figured, Maria's mother should be working herself free and calling her daughter. Batts laughed as he thought of his little scheme. He'd been passed over for promotions often in the past years, seeing other police officers who'd been there a shorter time than Eric make detectives. *If they only knew how smart I really am*, Eric thought, grinning again. He'd just eliminated Maria Da Silva from participating in the evening's activities. The less personnel familiar with this case, the better. She and her mother would be up all night waiting for him to return. Maria would refuse all of the chief's directives, and Eric knew the chief would let her stay home. He laughed one more time, spittle hitting the windshield. He'd never intended on going back. *I really am smarter than all these dopes.* He looked in the rearview mirror at himself; he could see intelligence in those eyes staring back at him. *They're all gonna learn just how smart I am.* A scowl crawled across his face. *But for some of them, it'll be too late!*

CHAPTER THIRTY-EIGHT

Vina yelped and pulled away as Maria pushed gently on her neck. "Mama, I don't think anything is broken," she said.

"It wasn't, until you started manhandling me," Vina grumbled. "If you assault all crime victims like that, you probably kill more people than you save."

Maria smiled. The grumbling meant her mother was getting back to normal. The two women sat on one of the little-used couches in the tiny living room. A crime investigative team would be taking a look at the bedroom and the kitchen upon their arrival. Meanwhile, Maria wanted to assure herself that the house was now secure and that her mother didn't need immediate medical care. She moved carefully through each room. No broken windows; deadbolts that should have been used earlier now secured front and back doors. She bit her tongue and refrained from saying anything to Vina like "I told you so." Her mother, almost too late, had learned a valuable lesson. Nothing she said now could improve on it, and it would only hurt her mother's pride.

Maria returned to the living room and sat down. Vina's eyes had a brightness to them that usually indicated anger. Two red splotches, high on her cheeks, confirmed it. Maria nodded to herself. If she could, Mama would take the would-be murderer apart. Maria wanted to get some ice from the fridge to put on her mother's neck, but that would have to wait until the investigation had been completed. They could, however, begin looking for other clues. The detective in her decided to move ahead. "Let's see if there's anything we might have missed the first time around," she said. Maria began taking Vina back through the whole incident, looking for some clue that might help them identify the intruder.

"Are you sure you never saw his face, Mama?"

Vina brushed the question away. "I've told you twice already, I couldn't see his face. I was blindfolded. And I couldn't make out anything from his voice. He always whispered." She shook her head in disgust. "I couldn't tell anything about that person, except that his sweat stank so much I nearly threw up."

Maria's head whipped around. "What did you say?"

"Well, it's the truth." Vina smiled. "I know it sounds disgusting, but that man had the worst smell about him I've ever . . ."

"Mama," Maria interrupted. "You may have just identified the assailant!" She picked up the phone and dialed the police station. "Detective Da Silva here. Let me talk with Shirl, if she's still there." A pause, then . . . "Shirl, Maria Da Silva. I'm fairly sure the man who broke into my house tonight and assaulted my mother was Eric Batts. Someone needs to head to his house and try to pick him up. Before you do that, let the chief know, if at all possible."

She paused to listen for a moment. "No, I'm staying right here for the night. Batts just might show up again." She looked toward Vina. "This time, his reception will be different."

Quiet ruled the corridor of the surgery center. After hours, the building held no one except the occupants of the small waiting room and adjacent holding area. A newspaper snapped faintly, the reader turning to a new section. A chair creaked from time to time as Hank Thompson shifted his considerable bulk, trying to stay comfortable. The walkie-talkie on the table beside him crackled to life and he looked up, wondering why the police station would be calling him. He wasn't supposed to be on duty at all. Nevertheless, he spoke into it.

"Go ahead, Shirl."

"Hank, the chief just radioed in. He knows it's not your shift, but he said you're one of the few he can trust. Jinx needs you to go over to Eric Batts' apartment now and pick him up."

Hank couldn't believe his ears. "Shirl, you called the chief 'Jinx'. You never do that!"

"Shut up and get going."

Surprise again! The dispatcher just didn't talk like that. But, what should he do? The sergeant scratched his head and thought. "Um, Shirl. I'm kind of guarding a couple of key witnesses right now. If I leave, they're unprotected."

"The person you're guarding them from is Eric Batts!" Shirl's voice rose in excitement. "Get him, and there's no need for protection."

"Would it be possible for Maria to bring him in? She can handle a guy like Batts."

Shirl's voice dropped in volume. "Hank, not everyone's supposed to know this, but someone broke into Maria's place tonight and mugged her mother. It may have been Batts. She's got her hands full right now and can't leave."

Hank sighed. "Okay, Shirl. If the chief ordered it, I'll get right on it."

"One more thing. The chief said to consider Eric armed and dangerous. He'll be sending backup for you, but you're in charge. Be careful, Hank."

The big sergeant got up from the chair. "Don't worry, Shirl. I want to be around to collect that big pension all us police offi-cers receive." He could hear Shirl chuckle as the call ended.

After updating Vincent and the others on what he planned to

do, Hank slipped out a side door to his patrol car and left quietly in pursuit of a patrolman who was looking more and more like a killer.

In the holding area, Vincent removed his revolver and quietly placed it beside him on the thin bed. His fingers trembled with even that simple effort. The detective shook his head in disgust. In the event action was needed, he'd be useless.

In the shadows, under the reception desk, Eric Batts smiled.

CHAPTER THIRTY-NINE

"Get his blood pressure stat." "I've found a vein. Give me some tubing." "What's the monitor reading?"

The EMS team worked quickly and efficiently. Within minutes of their arrival, Raymond had an oxygen mask and an I.V. started. Henry's custodian managed a weak grin around the mask as they carted him out to the waiting ambulance. "I knew you wouldn't let me down, Reverend."

Henry Watchman could barely understand the words. But he gave Raymond a reassuring pat on the shoulder. "You just get well. It looks like I may have found that helper you've been asking for. When you recover, you can train him while sitting in one of these pews you've polished for so many years."

Raymond gave a thumbs-up as the paramedics lifted him into the ambulance and closed the door. Henry watched the vehicle that represented the difference between life and death for an old friend speed away. "Thank you for sparing him, Lord," he prayed.

The church building looked almost forlorn in the darkness. The man who had cared for it for so many years now fought for his life. The only light came from the small spotlight directly over the pulpit. Henry moved into its circle of brightness and used his cell phone to call Jenna.

"Hello, this is Jenna Watchman. I can't come to the phone right now . . . "

Henry frowned. Something had to be wrong. His wife should be waiting by the phone for news about Raymond. He walked toward the light switch to turn off the spot and head back to the hospital.

CLICK!

Henry stopped as the door to the back of the auditorium opened and Jenna stumbled into the building. The pastor changed his mind and quickly flipped on two more lights.

"Jenna, what are you doing here?" he asked. "Who's taking care of Vincent and the others?"

In answer to his question, several others came into the church behind Jenna. First Israel, keeping his hand on Jenna's shoulder for guidance, then Wanda and Mary, supporting a weak Vincent between them. As if that weren't enough, Titus trooped into the sanctuary beside Wanda. The dog looked up adoringly into his new friend's face. But how had he gotten out of the pen, Henry wondered? Thank goodness Raymond couldn't see what Titus was doing to the custodian's mopped and polished floors!

Henry started for the group when one last figure came into view. Eric Batts, gun drawn and aimed at Jenna, closed the door behind him and motioned for the others to move forward.

"Judgment time, preacher," Batts rasped.

The preacher quickly looked over at the dog. Pointing toward Batts, he said, "Get 'em, Titus." In response, the dog moved closer to Wanda and wagged his tail. Henry Watchman sighed. A nice dog, but good for nothing! He eased over to his wife and tried to shield her from the potential line of fire.

"You can't protect her or anyone else, now," Batts said. A strange light had come into his eyes. Henry had seen that same look before when he'd fought professionally. The boxer who knew he was doomed to be defeated unless something changed dramatically would glance about in desperation, then go for broke, chancing everything because he had nothing left to lose.

Henry realized they were about to die.

"Eric," he said in a firm voice. "You don't want to do this. I can't believe you want to kill everyone here."

Batts waved the gun toward Vincent. "I don't. This high-and-mighty detective is the only one who needs to be taken out. If you'd stayed out of everything, preacher, no one else would have been hurt." Saliva flecked the corner of his mouth and he used the other hand to wipe it away. "Now, it's your fault alone that everyone has to die." He gave a savage grin. "The gun belongs to an ex con. He'll be charged with the murders. And, it serves him right. He should have stayed in jail anyway."

Vincent gathered what little strength he still possessed and lunged for the gunman. The round exploding out of the gun sounded enormous in the small church. The detective fell backwards as the bullet slammed into his shoulder. Batts whirled before Henry Watchman could move and aimed the gun at him. The pastor thought he could see heaven opening before him. Then . . .

The gun fired. Strangely, Henry felt nothing. Eric Batts, however, opened his mouth as if to say something. A fountain of blood spurted out instead and he sank slowly to the wooden floor. A thought, unbidden, popped into Henry's head: *Raymond's not going to be happy with blood on his wood floors.*

"That's the first time I've fired my gun at a person in over twenty years," said Jinx Monroe, moving into the church. "Sorry to have to end Batts' life in a place like this, Reverend." He bent over Eric Batts and checked for a pulse. Then he holstered his own weapon and picked up the gun Batts had stolen. Titus had shrunk against Wanda's leg. His tail drooped between his legs and he whimpered softly.

"Thank goodness you're here!" Mary exclaimed. "You came at just the right time."

Henry stood very still, his eyes never leaving Monroe. "It's not over yet, Mary," he said. "Tell them, Chief."

Monroe looked up in surprise. "What are you talking about, Pastor Watchman? I just saved your life."

The pastor shook his head. "No, you just saved your own skin. You did kill a murderer. I'm pretty sure Batts stabbed the librarian to death. But you killed the others."

Jenna gasped and her hand flew to her mouth.

Jinx Monroe gave the pastor a long look. "Watchman, you've been stuck in your study for too long, coming up with stories like that," he said.

"If that's true, you'll put down Eric's gun, Chief."

The others noticed belatedly that Jinx Monroe still held the gun loosely, aiming in their general direction.

"Come on, Pastor Watchman, I only have one holster! Don't get paranoid on me now." Israel stumbled forward a step. "Excuse me. Are you the chief of police?" he asked.

Monroe's eyes narrowed. "Yes, I am. Why do you ask?"

"Your voice! I've heard it before!"

With those words, Israel became the center of attention. For his part, the blind man stared sightlessly in the direction of Jinx Monroe, his eyes wide.

"The night of the car explosion. I heard your voice." He aimed a shaky, accusing finger at the chief. "You were the one who set the fire. So, you must have killed the club owner!"

The captain tilted his head and glanced toward the ceiling, as if in thought. "If I remember correctly – I'll have to look at my log later to make sure – I was at least fifteen minutes from there in a restaurant, with two local politicians, when it happened." He gave a cold smile. "You should be more careful who you point fingers at. Especially with your reputation of being a blind, drunken sot."

"Actually, he's got it right," Pastor Watchman said quietly. "I checked out the alleys behind the restaurant and the strip club. The pathway through there is strewn with garbage. At night it's probably not the best place to be, but anyone brave enough to poke around a bit would discover the two alleys connect by way of a couple of basements." His eyes pierced the captain. "Those basements had doors that were jimmied, so anyone could go into and out of them with no one seeing them. Of course, only someone intimately familiar with the area would know about them." The chief slumped some as the pastor continued to talk. "I did some further checking. It seems you had that particular area as your beat when you first joined the force." Henry Watchman took a step toward Monroe. "A pretty amazing coincidence, don't you think, Chief?"

A thick, greasy puddle of blackness oozed underneath the door. The demon reformed and the two snakes shot from its mouth into the head and heart of evil's tool, the chief of police. The demon cackled wildly. Time to end Watchman's influence in Hidden Beach. He would be promoted because of this! *"Kill them all,"* Shi'intor ordered.

Jinx Monroe sighed heavily. "You would have made a great detective, Preacher." He lifted the revolver and pointed it at the group. "And you're right, Batts killed the librarian. I told him she knew about a deal he'd tried to broker with a group of prostitutes. That wasn't true, but Batts didn't know it. He thought I wanted him to protect the reputation of the force. He saw a way to do that and frame Detective Anderson at the same time." Monroe waved the gun. "I'll do anything I have to in order to protect the force and this community. And, unfortunately, Anderson is bad for the force. I didn't want it to end like this. I'm sorry." He crouched slightly and gripped the gun in both hands.

"Hold it, chief!" Henry Watchman commanded. "You're not Eric Batts. I can't believe you'd kill all of us just to save yourself." He gestured toward the back door. "All your career, you've been fighting crime. You care deeply for this community. Do you really mean to tell me you'd turn your back on all that now?"

Sweat dripped from the chief's scalp and he reached up to wipe it away. Then he swung Batts' revolver in the direction of Israel. "I haven't worked all that out yet, preacher," he said. "But

I will do our community a favor and take care of this garbage." His finger began to tighten on the trigger.

"*No!*" Wanda jumped in front of Israel and clawed at the chief's arm. It was as if she had run into a stone wall. Jinx Monroe proved to be ready for almost anything. Unperturbed by the attack, he simply swatted Wanda aside with the gun. Blood spurted from her head and she fell awkwardly across a pew.

The chief didn't expect the brown streak that hit his arm. Sharp teeth began taking huge chunks out of his hand. Titus growled furiously and shook his head back and forth as he tried to separate Monroe's hand from its attached wrist. The chief yelled in agony, dropped the gun and punched the dog repeatedly with his other hand. Titus finally lost his grip and was flung against the pew beside Wanda.

Somewhere, a trumpet sounded. Silver notes seemed to fall upon the demon, staggering him. An angel burst through the church's roof. Shi'intor had only a moment to realize that now Toldin was bigger, stronger than any angel he'd ever seen. What had happened?

Then Shi'intor had no more time to think. Toldin, moving faster than he could follow, cuffed the demon to the floor, Off balance, the hideous creature could not react in time to pull away from the great sword that flashed downward. Wielded expertly by the protecting angel, it cut through the snakes and severed that portion of the demon's tongue completely. The two snakes writhed in agony on the floor before disappearing in an oily cloud of smoke.

"The prayers of God's children, heard by their Heavenly Father, can be powerful," Toldin proclaimed to the defeated enemy. "They give strength and power to us, God's servants."

Jinx Monroe bent over and quickly retrieved the gun. But as he stood back up, Henry Watchman pounced. The preacher knocked Batts' gun from his hand; Monroe countered with a powerful left aimed at Watchman's windpipe. Jinx Monroe might be big, but he was also quick. Henry Watchman, however, had fought big, quick men all his professional career in boxing. He managed to partially block Monroe's blow. For a fraction of a second, he stood facing his opponent, as if sizing him up. Then, he feinted at the chief's head, ducked under the parry and drove a fist into the chief's solar plexus. The big man began to fold. Henry reached over the lowered arms and slammed a hard right into the side of Monroe's neck. The chief fell awkwardly onto his back. But even as he fell, his hand clawed for the holstered gun.

Before he could get the gun halfway out, the pastor kicked it away. The gun skidded under a couple of pews and disappeared. Then Reverend Watchman opened the front door and threw the other gun into the hedges surrounding the entrance. "It's over, Chief," he said quietly. "Give it up."

Jinx Monroe looked around the church. Vincent lay on the floor, gasping for air. Jenna and Mary had run from the room. Even now they were probably calling 911. Monroe's eyes turned once more toward the pastor. Then he began to crawl backwards. He finally came up against the door. "If you don't want any more blood spilled in this church, Watchman, leave me alone."

Henry Watchman nodded. "Go home," he said. "There's nowhere else to run. The police will be by soon and we'll get you some help."

Jinx felt for the doorknob behind him. Still facing the preacher, he opened the door and slipped out.

Jenna called from the corridor. "I've called the police, Mr. Monroe. You might as well give up."

"He's gone, honey," Henry replied.

The two women trooped into the auditorium once more. In the distance, both police and ambulance sirens could be heard. The EMS would be having a busy night at Hidden Beach Community church.

"What do we do now?" Mary asked.

"The police will find him," the pastor responded. "He can't

run forever. And I don't believe he'll kill anyone else, now that the truth is coming out."

A wet nose rubbed against his hand. Henry reached down and patted Titus on the head. "Well," he said, "Titus, you finally did something right." The dog wagged his tail and looked around for a bucket of water to step in.

Israel made his way to Wanda. "How are you?" he asked. The former beggar laid a gentle hand on her shoulder.

"I've got a pretty bad headache," she answered. "If we can get the blood stopped, though, I'll be doing a lot better."

Jenna jumped up. "Shame on me! I'll get you a wet cloth. A little pressure should stop the flow and the cold will help the headache."

Israel sat down beside Wanda. "No one has ever risked their life for me before. Thank you," he said.

Wanda smiled in response. "We're in the same boat. I've never risked my life for someone else before." She thought for a moment, then said, "We've both been given a second chance, Israel. Maybe it's time to do something for God with our lives."

"You see, Israel," Henry said, "your new name is already sending you in a different direction."

The sound of multiple sirens grew in intensity as the police surrounded the church.

———

The angel dragged the limp body of the demon outside the church. This time, he would make sure Satan's servant did not escape. "You have failed," he said to the black mass of evil that trembled under his sword. "It's time for you to be gone from this place."

Hatred flowed from the demon. Shi'intor raised his head and looked the angel in the eyes, squinting against the celestial glow. "Leave me alone, and I won't send others. If you send me away, demons far more powerful than you can imagine will assault this town, this church, and your precious Henry Watch-man." Now outside the church, he could feel evil from the town beginning to strengthen him. If he could talk a little longer, buy some more time, he might yet be able to defeat . . .

The angel pressed harder on his sword and the demon winced. "You still don't understand," Toldin said. He gestured with his free hand, and suddenly hundreds of angels appeared around the demon, the parking lot and the church. "We are a team, a part of the community of God. These others have come straight from Heaven to help me, drawn by the prayers of many Christians. We stand together, and we will defeat anyone Satan sends in your place. No matter how strong you get, demon, you cannot hope to defeat all of us."

"Teamwork," the demon moaned. "How I hate teamwork!"

"Judgment time has come for you, Shi'intor." The angel glowed even brighter, and his captor began to wail bitterly. "In the name of our Lord Jesus Christ, I banish you to the Pit!"

And with one last, angry scream, the demon of Hidden Beach vanished from Earth forever.

———

Jinx Monroe seemed to wake, as from a bad dream. What had he been thinking? He looked around in bewilderment at the police officers aiming guns at him. There had to be a way out of this. Then he remembered what had started him down this path.

"It's not my fault," he shouted at the law enforcement officers. "Anderson doesn't deserve to be chief so soon. This is *my* town. I own it! I deserve to stay the chief!"

Now more revolvers pointed at him.

"I'm your chief, your boss. You *will* stand down immediately!"

Instead, Monroe watched as men and women with badges advanced grimly toward him. He looked around wildly. What could he do? Something glinted darkly in the lights of the parking lot. Monroe could see the revolver thrown from the church hanging in the hedges. He lunged for it.

The little group inside the church stopped at Jenna's insistence and prayed, thanking God for their miraculous deliverance.

"What will happen now?" Mary asked.

Henry looked out one of the windows. "I'm not sure, but I think Monroe is still out there. From the aggressive stance of several of the policemen, it looks like they have him cornered and he doesn't want to give up."

In response, a single shot rang out from the parking lot. Henry ran to the door and cautiously eased it open, but the only thing greeting him was the limp body of former chief Jinx Monroe. He must have recovered the gun from the hedges. Monroe's last shot executed the killer of three people. In the end, his suicide claimed a perverse sort of justice.

CHAPTER FORTY

"Okay, tell us how you knew about Batts and Chief Monroe."

The hospital room teemed with law enforcement personnel and Henry Watchman's friends. Vincent Anderson had been given the largest room in the facility, which happened to be the only reason the harried nurse assigned to Anderson had allowed everyone to stay.

"Admit it, Pastor Watchman, you had information no one else did."

Maria Da Silva smiled as she said it. Her muscled bulk made the huge room seem smaller. Vina sat on a chair right beside her. She'd made Maria bring her along to see the man who'd helped save her life. Maria's protests had been long and loud, but Vina had walked to the car and let herself in the passenger's side while the harangue continued. Maria, knowing she was whipped, had saved a little face by reaching across Vina and strapping her in tight.

Wanda, her head bandaged, and Mary stood next to Israel. Jenna had her arm around her husband. She didn't plan to leave his side for a long time. For his part, Henry didn't mind at all.

"Vincent, are you up to all this?"

The patient gave a wan smile and nodded. "The doc says my

shoulder should heal just fine. He got the bullet out and said I had no broken bones. So, I should be back at work sometime in the next couple of weeks."

Maria laughed and shook her head. "Listen, partner, it took me quite awhile to whip you into shape. I don't want to have to break someone else in because you ruined yourself coming back too soon."

Henry Watchman cleared his throat. Jenna smiled and said, "Just tell everyone to listen up."

Her husband blushed. "It seemed politer the other way," he protested.

The crowd in the room laughed. But they also turned their attention to the pastor.

"From the beginning," he began, "everyone on the case made a fundamental mistake. Maria, you and Vince figured the note found on the bodies was put there by a crazy who wanted to draw attention to his hatred of profanity. You believed he put the note face-down so that the words would be right next to the heart."

Watchman shook his head. "When you gave me the facts about the case, Vince, I immediately asked myself two questions. First, if I were the killer, how would I benefit from putting a message on a person I'd just killed where it couldn't easily be read? After all, supposedly I want publicity for my cause. Second, if I wanted to draw attention to my cause, why would I kill an unknown criminal?"

He ticked off the answers. "The only way I could benefit from a message face-down on a body would be if it kept the information about what I'd done from getting out. But, who would like to keep that kind of information away from the general public? The most obvious answer is, someone concerned about the image of the community and its ability to control law and order."

Henry looked around the room. His audience had locked onto his explanation. "Second, who would kill an unknown criminal to publicize his cause? Again, someone who cared about law and order. That person might decide that if he had to kill, it would only be a criminal who had already broken the law. Plus, an unknown con man would draw little, if any, attention. Again, this would be a plus to the person who cared about the image and stability of Hidden Beach.

"All those things pointed me toward a police officer as the guilty party," Pastor Watchman concluded.

Vincent raised his good hand. "Okay, I see how you got it narrowed down to one of us. But why the chief? I don't get it."

"That's because you were too close to it." Henry Watchman closed his eyes and, for just a moment, his shoulders drooped. It had, after all, been a long night. "I watched how the chief looked at you. I checked out your reputation. Everything pointed to a young man rising rapidly within the force. Before long, Jinx Monroe knew you'd be challenging him for the job. He wasn't ready to retire and give the position to a hot-shot like you." Henry grinned as he said these last words.

"But there's another thing. The timing of the first killing right after my sermon on profanity had to point to you, Vincent. Only someone who knew our link to each other would have been able to coordinate that and eventually set you up. I figured the chief's jealousy of your ability got the best of him."

"But the chief had an alibi for the night Robert Jamison, the owner of the strip club, was stabbed to death," Maria protested.

Henry shook his head. "Think about it, Maria. The steak-house where Monroe and his two friends ate is located only three blocks from the club. Someone who knew all the back alleys and shortcuts could move quickly and unseen from one place to the other without a problem. And, word got back to me that the politicians with Monroe that night hardly got to talk to him because he left the table multiple times for long periods. He said constant phone calls kept him occupied.. I suspect it was because of a murder he needed to commit that would implicate Vince even further."

Henry glanced at Wanda. She had turned pale as the events of that evening played out once more. "Monroe didn't like Jamison, but I believe he privately met with the strip club owner on a number of occasions to make Jamison believe they would soon be friends. In reality, the chief was just setting him up for the kill. He probably figured the killing rid the world of another predator. According to his twisted logic, he was really doing something *good*."

"The librarian doesn't fit that mode, reverend." Maria looked at Israel in surprise. She'd forgotten about him. Even Israel looked shocked that he'd spoken.

"You're right," Henry agreed, going on with his explanation. "And, that's where Eric Batts came in. The chief knew Batts had a reputation as someone who crossed the line from time to time – and Monroe hated a crooked cop worse than anything else. He also knew Batts disliked Vincent and was afraid the detective would discover Batts played both sides of the street. Monroe used that dislike to have the patrolman kill Ms. Danforth. He couldn't bring himself to kill her, because she'd committed no crime. But if he could get Batts to kill her, then he'd be justified in shooting Batts because of what he'd done."

"That's just sick," Jenna said.

Maria looked puzzled. "But why kill the woman in the first place?"

"Oh yes, I'd forgotten about that part." Henry turned to detective Da Silva. "Maria, remember when you said Ms. Danforth told you that law enforcement personnel had already been in the library looking for information? Not one person, but 'personnel;' plural! You thought her comments referred to Vince. But Jinx Monroe knew she'd remembered the chief's being there. That sealed her doom."

Henry Watchman pointed at the wounded detective. "Only the chief would have had access to your whereabouts at the library. Only he could have pulled all of this together. Shirl must have told him about the sermon I preached on profanity." The pastor grimaced as he reflected on the activities of the previous weeks. "The chief probably convinced Batts that by killing Ms. Danforth, they'd be able to frame Vince and get rid of him forever. It also gave the chief an alibi."

"And the note we found outside Israel's room," Vincent said. "Why did Batts leave it there?"

Pastor Watchman was shaking his head even as the detective was finishing up his question. "Batts didn't try to kill Israel; that was the chief."

Vincent looked puzzled. "That doesn't make any sense! After all, Monroe had just assigned a *guard* to stand outside Israel's room!"

"That was the genius of it," Henry explained. "Monroe knew he could get to the hospital a good ten minutes before anyone else would arrive. He probably opened the door just a crack to see if Israel was alone. Instead, Monroe saw me in the room and then decided to frame me even more by leaving the note and the knife in the hallway." The pastor shot a look at Vincent. "The fact that you also showed up unexpectedly helped add still another suspect to the killings."

Vincent, still stunned by the evening's events, shook his head in amazement.

"So why did Jinx Monroe kill Batts?" Jenna asked.

Maria raised her hand for attention. "I think I understand that one. Once Batts killed, the chief had him marked as a criminal in his mind. Again, it might be weird, but Monroe felt justified in shooting another murderer – even if he, himself, had recruited Batts to commit the murder. Plus, with Batts dead, everyone would assume the 'profanity killer' had been taken care of."

"Just like in Proverbs," Henry Watchman murmured. In response to several questioning looks, he spoke louder. "Sorry about that; just thinking out loud. In the first chapter of Proverbs, the author warns his son to stay away from people who believe they can get what they want through violence. Then he says, in effect, *'These people rush to commit murder, but they don't realize they are lying in wait for their own blood. They ambush themselves.'* We would save ourselves a lot of trouble and heartache if we'd only listen to and follow the Bible."

The door opened and Vince's nurse slipped in. "Sorry, but the doctor just called and said everyone needs to clear out."

Maria leaned over and gave Vincent a gentle hug. "I've still got quite a few reports to make on tonight's events. The deaths of two cops will be looked at closely by everyone."

The others came by the detective's bed one by one, wishing him a short time of recuperation.

Jenna and her husband stood back and let everyone else leave. Henry Watchman smiled at Jenna and motioned her to slip on out.

"Could you give me just a moment, nurse?" Henry asked.

The nurse nodded. "I'll give you some privacy," she agreed. "But you have to make it quick."

After she'd left, the pastor turned to Vincent. "God spared your life for a reason, Vince. You have some incredible gifts, but they'll be wasted unless you let go of events that happened years ago." His eyes bored into those of the wounded man. "Don't live in the past anymore. You can't move forward when you're chained to old memories."

The detective returned Pastor Watchman's look. Then he shifted his attention to the thin sheet covering him. "If it weren't for you," he said, "I'd be in the morgue right now, instead of recuperating in this hospital bed."

Vince squared his shoulders and raised his head. "The past we're talking about occurred when I was a small boy. I didn't understand everything that happened. I just knew it caused me a lot of pain. But tonight," he continued, "I saw a man risk his life for me. I watched you confront the possibility of death and not lose your cool." Vincent made a pushing motion with his good hand. "I've decided to leave the past where it belongs – in the past." He reached up and placed his hand on the pastor's shoulder. "I like the Henry Watchman I'm coming to know as an adult."

Henry breathed deeply for a moment. "That's good," he finally said. "I don't know many people as stubborn as I am. It would be nice to have someone like that as a friend. He could help Jenna keep me from making wrong decisions."

"Ditto."

Vincent lay back in his bed, smiling.

CHAPTER FORTY-ONE

The van moved across Hidden Beach toward the ocean and home. In the distance, a faint light could be seen as dawn made its appearance once more. A new day, a new life, Henry Watchman thought. Jenna rode beside him; her hand rested lightly on his leg. She seemed as calm as if none of the night's activities had ever occurred. "I don't deserve a wife as good as you," he whispered to her.

Jenna leaned close to her husband, placing her lips right next to his ear. "Of course you don't," she breathed. "It's called 'grace'."

They laughed. Tough times made good marriages even stronger.

"Reverend Watchman . . . ."

"Just call me 'Henry,' Israel."

"That's hard for me, sir." Israel admitted. "I'll call you 'Pastor' for right now, if you don't mind."

Wanda sat next to the blind man. From time-to-time, she braced him when Mary turned corners and slowed for stop signs.

"Whatever makes you comfortable," Henry said. "Israel, you sound as if something is worrying you. Am I right?"

"Yes, sir. I don't mean to be ungrateful for all you've already done for me. But . . . what now? What do I do? Where do I go? I've got to make some money."

Henry squeezed Jenna's hand, silently asking for prayer. Then he said, "Israel, our church needs a new custodian. Raymond has said that after he's out of the hospital, he can train you to take his place. There's a small house on the back of the property where you can live rent-free. The salary won't make you rich, but it will pay the bills."

Israel rubbed a hand through his hair. "Pastor, I can't do all that work." He sounded frustrated. "I'm blind! Plus, you don't want a drunk working for the church."

"I've already got a plan." Pastor Watchman glanced over at Wanda. Here's where it got tricky. "Wanda, Mary and I talked earlier this evening. She's enjoying your staying with her so much that she'd like to make it permanent."

A gasp from Wanda greeted his words. "I . . . I would love to do that," she said. "But, I'm like Israel, how do I earn a living?"

Henry smiled. "That's a part of my plan, and Mary's, as well. Raymond has been saying for a long time that we need another custodian to help with increased activities. I figured Raymond and Israel, working together, could take care of the inside. Raymond will be Israel's eyes. That will give Raymond the rest he needs. Besides, he'd love to have someone to boss around!" Henry glanced at Wanda in the rear view mirror. "You, on the other hand, would be in charge of all the trees, flowers and shrubs around the outside of the church. With Israel's ability to fix just about anything, and with your love of gardening, the two of you would be a formidable team."

Mary spoke up. "And when people see what a great job you're doing, you'll probably be as busy as you want helping them get their flowers in order. That, plus what you make at the church, should give you a pretty good income."

"A stripper and a drunk!" Wanda spoke the words, but her face showed the beginnings of hope.

Jenna turned in her seat to face the couple. "No," she

corrected. "Two people God created and for whom Christ died. Two people who have a bright, clean future before them. Both of you have had a hard life and you'll be able to help one another when you're tempted to slip back into old ways."

Henry spoke up. "Israel, you'll need to attend our Celebrate Recovery group meeting every week. It's for people with substance abuse problems, and it's led by a recovering alcohol-and-drug addict. If you want to keep working for us, you'll make that a regular part of your schedule." He softened his voice a bit. "You'll also find men and women there who have been where you are. They'll love you and support you."

"It sounds like a family," Israel said. "I've never had a family before."

"What's your answer, then?" Mary asked from the front.

Israel put his hand out for Wanda to shake. "I'm all for it, partner, if you are."

Wanda said nothing, but a huge smile transformed her face as she took Israel's hand and squeezed it.

CHAPTER FORTY-TWO

Sunday brought blue skies. A warm breeze tugged gently at Jenna's dress as she crossed the parking lot. Newspaper headlines about the previous week's goings-on had guaranteed a packed church this morning. Sure enough, every free bit of space had a car in it, with some even parked in the Watchmans' driveway.

Jenna stared in astonishment as she entered the building. The auditorium bulged at the seams, crammed to capacity. People even stood in the back, unable to find a place, yet unwilling to leave. A sense of expectancy filled Hidden Beach Community Church. Enthusiastic voices lifted psalms, hymns and spiritual songs up to Heaven. In this atmosphere, the power of God could change lives forever. Jenna prayed that God would use her husband mightily as he preached.

Pastor Henry Watchman walked up to the pulpit and opened his Bible. As he surveyed the crowd – and today, the term certainly fit, he noted – Henry thanked God once more for sparing him, his wife and their friends. It gave him one more opportunity to share the wonderful news of Christ's love. He cleared his throat and began to speak.

"What an eventful week in the life of our church! People's lives have been saved right where some of you are sitting. Others of you parked close to the place where a respected individual made a wrong, horrific choice." Earlier, Henry had talked with his church elders, as well as with Jenna. They'd decided not to ignore the shootings or the suicide. People knew about it, and someone needed to make sense out of all that had happened.

"Throughout the Bible," Pastor Watchman continued, "there is a history of humankind making wrong decisions. Inevitably, judgment followed those sins. However, both in the Old and New Testaments, we see God holding out a hand of hope and redemption, ready to forgive those who realize they need help."

Looking over the congregation, Henry Watchman saw Wanda and Mary on the second pew from the front. Farther back on the left, Vincent sat stiffly, supported on either side by Maria Da Silva and Shirl. Henry knew bandages covered most of the detective's upper body. He had to be uncomfortable. The doctor hadn't wanted to release him, but when Vincent put his mind to something, no one could stop him.

"Over the past weeks, several individuals did their best to frame Detective Vincent Anderson and me, making us look like murderers. Instead, God protected both of us and brought the guilty to justice." Pastor Watchman looked briefly at Maria, Shirl and Vincent, and smiled.

Then he shifted his attention to the other members of the congregation and said, "I challenged one of the participants in this ordeal to watch how God would work for His glory, despite the efforts of evil individuals, and make us better, stronger people. I called it an experiment." He paused for emphasis. "I ask that person, and anyone else here today who initially had doubts that God could bring good from bad, this question: Has God kept His word? Did my Heavenly Father pass the test?"

Wanda knew the words were for her. She'd forgotten Pastor Watchman's "experiment." He had certainly put God's reputation on the line at the darkest moment for both of them! But since that time, she could point to a warm friendship with Mary and a sun-dappled garden that thrilled and relaxed her every time she set foot in it. She had a new home that allowed her the freedom to grow into the person God had always wanted her to be. And, for Henry Watchman, the television, radio and newspapers had applauded his courage. She remembered Jenna's telling her that more than one hundred of the church's members had called or written, assuring Henry and his wife of their appreciation and support. Yes, God had definitely passed the test!

"One of the best stories about God's love comes from the lips of Jesus." Henry Watchman moved into the body of his sermon. "We call it 'The Prodigal Son.' This morning, I want to give the story a more personal name: 'Your Second Chance.' You see, the same opportunity the father gives his son in this account, God, our Heavenly Father, wants to give to each of us.

"The story begins with a young man making the first of what proved to be many foolish choices. He asks for his inheritance early. When the father honors this request, the son responds to this loving act by leaving his father and brother to work the farm by themselves. He decides to embark on a life of selfish pleasure." On the front row, Israel McFain nodded. He knew where a life like that could take a person.

"The money didn't last forever. And Jesus tells us that when it ran out, the partying ended, the fair-weather friends dried up and the willing women departed. The young man found himself far from home. And this time, he had no father to bail him out or give him food.

"As most of you know, wrong choices move us downward in life. The Prodigal Son now found himself forced to take a job feeding pigs in a pig pen. The job paid so little that he was tempted to eat the pigs' food!" Henry's eyes swept the back of the auditorium. His sharp vision caught a glimpse of David Jones. The man crouched behind several others, trying to remain unnoticed. His eyes had filled with tears and David unconsciously brushed them away as he listened to what could have been his own life.

"Finally," Henry continued, "the young man's situation got so bad that he began to closely examine his life. He couldn't blame his father, his brother or anyone else. The Prodigal Son realized the finger of blame for all his problems pointed directly at himself. In the mud and muck of the pigpen, something great happened. The former party animal admitted he'd been wrong. And once he'd gotten to that point, he began to look at home in a different way. But how could he ever go back?"

Henry looked over the congregation. "That's what some of you are asking yourself. The realization that you've ruined your life has hit you. But you wonder if life can ever hold more for you than what you've already experienced. In other words, many of you want to know if you can come home to God again."

Pastor Watchman opened his arms wide. "All of us need to put ourselves in the place of the Prodigal Son as we finish his story." Henry looked at his Bible once more. "The son who had made all the wrong choices finally made a right one. He decided to go back to his father and admit he'd acted selfishly. There would be no place in the family for him any more; of that, he was sure. But he no longer cared. He just wanted to be home with his father, even if he had to be the lowest of the slaves. So, gathering his courage and putting aside his pride, the son started for home.

"I can imagine him planning his speech. After all, the young man just knew his father would be furious. 'Father, I was wrong; please don't turn me away. All I want is to live here as your slave.' He probably rehearsed it over and over as he walked. His tension rose higher and his blood pressure got worse the closer he got to home. Would he be driven off? Would his father ridicule him for what he'd done?

"None of that happened. To his astonishment, before he could even get to the house, something occurred that completely overwhelmed the Prodigal Son. You see, unbeknownst to him, his father had been looking far down the road every day, hoping against hope to get a glimpse of his wayward child. And the Bible tells us that while the young man was still far away, the father saw him. Instead of anger, his face showed joy. In today's language, the father jumped off the porch and began running as fast as his legs would carry him." Pastor Watchman grinned at the congregation. "I can imagine him hitting the returning son at full speed, gathering him in his arms and giving him a big bear hug!

"The young man begins his rehearsed speech about being a slave in his father's house. He gets interrupted, however, by the father. 'A slave?' the overjoyed man says. 'A slave!!! No way! We're going to dress you in the best clothes and throw a party!' The father can see confusion in his son's eyes, so he explains his reaction. 'I'm ecstatic because the one who was lost has been found. I want to give you only the best! You'll not be a slave in my house. You're my son. You're an honored part of the family.'"

Pastor Henry Watchman paused again to look out over his people – his family – his friends. Midway back on the right side, Billy and Cherie Lawrence sat as close together as they could, shoulders touching and hands intertwined. They'd not missed a single Sunday since Wanda's lecture and the pastor's offer of a second chance. Sadly, Owen Stiller had decided to skip church once more. Henry sighed to himself before continuing. God had given humankind the freedom to say no to Jesus Christ. And, when a person like Owen put pride in front of change, it became a terrible freedom. Pastor Watchman focused once more on those who had come to hear of God's grace.

"Jesus uses this story to tell you that no matter how far you've strayed, no matter how many poor choices you've made, no matter how messed up your life is, today there exists a second chance. If you will simply admit you've done wrong, you're halfway home. Remember, Jesus Christ took your sins and paid for them on the cross. And when you lift your eyes to the cross and ask for forgiveness, you'll find a Heavenly Father who has been watching for your return all along. He will sweep you into His arms, forgive you of everything you've ever done and welcome you into His family." Henry closed his Bible. "Give Jesus Christ control of your life, and He will give you a new future, one that includes living forever with Him. You can . . ."

Henry Watchman stopped because of a commotion on the second row. Wanda Lemming had stood up. Tears streamed down her face and she said, "I can't wait any longer. I want to come home to God." She moved to the altar and, kneeling, continued to weep as she poured her heart out to her heavenly Father. Mary and Jenna came forward to comfort her.

Before Henry could step off the platform, others began to follow Wanda's example. Some, the pastor knew well. Many, however, were attending the church for the first time. Henry motioned to several of his members to help him talk with those who needed assistance.

"I want to live up to my name, Pastor." The words came from the blind, newly-named Israel on the front row. Henry sat down by the new custodian and grasped his hand. The hand shook violently, and his eyes were squeezed shut tightly, but Israel's voice sounded firm. "You've given me a new chance. This morning, for the first time, I've seen God in a new light. If He can love me even seeing what I've done with my life, then I want that kind of love." Israel kept his eyes closed, but raised his head. "I want a life with Christ in control of everything, Pastor."

Everywhere Henry Watchman looked, God seemed to be working. At the extreme end of the platform, almost around the corner of the piano, he could see David Jones on his knees, praying. As he watched, David's wife, Katherine, quietly moved to kneel beside him. Perhaps there would be a second chance for David's marriage, as well as for his relationship with God.

A host of angels ringed the inside of the worship center. Wings spread wide, they formed an unbroken circle of protection. As Wanda and others gave their lives to Christ, the angels raised their arms toward Heaven, and shouted, "Worthy is the Lamb, who was slain, to receive power and wealth and wisdom and strength and honor and glory and praise!"

The silver glow of heavenly power grew brighter, until the whole church fairly vibrated with God's presence.

Jenna raised her head and looked at Henry across a sea of people seeking God's love and forgiveness. She knew the magnitude of the victories God was bringing about on this day. For himself, Henry Watchman could feel something big and powerful happening in this church – and in his life. "Thank you, God, for allowing me to be a part of your work," he prayed. "Thank you for being faithful to Your word and touching people's lives through Jenna and me."

Then, Pastor Watchman focused once again on the hungry soul beside him and returned to his life's work, sharing the love of Christ.

The demon undertow of evil that had hurt so many lives was defeated . . . for the moment. In the coming months, the community of Hidden Beach would face darker, stronger spiritual forces. The angels that presently stood wing-to-wing protecting the church could see the tide of evil approaching. They would battle Satan's forces in God's strength, standing faithful.

And so would Henry Watchman.

The End

ABOUT THE AUTHOR

Mark and his wife, Donna, live in Central Florida, where he continues to author books, write blogs on ConqueringDepression.com, and oversee Mark Sutton Ministries. MSM is dedicated to helping the people of Haiti through building schools and houses, offering free education, feeding orphans and other children daily, educating pastors and planting churches.

Mark's previous books include: Pitfall (hope again books), Hope Again: A Lifetime Plan for Conquering Depression [with Dr. Bruce Hennigan], (hope again books), Hope Again: A 30 Day Plan for Conquering Depression (B&H Publishing), Conquering Depression [with Dr. Bruce Hennigan], (Broadman & Holman Publishing), God's Man [with Dr. Don Aycock] (Kregel Publishing), Still God's Man [with Dr. Don Aycock], (Kregel Publishing), 30 Days to a Better Marriage, (Ragged Edge Press).

For more information on Hope Again: A Lifetime Plan for Conquering Depression and the Conquering Depression Seminar go to www.conqueringdepression.com

ALSO BY MARK SUTTON

Pitfall,)Hope Again Books)

Hope Again: A Lifetime Plan for Conquering Depression, with Bruce
Hennigan, M.D., (Hope Again Books)

Hope Again: A 30 Day Plan for Conquering Depression (B&H
Publishing)

Conquering Depression [with Dr. Bruce Hennigan], (Broadman &
Holman Publishing)

God's Man [with Dr. Don Aycock] (Kregel Publishing)

Still God's Man [with Dr. Don Aycock], (Kregel Publishing)

30 Days to a Better Marriage, (Ragged Edge Press).